The Sleepover Clause

Barbara Barrett

CRIMSON
ROMANCE
Avon, Massachusetts

This edition published by
Crimson Romance
an imprint of F+W Media, Inc.
10151 Carver Road, Suite 200
Blue Ash, Ohio 45242

www.crimsonromance.com

Dedication

TO THE STATE OF IOWA, AND IN PARTICULAR, THE TOWN OF BURLINGTON, SITE OF MANY FOND MEMORIES FROM MY YOUTH, THANK YOU FOR PROVIDING THE PERFECT SETTING FOR THIS STORY.

TO MY FAMILY: MY MOTHER, EVELYN; MY SISTER, PEG; MY CHILDREN, LESLIE AND CHRISTOPHER; AND MY GRANDCHILDREN, SAMANTHA, ZACHARY, TURNER, JADEN, JACK AND SHELBIE THANK YOU FOR YOUR SUPPORT AND BELIEF IN ME.

TO MY WRITING PEERS: MY CRITIQUE PARTNERS, JUDY, JEANNINE AND SARAH, AND THE SPACECOAST AUTHORS OF ROMANCE CHAPTER OF ROMANCE WRITERS OF AMERICA, THANK YOU FOR SETTING THE BAR HIGH BY MAKING ME DIG DEEPER AND WORK HARDER TO TELL MY STORY AND FOR ALWAYS BEING THERE TO HELP.

TO JENNIFER LAWLER AND CRIMSON ROMANCE, THANK YOU FOR THIS OPPORTUNITY.

AND FINALLY, TO MY HUSBAND, VERYL, THANK YOU FOR YOUR NEVER-ENDING LOVE AND SUPPORT AND FOR GIVING ME THE SPACE TO PURSUE MY PASSION.

CHAPTER ONE

Though she rarely agreed with her mother about anything, Aubrey Carpenter had to admit the woman had been right this once. Iowa sucked.

Since she'd flown in from L.A. four hours earlier, the state had done its best to pull the welcome rug out from under her. Tornado warnings. A sudden rain shower flooding the engine of her rental car. Farm equipment clogging the roadway. And rain forest variety humidity seeping through what had been her best designer pantsuit.

To top things off, she'd just discovered that McKenna Custom Coaches, her destination and hideaway for the next four weeks, was housed in a converted firehouse. What more could an interior decorator on the run want? But then, what had she expected of the small southeastern Iowa town of Burlington? A barn?

She parked the car, telling herself things were going to be all right. Her life was on the mend. She just needed to lie low for a few weeks, attend to the unusual task ahead and she'd be back renovating homes in Beverly Hills in no time.

Finding the front door unlocked, she entered, expecting to find a bustling reception area or at least a clerk waiting to greet her. Nobody. The place looked like a dump with its aged, unmatched, dilapidated furniture.

A hollow knocking sound drew her farther inside to investigate.

As her eyes adjusted to the dim light, she made out a large, hulking object some twenty feet away. As she refocused, she was awestruck. The bus! Jenna's bus. The reason for this trek to the heartland. Sleek and black, the vehicle was bigger than she had imagined. Good. Four weeks of confinement within its close quarters had concerned her.

She glanced about, taking in the pristine starkness of the room. A huge cavern with no other furniture or other objects, except for the bus.

She sniffed the air, trying to identify the smells. One was slightly dank, like drying wood, and the other was the odor of oil. Definitely a garage. Just where she wanted to spend the next four weeks.

The knocking resumed. Directly in front of her. Under the bus? "Hello?" she called out.

The banging stopped momentarily. Near the floor, a deep male voice called out, "Who's there?"

Showtime! However, she hadn't expected to deliver her opening act to a mechanic. "Aubrey Carpenter. This is McKenna Custom Coaches, right? I didn't see a sign, but the address matches what I was given."

"Who?"

"Is this McKenna Custom Coaches or not? I'm way behind schedule, so if this is just some garage . . . "

The rest of the sentence froze in her mouth as a massive length of male frame shot out from under the coach. A thin shaft of sunbeams from the windows high off the floor streaked across his face, revealing a firm, square jaw, short, narrow nose, and a day's growth of beard. Under the beard? One of the most earth-shatteringly good-looking men she'd ever seen, and she'd seen more than her share in L.A.

He continued to lie there, suspended by some sort of wheeled contraption beneath him. A white T-shirt stained with oil and other grime hugged his chest. His legs were sheathed in blue denim. "You're in the right place."

Though she was accustomed to being around Hollywood hotties, this guy, this . . . mechanic . . . was making her nervous. The sound of her tapping foot reverberated throughout the massive interior. "Where is everybody, then? Don't they keep regular business hours?"

He sat up and wiped a screwdriver on a cloth he pulled from a back pocket. "Who did you say you were?"

"Aubrey Carpenter. I just flew in from Los Angeles. They should know I'm coming."

"Not me," he returned drily. "I'm Mitch McKenna, one-third owner."

"You're . . . you're McKenna?" She couldn't keep the incredulity out of her tone. Just what she needed. A dumb hunk to work with.

"What can I do for you, Ms. Carpenter?"

"Wrong way around, Mr. McKenna. It's what I can do for you." She glanced at her surroundings. "And none too soon. Charming place you've got here. Do you build fire engines on the side?"

He let her comment slide. "Just what do you think you can do for me?"

"For your company. I'm here to finish the DiFranco motor coach."

"What did you say?"

"You're building a touring coach for Jenna DiFranco, right? According to the contract schedule and recent email reports she's received from you, it's time to finish the interior. That's my job. I'm Ms. DiFranco's decorator."

"Decorator?" Mitch McKenna shot up, causing her to take a step back despite her intent to stand her ground. He towered well over six feet. Narrowing his eyes like those of a cat, he raked his long, workmanlike fingers through his more-than-adequate sandy brown hair. "News to me."

Darn Jenna! Aubrey knew her arrival would go over like this if her sister, Jenna DiFranco, didn't grease the skids first. Remind them who was in charge. But Jenna was more than a little preoccupied these days, since her divorce had become final and she'd decided to go back on the road with her concert tour. Well, the news was out now, and Mitch McKenna could just deal.

"Since you seem to be . . . preoccupied . . . tinkering with that thing, perhaps the other owners are aware of my arrival? Is this Ms. DiFranco's bus?"

"Motor coach."

She stepped toward the coach, but he slid into her path, blocking her way.

"The coach's off limits until we get this squared away."

That tore it. Hands on hips, foot tapping yet again, she gave in to the frustration that had beset her ever since landing in this corn-infested wasteland. "I've don't have time for this. I just spent three and a half hours on a bumpy flight from L.A. and four hours on the road trying to find this burg. I don't need to justify myself to a . . . to you."

His eyes took their measure of every one of her sixty-three inches. "I think you'd better meet my partners."

Now there was progress. "Great. Go get them."

"Gray! Geoff!" His voice came out a vicious snarl. "Get out here now! We've got company." He turned back to her, his face stone.

Within seconds, a taller version of Mitch McKenna appeared. When the man saw Aubrey, he gave her the smile his brother had withheld. Turning to Mitch, he lifted a brow and said, "Company, huh?" He extended a hand. "I'm Graham McKenna. And you're . . . ?"

"This is Aubrey Carpenter," Mitch supplied. "Says she's been sent to decorate the DiFranco coach."

Clad in a short-sleeved madras shirt and khaki slacks, Graham McKenna, Gray, his brother had called him, was thin, like a runner. His arms and shoulders lacked the powerful build of his brother. "Decorate? I thought . . . ?"

"That I'd pretty much completed the job? I was just about to tell the lady she was too late," Mitch said, giving her a meaningful look.

"There seems to be a bit of a misunderstanding here, Ms. Carpenter," Graham said. "I don't know why Ms. DiFranco thought she had to send her own decorator, but you're too late. Your services aren't needed."

"Carpet's installed, wall coverings are in. Only thing left is the furniture," Mitch added, one side of his lips curled up in a smug expression.

The two men moved together as if closing ranks against her. Two against one. She was up to the task. Good thing, though, that the other person he'd summoned didn't appear to be around. Three was a bit much. "I agree there's been a misunderstanding, Mr. McKenna. But on your part. Ms. DiFranco's contract gives her the right to bring in her own decorator."

The McKennas exchanged looks. Graham raised his brows toward Mitch, Mitch shrugged.

Graham put on a smile for her again. One of those fake, get-the-customer-on-your-side smiles that didn't reach his eyes. "What would you have us do, tear out everything we've installed? Surely you see how counterproductive that would be?"

She took a step closer and squared her shoulders. "What I see is an outfit unwilling to honor its commitments."

"No! No, that's not the case at all," Graham hurried to say. He clasped his hands, as if in supplication. "But your services are sure to raise the tab, which Ms. DiFranco wouldn't want."

"That's not your call, Mr. McKenna. Ms. DiFranco should make that decision."

Graham continued to rub his hands together. "Of course, but she should have contacted us first. We would have appreciated advance notice of your arrival."

She felt heat creep up her neck. Though she had every right to be here, Jenna's forgetfulness had put her at a disadvantage. But Aubrey wasn't going to give them the upper hand. She and Jenna had too much at stake. "Perhaps she was unable to get through, given your company's rather, uh, casual approach to business?"

She pivoted, deciding that a hasty, though dramatic, retreat was in her best interest. Before they made an even bigger deal about Jenna's not informing them. "Ms. DiFranco will be in touch. I'll be back tomorrow."

She took two steps into the semi-darkness and went flying. "Ooof!" Before she could catch herself, she landed on her backside, hands splayed at her sides.

"What the . . . !" Mitch called out.

Graham bent down to check her. "Are you okay?"

She could feel moisture welling up in her eyes. *Not again!* Hadn't she been humiliated enough recently? And she'd been so close to grasping the upper hand. "What . . . what happened?" On top of the pain shooting through her fanny, she also felt something cold and sticky oozing through her slacks.

Gingerly, Graham touched the area of the floor surrounding her. Examining his hand, he said, "You slipped on some oil." He shot his brother a scowl. "Oil someone was supposed to have cleaned up by now."

Mitch stood off to the side a few feet away, taking in her predicament. He bit a lip. "Would have, too. Except I was interrupted."

"That's no excuse," Graham replied. Turning back to Aubrey, he said, "Can you stand? Let me give you a hand."

"Stay away from me!" she spit out. Once again, she asked herself why she'd agreed to come to this godforsaken place. This was the last straw, after the string of annoyances she'd experienced since she'd been here.

She checked the oil spill for herself. This area of the garage was so dark, no wonder she hadn't seen the patch of oil. She fumed at Mitch. "This is dangerous! How can you work like this?"

"Don't . . . usually."

She struggled to her knees but couldn't get a purchase on the slick surface beneath her.

Mitch sprang to action, moving swiftly to her, pulling her up by the waist. He set her upright but continued to hold on. "Anything broken? Can you stand on your own?"

He released his hold on her so she could check, but he stayed close in case she started to slip again.

Despite the pungent odor of oil irritating her nostrils, the throbbing pain in her fanny, and her embarrassment coupled with anger over this entire situation, her attention was momentarily drawn to the scent of forest coming from her rescuer. Aftershave. Earth-shaking shock waves pummeled her body at his touch. What was happening to her? Never mind. She wasn't here for fun and games. Besides giving herself a breather from the alligator pit in L.A., she was on a mission.

She sucked in air, attempting to get her brain back on track. Stretching tentatively, she rolled her shoulders and rubbed her hind parts. Wincing, she cried out. "Oooh!"

Mitch moved toward her again. "You're okay, aren't you?"

"I'll survive. But don't count on a swift recovery." She held out her palms for inspection. "And look at these!" Black muck covered them.

Mitch appropriated his brother's clean handkerchief and began wiping at her hands himself. "This'll get the worst of the gunk off," he said as he swiped away.

"Thanks. I can finish," she said, taking over. While she worked at cleaning her hands, she bit her lip, nearly biting through skin, intent on dispelling the fireworks his ministrations had set off.

Mitch backed away. "Sure." He quickly put his own hands in his pants pockets.

She scrubbed away a bit longer, then handed the soiled cloth back to Graham. She nudged the strap of her purse higher on her shoulder. "So much for fast exits. I'll try again." Scanning the floor carefully for any further obstacles, she stumbled to the door she'd entered with as much dignity as she could muster. Stopping, she looked back over her shoulder. "To repeat, I'll return tomorrow morning."

"We'll talk to you, but don't plan on sticking around," Mitch added. "We don't work with subcontractors."

Aubrey was wise enough not to push harder. She'd save that task for Jenna.

*

"Do you believe that woman?" Mitch ranted once he'd assured himself Aubrey Carpenter had left the premises. Back in his office, he paced while Gray leaned against the desk. "Shows up without a word of warning. Announces she's taking over."

Gray gave him a strange look. "Have you been ingesting gas fumes, Mitch? That was one healthy woman. I don't see any harm in her working here temporarily. We could use the help."

Did Gray know about his problem? Or suspect? "Help us? She can't even exit a room without slipping and falling down."

"Like that accident was her fault?"

Mitch raised his eyebrows. "Okay. I meant to clean up that spill, but—"

"You got involved fixing something or other on that tour bus and forgot," Gray finished for him. "You've been preoccupied ever since things went sour with Dianne."

Mitch attempted to respond to the accusation, but settled for a *hurrumph* instead.

"We'll be lucky if she doesn't sue us for mental anguish and the price of that fancy pantsuit," Gray continued, "as if we could even afford that these days. I don't get you, Mitch. You knew that oil spill was there. You could have stopped her."

That cut. "No, I couldn't. She took off in such a snit, I didn't have a chance to warn her. With that condescending attitude, she probably wouldn't have listened if I had been able to warn her." He hadn't really set her up, had he? He'd felt an immediate dislike; no, distrust . . . well, some kind of strong reaction to her, but he didn't wish her ill.

Gray settled into one of the easy chairs they'd salvaged from their parents' home and picked up a report he'd laid on Mitch's desk earlier in the day. "Have you reviewed last month's profit and loss statement yet?"

"Haven't had time. More of the same, I assumed. No profit, all loss?"

Sighing, Gray flipped the report onto the desk, his face wrinkled in concern. "You got that right. A few more months of statements like these and we'll be out of business."

"You worry too much about finances, Gray. The DiFranco project will see us through, at least for a while. Then we've got another project coming up, plus a couple prospects close to committing."

"Close isn't signed on the dotted line. This DiFranco project could still go sour, if we don't meet the deadline." He set the report down and turned to his brother. "Sure, I'm worried about our finances. But you're worried too, Mitch. About something else. And I want to know what."

"Me? Worried?" Mitch shrugged, attempting to minimize Gray's concern. "That's just my usual negative attitude. I've been a real grouch these past months."

Gray fixed him a hard gaze, as if trying to penetrate his thoughts. "Maybe. But lately there's been something else. You hardly smile. The full-blown, carefree kind, at least."

"That's crazy. Here, I'm smiling now." Mitch attempted to widen his mouth, even show some teeth, but both he and Gray knew it was a forced effort.

Gray watched him and merely shook his head in confirmation of his assessment. "You've been working night and day on that bus."

"Motor coach."

"Motor coach. You're exhausted. It shows in your moodiness. Like with this Carpenter woman. She was doing her job, and you acted like she'd launched a personal attack against you."

She'd launched an attack, all right. An assault on his senses. Eyes that sparkled like the sapphires in his mother's good earrings, especially when she was occupied giving him what for. Reddish-brown hair that from the instant she'd walked into a shaft of sunlight had looked like burnished bronze. He hadn't noticed a woman in that way in months. Too bad he planned to evict the object of his interest the next day. "Sorry, I'll try to be more chipper."

"That's not my point." Gray narrowed his eyes, a worry line etched across his brow. "Your moods I can tolerate. They're understandable, given what you've been through with your fiancée walking out on you." He paused, as if seeking just the right words. "But I don't want whatever is bothering you seeping into your work. Too many things could go wrong, especially when you're under that monster vehicle."

"Don't worry about me. I'm careful."

"So far. But if you keep driving yourself like you have, who knows? It's difficult enough helping Geoff cope with his situation. We can't risk you having problems, too."

Mitch raked a hand through his hair in frustration. He wanted so much to tell his brothers he regretted putting his law career on hold to join them in this venture. But Gray was consumed with their financial affairs. And Geoff was still dealing with his condition. They shouldn't have to deal with their younger brother's self-doubts as well. "Don't worry about me. I'll be fine," he lied.

Gray leaned in. "This Carpenter woman could be a godsend. While she works on the interior, you're freed up to do other things. Things that will get this project done well before the due date and earn us that bonus."

Gray's point was hard to rebut. Just the same, Mitch had an uneasy feeling about Aubrey Carpenter. Maybe she could help them bring the coach in on time, but did he dare risk letting her so close to his work? So far, he'd managed to fool his brothers, but he doubted he could keep his inadequacies as a decorator from her. He didn't need complications like her in his life. "Do we have to talk about this now? I need to get back to the coach."

"No, we can put off discussing how to handle this woman for a few hours. But you heard her. She'll be back tomorrow. We need to be ready to deal with her." Gray rose and started for the door. Turning back, he added, "We'll talk later. Over supper."

Mitch was headed for the door himself when his phone rang. It was Orville Drummond's secretary asking if he could see her boss later that afternoon. What did Orville want? Mitch had closed that door three years prior and vowed not to reopen the subject until they got the business in the black.

Reluctantly, out of loyalty and for old time's sake, he agreed to the meeting. He'd lost enough time dealing with Aubrey Carpenter. Now he'd lose more to this appointment.

*

"I don't care about your costumes arriving in the wrong color, Jenna. You said you'd call these guys and let them know I was coming." Aubrey leaned back in the chaise lounge on the patio of the bed and breakfast she'd found for the duration of her stay. Her stained pantsuit now residing in the owner's trash barrel, she sank into the floral chintz cushion and sipped lemonade. She was cooler in the cotton short set, though her backside still ached.

"I tried, Aubrey. Really. But no one answered the first few times, and then, once my boxes arrived, I forgot. Can you imagine? They sent me, me, a perfect winter, tangerine and lime green!"

Aubrey breathed in deeply and exhaled slowly, her time-tested technique for dealing with Jenna. "Did you contact your costumer? Maybe he got the order wrong?"

"Of course, I called him. As soon as I examined the monstrosities he sent me."

"And?"

"And what?"

"What did he have to say about sending the wrong colors?"

"Mr. Helen apologized profusely. Then he checked his database. Can you imagine? Mr. Helen has discovered the computer. Amazing! Anyway, he checked his records and discovered my gowns had been shipped elsewhere. And I got Reba's."

Aubrey had to smile. Jenna had never met the great country

star but considered herself a sister under the skin because they'd both been on the road. Of course, Jenna was a concert pianist, not a country singer, but she glossed over that discrepancy. "So all is well with the tour?" She held her breath. There were usually ten things going wrong for Jenna for every one that went right.

"I guess. It doesn't come together until just a few hours before we take off."

"My point exactly. Your tour is going nowhere, Jenna, if your motor coach isn't ready."

"Not ready? That coach has to be finished one month from today. They assured me they could meet the deadline with no problems. If they want that bonus for early completion, they'd better come through."

"I know, Jenna. I told you when I agreed to this crazy assignment I had to start working on the interior as soon as I arrived if I was going to meet your deadline. And I needed absolute cooperation from these country bumpkins."

"Aubrey! The McKennas are anything but country bumpkins! Graham is a master designer. He's been written up in numerous trade journals, at least so he said. I'd kill to have Geoff on the road with me as my PR man. And Mitch knows every nook and cranny of that bus."

"That may be, but so far, my experience with them has not been amicable."

"Didn't you even try to get along with them?"

A pesky bee flitted around the glass of lemonade setting on the patio table. Aubrey waved her hand to discourage the insect from its course. "Why do you assume I'm the one who got miffed?"

"For starters, you didn't want to be there. Though you jumped at the chance to get out of L.A., we both know your feelings about the Midwest, especially Iowa. But don't knock the place, just because Mother has always bad-mouthed her hometown. She wasn't made for Iowa winters." Their mother, Iris Appleby, now lived with her third husband in Santa Barbara, but she'd grown up in the Midwest hating her surroundings and wanting more for, first herself, and after she'd become a mother, for Jenna as well. Aubrey had come along in the Hollywood, second-husband phase of her mother's checkered past. "Our mother wasn't made for a lot of things, but she was right about this place, Jen. Blah, boring and uninteresting."

"So you walked in there with a chip on your shoulder?"

"I didn't need to. Mitch McKenna already cornered the market on those."

"Mitch? He's usually the most reasonable one."

"Not today." She related the incident with the oil spill while guarding her drink from the bee, flicking her hand every so often.

"You don't think he meant you harm, do you?"

"No, he's mulish but not malicious."

"Well, take care of yourself from here on."

Like she needed her sister's counsel to know that. "Oh, I intend to."

There was no point continuing to press Jenna about calling the McKennas. She'd either remember or forget. "How's Paige? Still locked in her room?"

"No way! Her counselor advised me to humor these moods but not give in to them. She's not a happy camper, but she's going to classes every day."

"Classes? I thought school was out for the summer?"

"Summer school. She needs to stay occupied and keep her mind off this divorce. She wanted to go with her father to the East Coast, but I wanted her here with me as long as I was home."

Poor Paige. What fourteen-year-old only child wanted to see her world turned upside down by her parents? Jenna should be more tolerant; she'd been through the same thing with Aubrey's father and their mother. Aubrey regretted taking off and leaving her niece to fend for herself. But sticking around hadn't seemed like a very good idea. Jenna wanted her in Iowa and people in L.A. wanted her hide.

She'd have to deal with that last part soon. The world had grown smaller since the Internet and the cell phone. It wouldn't take long for them to catch up with her.

*

Though Mitch had been told he could go into Orville's office, he knocked just the same, in deference to his friend. Hearing a muted "come in," he opened the door and stood on the threshold, remembering. He hadn't been here in months. The memory cut too deep.

Orville sat behind his mammoth desk, head bent over some contract or brief. Behind him, sunlight streamed through the windows, revealing how the man's hair had thinned on top. He glanced up and smiled that smile that had tempered Mitch's anger more than once over the years. "Mitch! Thanks for coming. Have a seat."

Mitch did as requested and waited. His eyes focused on a pen lying on Orville's desk so that he wouldn't have to stare at the man nor eye anything else in the room. He didn't want to see law books, or blue-backed briefs, or legal pads. They brought back painful reminders of what he'd given up. Some might say *sacrificed*. He wouldn't go that far. His decision to give up the law had been his decision and his decision alone.

"How are you doing, son?" the old man asked. "And your brothers? Still building those fancy buses?"

"Motor coaches."

Drummond gave him a tolerant smile. "You always were a stickler for specificity."

Mitch shrugged and wondered where this was going and how soon they'd arrive. "We're finishing up our biggest project to date. For a pianist from Los Angeles who's going on tour."

"That's wonderful. The business seems to be growing faster

than I thought possible."

"Yeah, well, we've gotta finish this one first. Then we'll see. We're hoping this client will send more clients our way, providing she's happy with how her coach turns out."

"And why wouldn't she be? You fellas do good work."

If only he knew. But Mitch wasn't here to talk about his problems. Not even to his old friend. No one could know.

Drummond rose to look out his windows. Returning his attention to Mitch, he said, "I have a proposal for you. That's why I asked you to stop by today."

Mitch settled back in his chair, continuing to wait.

"My doctor tells me I have to slow down. Blood pressure is kicking up again."

Mitch rose from his seat. "Sorry to hear that. Will you need surgery?"

The older man shook his head, a look of disgust sweeping his face. "No. It's worse. I need to modify my diet, exercise more, and cut back on work." He sat and indicated Mitch should also. "That's where you come in, boy. How'd you like to take up the slack?"

Mitch's ears began to ring and his heart felt like it was pumping triple time. Had he heard correctly? "What did you say, Orville?" With a start, he realized he was grinning foolishly.

"I've never taken on a partner. Didn't feel I could get on with someone day after day. But you and I got along just fine when you clerked here. We agreed on the basic tenets of the law." He rose again, coming around to where Mitch sat. He placed a hand on Mitch's shoulder. "I trust you, boy. Eventually, I'd like to turn the firm over to you."

Mitch tried to breathe. Ever since he'd worked for Orville years before, this was what he wanted. To be part of a small firm, his own firm, someday. And now his old friend had placed the possibility in his lap. It was too much to take in.

"Mitch? Are you interested?" Though Orville's voice remained firm, calm, it was tinged with a bit of impatience.

Mitch blew out a breath. Tried to gather his thoughts. And in so doing, reality sank in. His shoulders slumped. "Orville, I can't tell you how much this offer means to me. You've been my role model. My mentor. I admire the type of law you practice."

The other man settled onto the desk. "Thanks. Your admiration does my heart good. Do we have a deal?"

Mitch shook his head. "I can't take you up on it, Orville. I've invested every penny in McKenna Custom Coaches. I can't afford to buy into your firm, let alone buy you out."

Drummond put up a hand. "I know that. If you recall, I'm the one who filed the partnership agreement you boys drew up. What I had in mind was a trade, of sorts. You put in time for me each week, and you earn a small piece of the business. I'm not planning to retire outright. Too much fun to give up all at once. So we let that small piece gather interest and grow. When I'm ready to quit entirely, you should have enough equity built up to buy me out."

Mitch had to smile. "You've already put pencil to paper on this one, haven't you?"

Drummond didn't deny it. "You've had to struggle financially the last few years, getting that business up and running. And we both know why you did it. I don't agree with your decision, but I certainly understand the brotherly concern that brought you to make it. But here's a way you can ease out of it, gradually, and get back to what you really want to do."

Mitch tried to speak, but his mouth was cotton. Orville's offer was overly generous, just like the man himself. But he knew, deep down, he couldn't accept. He had to immediately douse any fantasies that might have sprung up in his heart in response to the proposal. Because there was no way he could say yes. He'd promised Gray he'd always be there for Geoff.

He rose and started for the door. He had to get out of there before temptation overcame him. "I can't Orville. I just can't."

"But . . . if it's the financing, I told you, I figured out a mutually beneficial funding scheme. It'll work."

"Thanks for thinking of me. And for your faith in me. But I can't leave the guys. Not now. Not for some time. If ever."

Drummond followed him to the door. "Think about my offer. Talk to the guys about it. They'll understand."

The guys couldn't know about it. "This is my decision alone. Please, don't mention your offer to anyone else."

Drummond stared at him a moment, as if trying to come to grips with Mitch's refusal. "Don't say no today, Mitch. Give my offer some thought."

Mitch stood for several minutes in the corridor outside Orville's office, ostensibly reading a plaque on the wall. He wanted to run out of the building as fast as he could escape, but his legs had gone leaden. Perspiration streamed down his face even in air conditioning.

He couldn't let himself even think about it. He'd crossed that bridge three years ago. Put his dreams of the law out of his mind. Well, at least hidden away in the recesses of his mind. He didn't dare consider it. He couldn't leave the guys. They needed him.

That need—and brotherly love—was breaking his heart.

CHAPTER TWO

Mitch had barely returned to his office when Gray stuck his head in the door. "Done for the day? How about a little libation? It's time you gave yourself some time off."

"Huh? Okay, sure." Did he sound as disoriented as he felt? Orville's offer still had his head ringing.

The two made their way to their second floor quarters. Gray opened the fridge and took out a couple beers. He offered a cold one to his younger sibling. "Here. Start with this."

Though Mitch accepted the can and pulled a draw, he hardly noticed he was drinking. He tried not to think about the events of the last hour. If Gray picked up on his distraction, he wouldn't quit until he knew all the details.

Gray scavenged a can of peanuts and bag of chips, then flopped into the chair next to him. "Thought any more about our visitor from California?"

Mitch cocked his head and frowned. "That again?"

"We've only got tonight to decide how we're going to handle her."

"Other than sending her back to the West Coast?" Though the idea had certain appeal, it was probably out of the question. "Think of the havoc she'll wreak."

"What's the worst that could come of her being here?"

"We don't do business that way."

"We haven't so far," Gray conceded. "But what would be so awful if we did?"

"She'll slow us down. We won't meet our completion date, then we'll lose the bonus money and have to pay that penalty Jenna DiFranco insisted on." A new idea hit. "Maybe she sent this Carpenter woman here for that express purpose?"

Gray's words finally sank in. "Plan? What do you mean?"

Gray got up and joined him at the sink. "We probably can't stop her. But we can play hardball negotiating her work arrangements."

Mitch mulled the idea. It had its merits. And Gray was right. In the end, they wouldn't be able to prevent her from staying. So they might as well paint her into as much of a corner as they could before she prevailed. "What did you have in mind?"

Gray scratched his head. "Let me think." He thrummed his fingers on the countertop. "For starters, we establish ground rules." He smiled crookedly as if warming to the idea. "Good plan, even if it is my own. For instance, she can only be here certain hours of the day. We'll figure out when later."

"You mean like between two and six in the morning?"

Gray chuckled. "Not bad, bro, but I don't think so. We've got to have a logical business reason for everything we get her to agree to. At least appear to have one."

Mitch opened the dishwasher and placed the dirty plate inside. "How 'bout she has to use her own cell to make all her business calls?"

"I'm sure she has one. I think it's now a state law in California."

"Charge her rent?" He was only half serious, but this was the most fun he'd had all day.

His brother grinned. "For this place? She should be charging us to enter it." He continued to stand there, the lines of his face creased in thought. "Try this on for size. Someone has to be with her the entire time she's inside the motor coach."

Mitch slapped his brother on the back. "That's brilliant! We'll be underfoot so much, she'll finish her business in no time just to get away from us."

"I do have my days. Hungry?"

"Just had a sandwich. And two beers."

"Got room for pizza? I say we celebrate and think up some more conditions for our little arrangement."

What the hell? It was the end of the day. He'd run an extra mile in the morning.

They were almost at the door when the phone rang.

"Should I?" Gray asked.

"Can't avoid her forever."

He rejoined Mitch a few minutes later. "As anticipated, that was Jenna DiFranco. Consider ourselves properly reminded of our contractual obligations. Ms. Aubrey Carpenter is to begin her work here tomorrow morning."

*

The next morning, Graham ushered a vindicated Aubrey to Mitch's office.

Whoa! She was expecting an office, not a man cave. The room was huge, twenty by twenty, she estimated. And filled with exercise equipment, a foosball table, a dart game and two leather couches. Did the guy ever work?

"Ms. Carpenter," was all Mitch McKenna said from the other side of the room. The sight of him was enough to charge her insides. The denim jeans and T-shirt had been replaced today with a soft yellow knit shirt and khakis. He did clean up well.

He was seated on the side of the room that resembled an office. At least there was a desk, of sorts. More like a long table with another long table behind loaded down with computer equipment. Mitch was stretched out in an office chair behind the table, his feet up. He made no effort to rise.

Another man stood at one end of the desk. Shorter and blonder than Mitch and Graham, he had the same yellow-green eyes as Mitch, set wider apart. Smiling broadly, he said, "Ms. Carpenter. I'm sorry I missed you yesterday. I understand you had a slight accident."

Though she extended her hand, she wasn't ready to be gracious. "Perhaps if you'd been here, my best pantsuit would still be part of my wardrobe."

The man winced, as if she'd socked him. It was then that she noticed the cane.

"I'm Geoffrey McKenna; Geoff, the middle brother," he said, recovering and shaking her hand. "I've spent my life keeping these two out of trouble, but yesterday got by me. Have a seat, won't you? We have a few ideas we'd like to run by you."

This was more like it. Jenna must have really come down hard on them. She sat in the chair Graham offered. "Ideas? Not really necessary. That's why I'm here."

"Oh, we know," Graham said, settling himself against the other side of the desk. "But since you're not familiar with Iowa or this business, we thought a little structure would help you settle in."

Structure? What were they up to? She inched her spine higher. *Be gracious, girl.* She widened her mouth into a smile, jaw muscles that she didn't know existed clenching. Nothing was more disarming to a group of men than a woman who could smile while she cut the floor out from under them. "Structure. Tell me more."

"We're working on a finely tuned completion schedule here," Geoff McKenna said.

"The vehicle has to be in L.A. ready to go on July 22," Graham added. "That gives us six weeks to do everything, including test driving and delivering it. That allows you no more than four weeks, starting now, to finish your part. Were you aware of those deadlines?"

Was she aware of them? If they only knew what she'd been hammering out on her computer at two this morning. The timeline was so tight, her work was almost planned down to the hour. She lifted her eyes to Graham McKenna's. "Yes, I was. And I'm prepared to meet them." She thought to add, "With suitable working arrangements."

"Our point exactly," Mitch said. His nostrils flared just the slightest, reminding her of a race horse itching to hit the track. A stallion. A sleek, sandy thoroughbred.

"Fine. Why don't you tell me what you have in mind, and we'll see how *your* ideas play into *my* plans."

The three exchanged glances. Guilty ones. Her skin prickled. Something was definitely going down here, and probably not to her liking. She had to be on guard.

Good thing she was, too. For the next half hour, they negotiated about every possible action she might take while working under their roof. When she could be there, how long she could work, no music, no hotplates—like she ever cooked—and no shorts or tank tops. She shook her head, said "No" more than once, and actually snorted on one item. She saw through their machinations and wasn't going to let them snow her.

Finally, her tolerance exhausted, she asked, "How many items are left on that list?" The three men went into a huddle and compared notes.

"I think we're done," Graham said at last. He read off the lengthy list of conditions.

"And, you can have access to the vehicle at hours other than what we've agreed to, with our advance approval," Geoff added. He looked at his brothers. "Anything else, guys?"

The other two shook their heads and started putting their notes away.

Aubrey waited a beat and then unzipped her leather carryall and removed a folder. "Now, I have a few ideas of my own I'd like to discuss."

Already standing in anticipation of her departure, Mitch said, "What?"

"My list," she said innocently. "I've been patient and flexible about your stipulations. But I have a few concerns of my own to discuss. Starting with my office."

"Office?" all three men replied, once again exchanging looks.

She was hoping for that effect. "Yes. I don't need much space, but I do need a place to work on my laptop, make private phone calls, and store my files." With a sweep of her hand, she said,

"Surely you can spare me a few extra square feet?"

Geoff raised his brows, Graham shrugged, and Mitch emitted a sound like a low growl.

After a bit, in a sort of last resort tone, Mitch said, "I guess . . . we could put her in the accountant's office?"

"The what?" Geoff replied.

"You know? The room on the other side of the building?"

"There are just storerooms over there," Graham said. "And the . . . " He shut his mouth, cocked his head, and turned toward his brother so Aubrey couldn't see the exchange. "Right! The *accountant's* room. That's a great idea."

"Okay, that's settled," Mitch announced. "Anything else?"

"My environment has to be safe and efficient. No more slipping on oil spills because someone forgot to mop them up," she shot a glance at Mitch, "and because it's too dark in the garage."

The men looked at each other and shrugged.

"Okay," Graham agreed, "whatever."

"Good," she said. "One last point. Some days, I'll need to be here twenty-four/seven. I'll need a place to sleep at those times. I don't want to be traveling back and forth between here and my lodging in the wee hours of the morning."

Mitch was out of his chair again. "You want to stay here . . . overnight? You do know we live here, don't you?"

"No, I didn't. But I don't think that would be a problem."

"*You* don't think it'll be a problem. Well, what a relief. Wouldn't want *you* to be troubled about *our* living arrangements." Mitch nearly snarled the words.

"I don't need a fully functional bedroom. Just a private place to catch a few hours' sleep. Maybe I could use the accountant's office?"

"Uh . . . " Geoff mumbled. "Not a good idea."

"Surely you could find a cot or air mattress to put in there?" she asked.

"The room's not very large. And the bathroom, uh, is way across the building, over here by our offices," Graham said, tapping his fingers on the desk.

"No shower or bathtub," Geoff added. "At least down here."

She lifted a brow. "But there's one somewhere in the building?"

Mitch raked a hand through his hair. "Well, yeah. I have one and so does Graham. But those are our private quarters."

Why were they having so much difficulty with this? Most of the men she worked with would have offered up their own beds, let alone showers, for a woman. She gave them a perplexed look. Who could possibly resist her request for a bed and shower? She even batted her eyelashes once, twice.

"Ah, for Pete's sake, guys," Graham said, "this isn't such a big deal. We'll find an air mattress and you can use my shower whenever you need one."

"Thanks," she smiled at him, feeling in control once again.

He merely nodded, not looking at either brother.

Mitch stood, hands on his hips. "That the end of your list? We're running out of time and patience," he said, repeating her words.

Poor thing. You know you've been bested, but you're not about to admit it. She closed the folder she'd been perusing and stuck it back in her bag. Wouldn't do for them to know she'd been using her grocery list as her source of improvised demands.

*

Geoff drew the short straw, so had to show Aubrey her *office*. Mitch and Gray waited until they could hear the two of them on the other side of the building before reacting to the meeting just ended. "What just went on here?" Gray asked.

Mitch sank into his desk chair and rubbed his temples. "Checkmate. The lady didn't like our rules. She retaliated by making up some of her own."

"You mean she never intended to make those demands until

our lists came out?"

"I suspect." Mitch rose and closed the door before continuing. "She's quick. When she saw our hand, she played along, gave in a little here, held out a little there. Then she threw in the whammy."

Gray stood and put his hands in his pants pockets. "Whammy? Explain."

"Think about it. Besides what we did to ourselves, tying ourselves down so one of us has to be here whenever she's in the coach, we also agreed to give her free office space, access to our office equipment, and free lodging whenever she wants. Including use of our bathrooms."

"Well . . ." Gray blew out a puff of air.

"Remember the game plan, bro? Pin her down with our rules? Discourage her with all the limitations we were going to place on her?"

"Right. So?"

"She turned the tables on us."

Gray peeked out the door. "At least we stuck her with an unworkable office. That was brilliant, by the way. Since I'm the accountant, who also does the laundry. I can't wait to hear her reaction to being cooped up in that tiny, poorly ventilated room with the washer and dryer going at the same time."

"Should be any minute now," Mitch predicted. "Though I bet she avoids a direct frontal attack. She won't admit to being had. She'll wait until she finds some small way to get back at us and then we'll live to regret our cunning."

Gray turned to his brother. "She's really got you cowed. Where's your spirit, man?"

That's what Mitch wondered. He played back the last forty-five minutes in his head. At some point during that time, his brain had apparently checked out. She'd countered every move and initiated twice as many of her own. She was smart, which meant she'd be on to him in no time. He searched his desk drawer for antacid tablets.

"So now what do we do?" Gray wondered out loud.

"Our work, of course. Jenna DiFranco has made sure we have no other option."

Mitch pulled his car keys out of his pocket and started for the door.

"Where are you going?" A note of horror crept into Gray's voice. "You're not leaving us alone with her?"

"Gotta check on the parts for the coolant system." Mitch had already decided how he personally was going to handle this Carpenter woman: keep his distance. Let Gray and Geoff babysit her. If he wasn't around much, maybe she wouldn't pick up on his secret.

Gray shot in front of him just as Mitch arrived at the door. "I don't think so. No sneaking out for you. We're all in this together."

He was losing his touch. He was usually two steps ahead of Gray. A survival skill he'd honed to a fine art form growing up the youngest of three boys.

"C'mon, Gray. You don't need me here all day. If we don't get that unit up and working, it'll be an inferno inside that . . . " He broke off as the thought sank in.

"What?"

Backing away a few steps from his brother, Mitch asked, "Was there anything in our agreement requiring us to provide a comfortable environment for her to work in?"

"Comfortable . . . ? No. She said *safe and efficient*." A broad smile slid across Gray's face. "You wouldn't?"

"I figure it's good for about a day before she hits the fan . . . literally."

"She's not going to like this."

"And your point is?"

"Okay. You won't get much of an argument from me."

Mitch retraced his steps to his desk and settled back into his chair. "I have paperwork to complete. I'll be holed up in here the rest of the day."

Shaking his head, his brother chuckled. "That tactic will work for a while. But Geoff has to get back to the doctor's office this afternoon. And I told him I'd go with him. That leaves you in charge of our guest."

When Mitch groaned, Gray added, "My guess is, she'll spend the better part of the day getting to know the inside of that bus. According to our ground rules, you'll be joining her."

"Geez!"

"In the heat," Gray said just before he escaped out the door.

*

Aubrey examined her new office. She'd suspected the trio was up to something, but she never imagined they would put her in their laundry room. But there was no way she would let them know they'd gotten the better of her.

"It's sort of a utility room," Geoff explained blandly. "There's a little bit of everything in here." He quickly added, "But I'm sure we can fit you in."

"What does a business that customizes motor coaches need with a washer and dryer?"

Geoff leaned against the dryer. "Actually, these appliances go with the two apartments upstairs. There's no room up there."

"You mean this is where you do your personal laundry?" She tried to keep her tone light and her amazement out of it.

"Uh, yeah." Geoff gave an embarrassed chuckle. "But don't worry. While you're here, we'll juggle our laundry hours with your schedule."

What could she say? He seemed ready to compromise. She'd have to do likewise, at least until she figured out how to work these arrangements to her advantage.

Geoff headed for the door. "I've got to get going. If you're ready to see the insides of the bus, I'll get Mitch to let you in."

Mitch? Why did he have to be involved in this? Geoff was so much nicer to deal with. "Yes, I'm anxious to see the interior. Are you sure you can't stay?"

He held out his cane. "I've been having to rely on this more frequently of late, which isn't good. Gotta see a doctor about some blood tests. I have MS."

Multiple sclerosis. That explained some things. "Oh. I didn't realize. How . . . how long have you had it?"

"Probably since my early twenties, but they actually diagnosed the condition three years ago. It's progressive, but they don't know how far or how fast I'll deteriorate."

"I see."

His face went slightly red. "Since you're going to be part of the family for a while, so to speak, I thought you should know. You won't have to perform first aid or anything. My hovering brothers claim that honor."

"Thank you for telling me." She recalled something from his earlier statement. "You said there were two apartments upstairs. You don't live here?"

"No. I live about ten minutes away. There's not enough room for the three of us up there, and . . . sometimes I have difficulty getting up and down the stairs."

"Oh." The one who'd been most friendly to her so far would be here the least. Not good news.

*

When Mitch arrived ten minutes later, he found her engrossed in setting up her headquarters. Laundry baskets were stacked on top of the two appliances. That had freed up a space where she'd placed a card table. Where had that come from? She'd also located a cushion somewhere, wrapping it in her shawl. It looked pretty spiffy. Well, she was a decorator.

"Follow me, if you want to see the coach." He was being curt, but this was the best he could do. The sooner he got through this, the better. He still hoped to dissuade her from doing this job.

She looked up from her laptop and smiled. "Okay. Let me grab my notebook."

He headed off, deliberately leaving her behind. His conscience pricked him, but that was minor. He'd get over it. He wasn't giving an inch more until she realized who was in charge.

He waited for her by the open door at the front of the motor coach.

"There you are," she said, catching up.

"Since we didn't know you were coming, we finished off what we could. To the eyes of the uninitiated, the interior is ready to roll."

"Really?"

He reached inside and flipped on lights. In a momentary return of conscience, he offered her his hand and helped her up the two steps leading to the door.

The interior of the X-100 had been finished in a tan-colored fiber wallpaper. The fiber helped the acoustics. The flooring was a low-rise coffee brown berber. Throughout there were accents of brass hardware. Very basic, very utilitarian. Very dull. He held his breath, hoping the impossible, that she'd like what he'd done and build on that.

"What do you think?" He tried to keep his expression noncommittal.

She chewed a lip. "I'd like to see the rest."

Glutton for punishment. "This way." He moved off toward the two rooms in the back, a spacious bedroom and private bath. The bedroom looked larger than it actually was, thanks to the floor-to-ceiling mirrors on the walls. One of his ideas.

"Whoa!" She pulled back immediately upon noticing them. "These have to go."

"They make it look bigger. We do this a lot with this model."

"Not this particular model. Jenna's avoiding mirrors these days."

Their client was certainly a strange one. "Superstitious?"

"No, recently divorced. Her husband didn't leave her for another woman, but he found a replacement before the ink was dry on the decree."

That he understood. Shades of Dianne.

Aubrey moved around the room opening doors, flipping on lights, peeking out the windows. She disappeared for a few minutes to check out the private bath. "Not bad for a movable spa," she said, returning. "We'll keep the tub and shower unit."

"Keep them?" He was now almost shouting. "Of course, you'll keep them. Replacing them at this time would be a real pain."

She fixed him with an ingenuous gaze. "I said, we'd keep them." Sliding past him, she headed back to the front. "Missed some features out here."

He followed her, finding a spot by the kitchen counter to lean on. He wasn't about to leave her to her own devices, even for a minute. "Aren't you going to take notes?"

She turned her head his direction, giving him a wisp of a smile. "I'll do that on the next pass through. Right now, I want to get a feel for the place."

"Ah." This was going to take longer than he planned. Folding his arms across his chest, he settled in for a spell.

"If you have something to do in your office, I'll be fine here." *I'm sure you will, lady.* "That's okay. Take your time."

"At least get some coffee or a soft drink. You must be terribly bored."

That he was. But she wasn't shaking him loose that easy. She'd have to be more inventive. He waited for the inevitable putdown of his decorating efforts. "I'm fine. Go ahead with your routine. I'll practice my Zen."

"Suit yourself." She swiped a hand across her forehead. "It's warm in here." She removed the light pink summer sweater she wore with her khakis, revealing a white knit tee.

Now it was his turn to stare, though he tried not to. He attempted to focus his eyes on the wall across the room. When that didn't work, he examined his hands.

Unbidden, his gaze kept returning to the knit top that hugged her chest. And the back of her khakis when she bent over. *Clean up the act, McKenna.* So he took in her hair, brownish with a tinge of red, cut smooth around the shoulders. It framed an elegant column of neck, the kind of place where a man's hot breath and kisses could linger for hours.

Without warning, she lay down on the carpet, fixing her sight on the ceiling light above.

He jerked upright. "You okay?"

She rolled her eyes. "Relax, Bus Man. I want to see the place from every possible angle."

Bus Man? "It's not a . . . "

She raised her brows.

"Never mind."

"I don't usually let anyone else in on my floor show. Don't mind my gyrations."

Mind? "Have no fear," he bluffed. "Just curious."

Her acrobatics went on for another twenty minutes. She pulled at the collar of her tee. "Whew. That must have been more strenuous than usual. I'm perspiring like crazy."

He ignored the bead of sweat that rolled down his own neck. "Maybe you should call it a day?" His question held just a tad too much enthusiasm.

"I'd like to, but can't. Too many details yet to record."

While she was preoccupied in the kitchenette area, he checked the inside temp on the controls. Seventy-eight degrees. Still bearable. When it got to eighty, he'd stop things for the day.

She rubbed the back of her neck. "You sure you're not warm? I'm burning up." She scanned the walls. When she spied the environmental system, she charged over to it. "Seventy-nine! Is the air even on?"

"The blower is. Not the AC." He'd been waiting for over half an hour to say that. It felt good even though the heat was starting to get to him, too.

She was in front of him in a flash. "There's no air conditioning in here? Do you wait until some magic number, like frying-eggs-hot, to turn it on?"

"Still need a part for the coolant system before the air will kick in. It's on order."

"And you didn't bother to mention that detail because . . . ?"

"You wanted to see the interior today, come hell or high water. The former won."

She grabbed for her sweater. "Like I need this." She stomped off, if that was possible to do inside a motor coach. "I'll be in my office. Cooling off."

He certainly hoped so. Or did he?

*

Aubrey settled on top of the clothes dryer and went into her breathing exercises. In-two-three, out-two-three, and so on. She'd encountered the Iowa version of the Three Stooges. She could almost picture them exchanging elbow nudges back in Mitch's office. "Nyuk-nyuk! Got her good with that heat business, guys. You shoulda seen her sweat! Nyuk-nyuk."

She . . . in-two-three . . . wasn't . . . out-two-three . . . going to let them . . . in-two-three . . . get the best of her . . . out-two-three. She could mix it up with the best jokers L.A. had to offer. She wasn't afraid of going head-to-head with these guys. As the opposing team, she'd wisely called a time out after the opening salvo from the home team. Now she needed a new strategy.

Think, Aubrey. Play to your strengths. Well, she had connections. She just had to work them. Although, that might be a bit of a challenge at the moment, since she was supposed to be lying low in her Midwestern hideaway. For the thousandth time, she asked herself what had possessed her to agree to transforming Heidi Buxbaum's cabin in the woods into a Louis XIV getaway. How was she supposed to know the place really belonged to Heidi's estranged husband, Cyril?

Okay, she should have checked it out. Especially in L.A. One never knew who had possession of what from day to day. But she'd been intent on making a deal on those antiques so she could establish an in with the dealer. So Mr. Macho didn't like Louis XIV.

Couldn't think of that now. A few weeks here in Hicksville and all would be forgotten. She could go home.

She pulled out her cell and began punching in numbers. She was glad her mother had no idea where she was or what she was up to. The last thing the woman needed to know was that her younger daughter's current office was a laundry room. The points she'd scored for establishing an upscale L.A. clientele would go down the tube quicker than her mother's mercurial moods.

CHAPTER THREE

The next morning, as Aubrey unpacked the last box in her office, door ajar, she heard a minor explosion in the garage that sounded like, "What's this?" Someone had found her first *improvement*. She hoped it was Mitch. It would be wasted on the other two.

She got her wish. Mitch was at her door immediately, a small stick in his hand. It was one of the several reflector poles she'd placed throughout the garage. "This is your doing, isn't it?"

"Uh-huh. As soon as you thank me for my resourcefulness, you can return it to where you found it. Just push down on the suction cup on the bottom."

He held it out to her while he continued to eye her skeptically. "What's it for?"

"My safety. I don't want to skate over any more grease spots. Yesterday, I did a little walk-through and mapped out this temple of doom."

"Temple of . . . ? Very funny. We don't need these." He threw the pole onto the washer. "I'll turn the overhead lights up higher and you'll be perfectly safe."

He was almost out the door when she called out, "Just a minute, Mr. McKenna!"

He stopped but didn't turn around. He seemed to be gathering his patience. "Yes?"

"I have every right to preserve my safety. It's part of our agreement."

"Part of . . . ? You mean that list of demands you came in with yesterday?"

"I mean the few concerns I brought to your attention after you and your brothers bombarded me with your rules."

"Good morning," Graham said, arriving at that moment. "I found this out on the floor. What a great idea! This little reflector flag glows in the dark to mark the hazards. Did you install these, Mitch?"

Mitch blew out a puff of air. "No! I did not. You can thank Miss Fix-it here."

"You brought these in, Aubrey?" Graham asked, a note of amazement creeping into his tone. When she nodded, he said, "Thanks. We should have better lighting in here, but . . . "

"I meant to speak to you about that," she interrupted. "The reflector poles are temporary. I have portable lights arriving in a few days. They'll be here while I'm here."

"Portable lights?" Graham's voice rose.

"Great idea, huh, bro?" Mitch cut in sarcastically.

"But Aubrey, we cut back on the overhead lights to offset our electric bill."

"Yes, I know that, Graham. I checked out your lighting yesterday when I was locating the hot spots on the floor. By not using it frequently, it's become old and dilapidated. I wasn't sure what you'd want to do about that, so I only took care of it temporarily."

Mitch shot a look at his brother. "Did you hear that, Graham? She only took care of it . . . temporarily." His voice held an edge.

Graham didn't answer. He was spluttering.

Mitch took in her handiwork in the laundry room. A bright blue bi-fold screen cut off the view of the two appliances. A green and blue rag rug, thrown at an angle, hugged the floor. Yesterday's card table had been replaced with a honey oak portable writing table. More computer equipment, including a fax and copy machine, lined the other wall.

He spun around slowly in the center of the room. "Lady, I've got to hand it to you. When you get busy, you kick up a dust storm. Did you sleep at all last night?"

"I slept quite well."

"When?" Graham asked from the back corner, examining a huge pot of geraniums she'd stuck there. "It had to take an hour or so just lugging all this in."

She smiled proudly. "While I was touring the place yesterday, I found a dolly and a cart in a storage closet. They made the job easier."

Mitch ambled over to her new desk and ran a hand along the edge. "Nice." Turning back to her, he said, "You don't let much get to you, do you?"

Startled by his candor, she blinked and replied, "There's always a way to make things better. So I did. That's all."

The two men headed for the door. Mitch pivoted, as if a new idea had just hit. "This is it, right? We've seen all of your handiwork?"

She gave him a smug smile. "Most of it, yes. I also cooled down the motor coach. I can't work in those conditions. And I've got a lot of work to do today."

Mitch narrowed his brows. "How'd you do that? I still have to . . ." His voice trailed off.

"You still have to install the part for the compressor?"

"How'd—how'd you know about that?"

"I called a local supplier to ask what might be wrong. As soon as he realized I was talking about the custom job here, he asked if you were ever going to pick up your part."

"I guess it slipped my mind. I'll get right on it."

"Take your time," Aubrey called to their disappearing backs. "I'm doing just fine . . . today."

*

Between their respective offices, a small area, formerly a storage closet, served as their break room. Mitch opened the thirty-year-old fridge and pulled out a bottle of water. Gray poured himself a cup of coffee. "She's good, Mitch. She hasn't painted a wall or put up one picture yet, but she's managed to best us at every turn."

Mitch shook his head, overwhelmed by her ingenuity. "It's like she made up a list of complaints and then fixed them, item by item."

"Pretty sharp."

"Pretty scary."

Gray tore open a packet of sweetener and shook the contents into his coffee. "The only scary thing about her is that she's got you scared. You can't figure her out." He placed a brotherly hand on Mitch's shoulder. "And that bugs you."

Mitch swung away. "In three days she's managed to tinker with everything in her path."

"Including you?"

"Me? Of course not!"

"You've been breathing fire ever since she arrived. You'd think Jenna DiFranco's decision to bring in her own designer was a personal affront to your ability to pull off this job."

"I . . . " Mitch slammed his bottle of water on the counter. "Stop playing psychoanalyst. I haven't liked her attitude. Bursting in here thinking we'd drop everything. Just for the privilege of having a real L.A. professional on the premises."

He took another swig while he considered how to get Gray off this topic. His brother was getting too close to home.

"She thought we knew she was coming. Can you blame her for being a little testy?"

"Don't you find her condescending attitude a pain?"

"Condescending? She's really got you spooked, hasn't she? Just because she found a way to light up the place and cool down the bus—coach—doesn't mean she's rubbing her inventiveness in your nose."

Mitch decided to let it drop. She obviously had Gray snowed.

"You know, we should have her over for dinner. She must be getting lonely."

"Lonely? When's she had time?"

"C'mon, Mitch. Give the hostility a rest. I'm going to ask her for tonight. I'll even cook."

"Tuna casserole again?" Mitch let down his guard long enough to goad his brother. Gray's cooking abilities were limited to taking out and heating up.

Gray groaned. "No. I'll surprise you. Just curb that tongue."

"I get the message. I'd be a lot more charming if you'd help me babysit her today."

"No can do," Gray replied, on his way out. "Got appointments 'til four."

"Must be pedicure day," Mitch speculated, once his brother was out of hearing.

*

"Aren't you falling behind in your regular work?" Aubrey commented as she and Mitch climbed into the motor coach. It was a half hour after she'd accepted Gray's dinner invite.

"Yeah, well, of the three of us, my schedule was the most flexible today." Give the hostility a rest, Gray had advised. Sure, bro. Easier said than done. But he'd give it try. As long as she didn't goad him further. Her *little touches* earlier that morning still grated.

She moved away from the huge floor fan she'd brought in and rubbed her arms. "Wow. What a difference a day makes. It's actually chilly in here now."

So much for being Mr. Nice Guy. She'd already reverted to her smart aleck routine.

"Did you really think I wouldn't figure out what was going on?"

Shrugging, he settled himself into a corner in the living room area.

She eyed him as if she was expecting some sort of reply. When he didn't follow through, she put her satchel down on the floor and moved closer. "Why don't you want me here? You're on a tight timeline. I can help you shave a few days off your schedule."

He bit his lower lip. He was supposed to get along with her. But she bugged him. "You've already cost me the better part of two days. Tell me how that's going to help."

She narrowed her dark blue eyes. "I'm not the one keeping

you here. You're falling behind because you're here monitoring my every move."

"Yeah, well . . . "

"It's that silly agreement. I saw right through it, you know. You were ticked off that I set Jenna DiFranco on you and wanted to get the upper hand. So you made up those stupid rules."

"They're not stupid!" Why had he said that? They obviously were.

She held up her palms, indicating surrender. "Fine. Have it your way. But I bet if I wasn't from L.A. you'd give me a break."

He raised a brow.

"You've had it in for me ever since you slid out from under this thing the other day. It couldn't be my work, because you haven't seen me do my thing yet."

He sighed. What was he supposed to say? Tell her she was a hundred percent correct and watch her gloat the rest of the day? Or plead innocence, only to be tripped up the next time he said anything? "Do we have to go through this? Chalk it up to bad chemistry. Poor timing."

She looked like he'd struck her. He admitted what she'd been trying to get him to say, and as his reward, she turned female on him. Hurt. Miffed.

"Nothing personal."

"Nothing personal? What do you call *bad chemistry? Poor timing?*"

She wasn't going to cry, was she? He hadn't meant to hurt her. Just make her stop talking. If she'd gone on much longer, she might have stumbled over the fact that he didn't want a professional interior decorator seeing through his amateurish efforts. "What I meant," he continued, feeling his way through this minefield, "is that you caught me at a bad time."

She cocked her head and looked expectant, waiting for him to explain.

Now what? Give her some cock and bull story about the shambles his life was in? No way! No one could know how he felt about this job.

"Because of your brother?"

"Gray?"

"No, Geoff. His MS? He told me how you and Graham are so concerned about him."

"He did?" He didn't think Geoff saw through that. They tried to be subtle.

She nodded.

"Yeah. It's Geoff." So he was grasping at straws. It was partially correct. He was concerned about Geoff's condition. If he hadn't been, he'd never be here instead of a law office.

Her eyes softened. She plopped down next to him on the carpet and touched his forearm. "It must have affected the whole family."

The brief contact left him momentarily breathless. "There's just Gray and me. Our parents are deceased."

"I'm sorry. I didn't know." She sounded sincere.

"We inherited this business from our dad. He'd planned to build RVs after he retired. Got as far as buying the place at an auction. Then a heart attack kept him from his dream."

"So the three of you are carrying on for your dad?"

He didn't want to talk about the business. He jumped up and moved over to the fan, pretending to check it. "Sort of. We decided motor coaches would be more lucrative than RVs." He skipped the part about it being four years between their dad's death and their decision to go into business together. Prompted by Geoff's illness. And how that changed his life forever.

He settled on a spot across the room from her. Leaning against the wall, he stretched up against it to work the kinks out of his back. "Think I'll bring a few chairs in here later. This gets uncomfortable fast. That is, if you don't think they'll damage the carpet."

She blinked. "Uh, the carpet. I've been meaning to talk to you about that."

"What about the carpet?" Apprehension was palpable in his throat.

She lifted her brows and pursed her lips. "It's gotta go."

Here it was. The start of her digs about his decorating skills. "What's wrong with it? And who's going to pay for new carpeting?"

"Nothing's wrong with it. Except the color will depress Jen . . . Ms. DiFranco. She's a winter. Dark brown is a fall."

Winter? Fall? "What are you talking about?" She'd returned to L.A.-speak.

"Colors," she said patiently. "People get their colors done to determine the best ones to wear. Hers don't include dark brown."

"Okay, I get that. But what about the extra expense?"

"It's covered. I have my own budget, outside what she's paying you."

Mitch ran a hand through his hair. That was a surprise. Jenna DiFranco had negotiated a mean price for the coach. She'd led them to believe she was strapped. "But what about . . . ?"

"What about this carpet? And the other money you were going to spend on the interior?" she anticipated for him. She hesitated. "I wasn't supposed to mention it until I was further along. But, whatever you've budgeted for it is yours to keep. If you meet her deadline."

Mitch was speechless, his heart was tap-dancing. Did she realize what she'd just told him? Admittedly, there wasn't that large a budget for the interior, but every penny counted. They were that close to bankruptcy. Gray would be ecstatic.

Aubrey eyed him cautiously. "Enough small talk. I need to get these measurements recorded or I really will get behind schedule."

For the next half hour, he held the tape measure and she drew it out to a myriad of reference points and jotted down coordinates. After a while, she glanced up from her notepad to check on him. "This has to be a bore. Why don't you take a break for a while?"

"How about you? C'mon. I'll show you our fabulous break room."

*

She was about to turn him down, when a crick in her neck

reminded her how long she'd been stooped over. "Okay. You talked me into it."

The *fabulous* break room turned out to be little more than a hole in the wall, no bigger than an oversized closet. As soon as she walked through the doorway, a tightness in her chest seized her. Oh, no! Not now. She'd managed so well in the confined space of the coach. *I can do this. At least for the few minutes I'll be here.*

"Here you go." He handed her an ice-cold can of soda. He must have noted her surreptitious scrutiny of the room, because he added, "It's not much, but every time we talk about enlarging this space, we get all territorial. None of us wants to lose our own office space."

She started to leave, but he called her back. "Why the rush?"

She stopped, but kept moving about the room to stave off the nausea that had started.

They sipped their beverages without further talk. When the silence grew too thick, Aubrey sought a plausible topic of conversation. Anything to keep her mind occupied. She noticed how the door hung slightly askew and decided to investigate. "You know, it wouldn't take much to cut back the door jamb so this door would hang straight."

"Uh . . . "

All she meant to do was to shut the door to see how it closed, then open it again. She could hardly afford to feel even more confined. But as soon as the door closed, she heard a tell-tale click. "What the . . . ?"

Mitch remained where he'd been standing, toward the back of the room. His expression was a cross between smug and astonished. "The lock tends to engage when the door's straight up. That's why it hung crooked."

"You mean . . . it's locked?"

"Picked right up on that?"

"You have a key, I hope." She tried to keep the galloping desperation she was feeling from creeping into her voice. This couldn't be happening. She protected herself from these situations by always keeping the door ajar. Standing near the door. Locating an escape route.

"Key? If I had one, I'd be over there getting us out of here, pronto." He didn't smile, but he did seem slightly amused.

She swept the room with her eyes. Maybe six feet across and ten or so feet long. Much worse than inside the motor coach. Keeping her claustrophobic tendencies in check there had been challenge enough. "What are we going to do?"

He rubbed his chin. "Haven't figured that out? You had all the answers a minute ago."

"I'm sorry. I do that. I see something that needs fixing and take care of it without further thought."

"I've noticed." His tone was laconic. "I'm more the 'don't-fix-what-ain't-broke' type. Or in this case, don't fix what's already broke." His joke made him chuckle.

"Why is that?" She inhaled deeply several times, willing her heart from beating so fast.

"The fact that I'm not trying to improve on everything I come in contact with?"

"I'm not that bad!"

He raised a brow in her direction, suggesting she might want to rethink that statement.

She let her eyes roam the room.

"What are you doing?"

"Looking for something to occupy my attention until someone finds us." She unplugged the coffeemaker. Remove that catastrophe-waiting-to-happen at least. She tried not to think about how fast an overheated appliance could ignite. She risked a glance at Mitch. Hopefully, he wouldn't see the beads of perspiration lining up across her forehead.

"Why did you do that?"

"Makes me uneasy. A heat-producing appliance in these small

quarters while we have no means of escape."

He rolled his eyes. "Maybe you should check to see if the refrigerator plug is frayed?"

She straightened her shoulders. "This isn't funny. I'm surprised you haven't been cited."

"We don't hold social functions in here. People in large cities have smaller apartments."

The room was starting to spin. "Are there any chairs?"

He glanced about the room. "And we'd put them . . . where?"

"Forget it." She found an open area of wall to scoot up against and lowered herself to the floor. She wasn't going to let the room get to her. She'd will away the feeling that the walls were closing in. "It looks like we'll be here for a while. Got any ideas for passing the time?"

He gave her a curious look, then sidled over and flopped down beside her. "Bring your notepad? We can work on floor plans."

"No. I left it back in the motor coach."

"So much for that." He felt his shirt pockets, then his pants pockets, his efforts producing a small eraserless pencil. "Here." He popped up and searched the counter, returning with several white paper napkins. "And here's your paper."

Forcing herself to breathe more evenly, she kept her eyes focused on the olive green shag carpet. "What if you were to switch this room with the laundry room? It's double the size of this. You could stack the washer and dryer along that exterior wall and vent them from there."

He regarded her with a very strange expression. "Is it a sickness or an obsession?"

"What?" Had he picked up on her phobia?

"You can't leave anything alone."

She sniffed. "I was just trying to help."

He gave her a half smile. "I know. That's the ironic part."

She wanted to shoot back a pithy retort, but that smile disarmed her. "How . . . how come you're not angry with me? At least you don't appear to be."

He grimaced, rolling his shoulders. "Too much effort."

"Oh." Her voice sounded flat.

"Oh, what?"

"I just thought . . . maybe you'd . . . changed your mind about me?"

"You mean that you're opinionated and pushy?"

She widened her eyes. "Not at a loss for words, are you?"

"You asked." However, the corners of his eyes crinkled. "I guess I'm getting used to it."

"You're mellowing?"

"Wouldn't go that far. You caught me at a bad time the other day. I was edgy about being off schedule."

"I should be able to help you there."

He angled his head and stared at her.

"Okay, getting stuck in here isn't helping. But you can use my skills. No offense, but that interior is pretty blah."

Abruptly, he rose and went to the small refrigerator across the room. Opening the door, he stuck his head in to check the contents. "No food."

"That's okay. I'm not really hungry." Her stomach was roiling.

He continued to forage through the boxes and containers on the counter, discovering at last a box of snack bars. He returned with two, offering her one, which she refused.

"You want to discuss what needs to be done with the interior?" she continued.

He studied the laces on his sneakers, pulling them open and retying them. "How about we talk about a new break room instead? Tell me what you'd do."

They spent the next half hour kicking around ideas, arguing about untended coffeemakers and whether to include a davenport ("Like my brothers need any more excuses to nap on the job!"). At one point, Aubrey looked up from her sketch and tilted her head to listen. "Did you hear something? Is Graham back? Or Geoff?"

Mitch strained to listen. He checked his watch. "They should've found us by now. Neither can go this long without coffee or something to eat." He went to the door and banged on it several times. "Hey! We're in here, you guys. Get us out of here!" He turned back to where she continued to sit. "Help me here, Aubrey!"

Reluctantly, she pulled herself up and joined him. Her legs felt rubbery, like they weren't totally connected to the rest of her body. She took turns with him hitting the door and calling out for help. Her panic increased as she grew more fearful that no one was ever going to show up. The physical effort stirred the nausea that had been building. Holding her stomach, she folded into herself. Mitch caught her just before she hit the floor.

"Aubrey? What's the matter?"

She allowed him to lay her down, unable to respond to his question because her breathing had become labored.

He grabbed a handful of napkins and doused them with the liquid left in his bottle of water and used them to pat down her forehead. "Aubrey, say something!"

She struggled. Nothing came out except gasping sounds.

"What is with you, lady? One of those exotic Hollywood diets?"

She closed her eyes and tried to follow the few Zen breathing techniques she knew. When she opened her eyes again, she found him staring down at her, confused.

"Sor-ry," she managed to get out. "Room . . . got . . . to me."

"The room?" Mitch lifted his head and looked around. "It's a little warm in here, but . . . "

"Claus . . . "

"Claustrophobia? My God, Aubrey, why didn't you say something?"

Even in her weakened state, she wondered when he'd realize the folly of that question. "What would you have done? Knocked the door down?"

He leaned over her and felt her forehead. "You don't seem warm." He gripped her chin and turned her face. "Look at me.

Let me see your eyes."

The touch of his hand had a settling effect despite the fact that it sent her stomach spinning in new directions. Did he actually care how she felt?

Instinctively, she reached for his hand. It was warm and large. Her own hand disappeared within it. Even the calluses were reassuring.

His eyes widened in surprise, and he took a deep intake of breath. "Your eyes look okay. Does this happen often?"

"No. Not very."

"What do you normally do?"

She tried to smile. "Get out in the open."

He thunked his forehead with his free palm. "That's not an option at the moment. What else?"

Her breathing was becoming more normal. "I guess lie down, like I'm doing. I'm sorry, Mitch. I should have said something as the nausea built, but . . . "

"But what?"

"I thought you'd use it against me. To keep me from working on the coach."

His face screwed up. "Have I been that big an ogre?"

She didn't say anything, discretion being the better part of valor.

Mitch didn't say anything either, but the scowl on his face didn't fade easily. Finally, he said, "Stay there. Gray should be here any time." He peeled off his jacket and laid it over her.

She closed her eyes again. Within minutes, she dozed off.

No one came to their rescue. Not for an hour. Not for two hours. And Aubrey slept on.

She awoke to a gentle chirping noise. Her cell phone. Automatically, she reached for it in the side pocket of her slacks.

"Aunt Aubrey?" the caller said.

"Paige? Is that you?"

"Mom said you were away on business and not to bother

you. She wouldn't tell me where you'd gone. I called your private phone. The one you don't use for clients."

She rubbed her eyes and shifted position in an effort to release the kinks. "What's up?"

"Mom insists on taking this concert tour. You have to convince her to stay home."

"She needs to do this, Paige." She didn't add that Jenna had staked almost all her fortune, other than college tuition for Paige, on this tour.

"Then why won't she let me stay with Dad? If she doesn't want me, he will."

If only she knew, Aubrey thought. But that would break her heart. "These are difficult times for your parents. They want your life to go as smoothly as ever, which means they need a little space for a while." There, that sounded reasonable, and true, from Jenna's perspective.

"Will you talk to her for me?"

Paige was relentless. "I'll suggest she talk to you. I can't ask her to change her plans."

"Okay. Thanks, Aunt Aubrey." Her words were resigned but petulant.

Aubrey hit "End" and sighed. She didn't need additional complications on this project. But she ached for her niece's hurt feelings and mistaken conclusions about her mother.

Mitch was giving her an odd look. Had she been snoring? How long had she been out?

"What? I'm sorry you had to hear that, but it was unavoidable."

"When were you going to tell me you had a cell phone on you?"

"When was I . . . ? Oh, my gosh!" She'd had the means of escape in her possession all along. "You don't think I kept quiet deliberately, do you? I'd totally forgotten about it."

"Right." He didn't sound convinced. A vein in his neck twitched.

"Really! I have two cell phones. One for business. I use it the most. In fact, I hardly ever use this one. Just for family emergencies. Which, as you could tell, that call was about. It didn't occur to me that I was still carrying this one."

"Hand me the phone." It wasn't a request. He punched in a number. "Gray? Yeah, it's me." He listened for some time. "I know we're late. What time is it, anyhow?" He looked at his watch. "Holy . . . ! Yeah, she's with me. No, we didn't have an accident. Well, not exactly."

He listened some more. Graham must be furious with them. "Gray. Stop talking. Come downstairs. Find the break room key and bring it over here." More talk from Graham. "Yeah, we're both in here. Yeah, I know that's a tricky door. But Aubrey didn't. She shut it before I could stop her."

Within minutes, Graham had located the key and released them.

The oily-odored garage had never smelled so good. She couldn't help doing a pirouette or two to celebrate her release. "It feels so good to get out of that heat."

"Heat?" Graham gave his brother a deep, penetrating stare.

Mitch rolled his eyes. "It gets pretty hot in there when you're cooped up for hours."

Graham turned to Aubrey. "Did you get anything to eat? It's way past dinner time."

"And we missed your special meal," she apologized.

"Wasn't intentional," he said, dismissing her concern.

"Where were you all that time?" Mitch asked him. "Didn't you hear us calling for help?"

Graham gave his brother a tolerant look. "If I'd heard you, I would have been here right away. I got back around three, went upstairs immediately to get ready for tonight." He turned back to Aubrey. "I got some stuff from the deli, to protect you from my cooking. It needed to be warmed and mixed together."

"Where's Geoff? Didn't he ever come back?"

"Don't know. Haven't heard from him, which, now that I think of it, is strange."

"He's probably left us both messages we haven't retrieved," Mitch surmised. "I'm famished. Let's eat that meal that's been waiting for us."

Graham gave them a sheepish look.

"What?" Mitch asked. "You burned it?"

"I . . . ate it."

"All of it?" Mitch asked in disbelief.

"Well . . . yeah. I eat when I'm nervous. And I worried when you didn't show up. I thought you were ditching me in favor of a restaurant."

Mitch shook his head. "Gray, you take the cake . . . literally! So what do we do about a meal? We're both starving."

"At eleven o'clock at night?" Aubrey said, laughing for the first time in hours. "I don't know which will do more damage to my stomach. Missing dinner or eating it at midnight!"

Graham touched her hand. "Please, I feel bad enough I didn't figure out what had happened. Don't leave the fact that I didn't feed you hanging over me as well."

Lowering his voice, Mitch asked her, "Are you feeling up to it?"

Actually, she was. It was amazing how a little fresh air and wide open spaces could revive her. "Okay, you convinced me. What are you going to whip up for us?"

"How do you like your pizza?" Graham asked. "With or without sausage?"

CHAPTER FOUR

Sometime around two, Aubrey thought to check her watch. "Gosh! Look what time it is. I need to be leaving." She stood and sought her purse.

Mitch rose and came over to her. "One of us will drive you."

"Better yet," Graham cut in, "stay here tonight."

"What?" Both Aubrey and Mitch spoke at once.

"Remember that *sleepover clause* Aubrey wanted in her agreement?"

"I don't recall that particular title," Aubrey replied.

"But you know what I'm referring to. We brought in an air mattress yesterday. Along with plenty of clean sheets and towels. Why don't you test it out tonight?"

She started to refuse. She hadn't really been serious. On the other hand . . . her eyes were staying open only about half the time. Driving was not a good idea.

She saw Mitch raise his brows in reaction to his brother's suggestion. Perhaps she should take him up on his offer to drive her back to the B&B? But when those brows came down, she noted the eyelids were just as heavy as hers.

"We're all tired. I'll stay, if you're both okay with it."

"I'll stay downstairs long enough for you to get settled," Graham volunteered. "And I'll keep some lights on in the garage, even though you've taken care of that with your reflectors."

It was an effort even to smile, she was that tired.

Ten minutes later, Graham called, "Good night, Aubrey," as he started up the stairs. "Sleep well."

"No problem there," she said to herself as she flipped off the room light and collapsed on the mattress. She crawled under the blankets and fell asleep immediately.

Sometime later, an unknown noise caused her to open her eyes. Tiny pinpricks of light striped the room. It must be a little after dawn. Then she heard it again, a tiny popping, scratching sound. At first, it was more an irritant than anything else, because concentrating on it kept her from going back to sleep. She obsessed over figuring out what it was.

Reluctantly, she pulled herself up and eventually located the light switch. Her eyes were still focusing when brightness hit, but in the haze, she still managed to discern the movement of a couple of black dots scurrying for cover. Yuck! Even with foggy vision, she knew what they were, and she was repulsed. Cockroaches! Then she remembered the sound she'd heard. Ooh! Ick! How close had they been to her head? Had they been in her bed? Ooh, ooh, ooh!

Gasping, she covered her mouth to stifle the scream that threatened to emerge. No need to alert the men. She could fend for herself against the Big Bad Bugs. They disgusted her but didn't scare her. But she had to get out of there. Find another place to crash for a few hours. She gave fleeting thought to driving back to the B&B, then dismissed it. She was still too exhausted.

She made her way slowly across the garage. There was only a trickle of light coming from the few bulbs Graham had left burning, but enough to locate the string of offices. At least, that's what she thought until she walked smack into a hard, hairy chest.

"Oh!" she exclaimed, not quite sure who it was.

"It's me, Aubrey," Mitch whispered.

"What are you doing down here at this hour?" Though barely conscious, she was awake enough to have taken in that manly scent. Something that reminded her of pine cones. He was shirtless. He must have quickly pulled on his jeans over . . . oh, my, he hadn't entirely zipped up. She wrenched her eyes upward, telling herself to keep them above shoulder level.

"I . . . I woke up and thought I heard a noise. I came to investigate."

"You thought I was redoing the garage, didn't you?"

"The thought did cross my mind," he whispered drily. "What are you doing up?"

"Me?" She rubbed her eyes and attempted to beat the wrinkles from her shirt. "I was chased out of my room."

"*Chased out?*"

She ran a hand through her tousled do and paused, considering how to put it. "I know I'm a freeloader, so I shouldn't complain. But I can't cohabitate with the critters in there."

"Critters?"

"Cockroaches." She kept her voice intentionally flat.

"Cockroaches?" He scratched his head. "Wait! There's a drain in the laundry room, although there shouldn't be any standing water. I'll bet you saw June bugs."

"June bugs?"

"Technically, they're cockroaches. They appear every year around this time. How many were there? Twenty? Ten?"

"Two."

"Two? Two little bugs forced you to flee?" He turned to go.

"Wait! They skittered away from my mattress when I turned on the light. I have no idea if there were more *on* the mattress, because I took off immediately. I didn't want to wake you and Graham, so I came out here looking for another place to sleep."

He considered her statement, finally saying, "You can use the sofa in my office. There's a throw you can burrow under if you get cold. I'll call the exterminator first thing in the morning."

"Based on just two June bugs?"

*

He didn't want to tell her she'd probably been smart to clear out. Two on the surface usually meant a nest nearby. "If you're going to be working in there, I want to make sure you won't be . . . interrupted. And you might need to stay overnight again. You'll sleep better knowing they've been snuffed out."

"I could always borrow your sofa."

"That's my point. We'll clean up your room so you don't have to." Something told him that if he let her, she'd take over his office in a heartbeat. He might be getting accustomed to having her around, but not in his space.

He escorted her to his office, telling himself he wanted to make sure she didn't walk into anything else. Especially not him again. She'd caught him off guard. He'd been wandering around the garage, debating if he should check on her after hearing a sound of some sort. He'd quickly donned a pair of jeans and headed downstairs to investigate.

He'd been standing there in the dark trying to discern the soft padding sound he'd heard when she bumped into him. Though she was still fully clothed, her rumpled appearance and her semi-awake state taunted him. She had no idea how absurdly disarming she looked. Not with June bugs on her mind.

Once in his office, he helped her get settled, tucked the throw over her, and watched her almost sink into sleep before his eyes. "See you in a few hours."

"Uh-hmmn." She snuggled further into the couch.

He stood there watching her a few seconds more, then better sense took hold. Silently, he crept back upstairs to his own bed, which now seemed overly large and lonely.

The next morning, Gray continued to atone for the meal they'd missed. "Morning. Seen Aubrey?" he asked as Mitch walked into the kitchen. "Thought she might like pancakes." Unlike Mitch, who'd thrown a ratty old robe over his shorts and T-shirt, Gray was fresh from the shower, fully clothed in slacks and a long-sleeved shirt.

"Pancakes? After all that pizza just a few hours ago?"

"I'm hungry again. Ravenous, actually."

"Aubrey's on the couch in my office. We've got June bugs in the laundry room."

"Really? Is she all right?"

"Other than having to play musical beds in the middle of the night, she's fine."

"We'd better get an exterminator in here right away."

"I'm already on that." Mitch took another sip of coffee. "Most women would have screamed, demanded we kill every bug in sight immediately."

"Sounds like she's growing on you. Have the two of your struck a truce?"

Mitch tightened his grip on the coffee mug. "I suppose. She's not as flaky as I thought at first. Just mouthy."

"That's progress." Gray busied himself removing pancake mix and the rest of the fixings from the cabinets and refrigerator. He turned to Mitch, a smile on his face. "We should invite her to stay here for the whole project. Save her the price of that B&B."

Mitch almost choked on the coffee. "Whoa! She can't stay in that laundry room. Even clearing the place of those bugs isn't going to make it habitable twenty-four/seven."

"Then we'll find somewhere else to put her."

Mitch narrowed his eyes. "Are you sure you're not the one she's growing on?"

Gray gave him a shy smile. "She is something, isn't she?"

Mitch didn't know how to reply. This conversation was heading a direction he definitely didn't want to go. "She's unique, that's for sure."

"As for anything romantic happening, she treats me like the sister we never had."

"Sister? That I hadn't noticed," Mitch mused. Only a few hours ago, he'd felt anything but brotherly feelings for her when he'd helped her to bed in his office.

"So, what do you think? Should we invite her to stay with us?"

Where would they put her? And how many nights would he put himself on guard duty when the real danger to guard against was her? "Why don't we see what Geoff thinks first?"

Gray poured six dots of batter onto the heated griddle. "Not a bad idea. But I'm starting to worry about him. He hasn't been here for two days."

"He called yesterday and left me a message. Said the heat was getting to him and he was going to stay in bed for the rest of the day."

Gray shuttled the butter dish and bottle of maple syrup to the table. "The same has happened the last couple summers."

Mitch considered. "He wasn't away as long, though. Usually, a long nap took care of it."

"If he's not here by the time we finish breakfast, I'll call." Gray flipped the pancakes, which had turned a picture-perfect tan, and shortly after brought the first batch to the table.

"Good morning." Aubrey stood in the kitchen doorway, wearing a heavy-lidded, dewy look. "I smelled those flapjacks all the way downstairs and couldn't resist. Got extras?"

"I made enough for all of us," Gray told her, smiling happily. "Have a seat."

"Thanks! Mmmm, they smell wonderful, Graham. I haven't had homemade flapjacks in . . . well, I don't remember the last time." She helped herself to three and dug in.

"What's up for today?" Gray asked, joining them. "When does the artwork arrive?"

"Artwork?" Wrinkling her brow, she gave him a curious look.

"Isn't that what you'll be doing? Figuring out knickknacks to place around the motor coach? Things Ms. DiFranco likes to surround herself with?"

Mitch rolled his eyes and busied himself cutting up another three cakes. Gray had dug himself in deep now. He couldn't wait to hear Aubrey put him in his place.

But instead, she merely said, "I guess there are a couple pieces of artwork I have in mind. But my main job is to decide on the colors to surround Ms. DiFranco with."

"Colors again?" That got Mitch's attention. He'd been bumped off the finish crew because he didn't know Jenna DiFranco's palette as well as Aubrey?

Aubrey turned to him. "You probably think that's more California doubletalk. But with Jenna—Ms. DiFranco—it's very important that she be in the right frame of mind before each concert and afterwards so she can rest her brain and power down. Color helps do that."

Aubrey filled in the silence that ensued. "Actually, Graham, today I need to rough out some sketches. I woke up refreshed, brimming with ideas I need to get down on paper. Must have been Mitch's sofa."

"That's right!" Gray said. "Sorry about that. I should have remembered that we tend to get visitors in the laundry room this time of year."

"Which reminds me," Mitch cut in, "The exterminator will be here soon. You'll need to move your things out for a few hours."

Keeping his eyes on Mitch, Gray said, "Actually, Mitch and I have been exploring the idea of moving you out of there, period." He quickly added, "And finding you new space."

Aubrey appeared about to refuse the offer. Before she opened her mouth, Gray added, "And we think . . . " he kept his gaze on Mitch, "you should stay here while you're in town."

His eyes bored into Mitch, urging him to say something as well. The best Mitch could offer was a half-smile. Even that took effort.

Eyes wide, Aubrey appeared to be speechless . . . for once. Furrowing her brow, she turned toward Mitch. "Are you sure, Graham? I don't want to put you out."

Mitch fumed inwardly. Now he'd have to say something hospitable. "Sounds like a good idea, as soon as we figure out where to put you." He shot Gray a pointed look.

"Oh," she said, apparently not quite sure how to interpret his words.

"Geoff may not be in for a while," Gray said. "Maybe we could convert his office?"

Mitch's expression hardened into a glare. "We don't know what's going on with him."

"Something's up with Geoff?" Aubrey asked, concern coming onto her face.

"We're not sure," Mitch replied. "He's been a little run down lately."

Gray added, "Heat sometimes triggers a reaction. He's been feeling weak and dizzy the past few days."

"Is he okay? Has he called in yet today?" Aubrey asked.

The two men exchanged looks.

"He usually sleeps late," Gray offered. "But I'll check. To relieve our concerns."

While he was out of the room, Aubrey turned back to Mitch, who'd gone for a bottle of water. He usually stayed away from maple syrup, but today it had been too tempting.

"I appreciate the offer to stay here. But, given the circumstances . . . "

"You mean Geoff? He'll be fine. We've gone through this before. And he'd feel terrible knowing you'd stayed away because of him." A new thought hit. "Actually, your being here might be therapeutic. The two of them will knock themselves out seeing to your comfort and forget about Geoff's condition."

"To his detriment?"

"Nah." He dismissed her concern, though a small, niggling thought at the back of his brain wouldn't go away. There might be more to Geoff's ailments this time.

She was silent a moment, obviously thinking through their proposal. Then, her eyes brightening, she said, "Okay. I'll accept. But I'm not a guest. I'm a boarder. I'll take my turn with meals and cleaning and contribute to the groceries."

So, they had a house guest. And he'd been the one to clinch the deal.

*

When Geoff hadn't shown up by ten, Mitch called him instead of Gray. "How's it goin', old man?" he asked when Geoff finally picked up after six rings.

"Not so good." Geoff answered in a slightly slurry voice.

Mitch tried to keep his tone casual and not let his brother hear the worry mounting within him. "What's up? Too much partying lately?"

"Dond I wiss."

"I'm coming over."

"Naw ne'cery."

"I'm sure it isn't," Mitch lied, "but Gray made pancakes this morning. Thought you'd like the leftovers."

"Pancakes? Waaz the occasion?"

"Aubrey stayed over last night. And before you jump to any nasty conclusions, it was because the three of us stayed up past two drinking wine, eating pizza, and talking."

"And you dint call me?" Geoff was attempting to return the humor.

"Way past your bedtime, bro. Next time." Mitch clicked off his cell phone and scowled.

"Trouble?" Aubrey stood in the open door to Mitch's office. "Sorry. I couldn't help overhearing your conversation. Geoff?"

Mitch was too preoccupied with his brother's condition to be offended by her eavesdropping. "Yeah. I'm going over there for a while. If you want to work inside the motor coach, go ahead without me."

"Really?"

The note of surprise in her voice made him look up. He'd been so caught up in Geoff's situation, he hadn't given much thought to what he'd said. Her question made him realize he'd turned a corner, of sorts. He trusted her with his precious project.

"I'll only be gone an hour or so. You can't do much damage in that time." Couldn't let her think she'd won him over. "As long as you stay away from the break room."

*

Later, alone for the first time in the motor coach, Aubrey frowned at the sketch she'd drawn. It still wasn't coming out on paper like she pictured in her head. Her cell phone buzzed. Jenna.

"No time to chat, but how's it going? Still at war with the Brothers McKenna?"

"We seem to have come to a truce. They even suggested I stay here while I'm working on the project."

"Stay there, as in *overnight*?" Jenna's voice rose. Then her end of the line went silent, as if she was deciding what to say next.

Aubrey dumped the contents of the portfolio she'd brought with her onto the ugly brown carpet. A travel book of Greece. A sky blue scarf. Several carpet samples and paint chips. "You're okay with that arrangement, aren't you?" As if, at twenty-six, she needed her big sister's approval.

"I guess it will be okay."

"But . . . ?"

"Are you sure you're . . . safe . . . staying there with three men? I know the McKennas' business reputation is flawless. I checked it out. But I don't know them personally."

"They're perfect gentlemen. Well, two are gentlemen. Mitch has his moments."

"What does that mean?"

"Nothing, really," she said dismissively. "Just that every time I think we're finally communicating on the same wave length, he goes all prickly."

"Mitch? I've always found him charming when I've spoken to him, but then, I usually deal with the older brother, Graham. Talk about prickly!"

Now it was Aubrey's turn to be surprised. "Graham? He may be a little stiff, but other than that, he's been quite sweet to me. Maybe you've got them mixed up?"

"I don't think so. It was Graham I spoke to Monday night when I spelled out their contract obligations. He got quite defensive."

Aubrey selected an off-white carpet sample from the pile before her and held it up to the light. "Speaking of older children . . . how's yours? Your only one, that is."

Another pause on Jenna's end. Finally, "Paige wants to go with me on this tour."

"I know. She called yesterday and tried to get me to go to bat for her."

"She did? She hasn't mentioned that. Why didn't you call me?"

Aubrey debated how much to reveal about her conversation with Paige. She loved both of them dearly, and it troubled her that the two of them were at odds. "Because Paige needs to talk to you about this herself. Have you mentioned the tour to her recently? Since yesterday?"

"No. I've been in rehearsals all week. I'm calling from there now. She's at one of her summer school classes today."

No wonder Paige was upset. She was probably rebelling at having every waking minute of her summer vacation scheduled for her. But it would be no use mentioning that to Jenna. She was the mom. She knew better.

"I think she's got something like separation anxiety. I know you have to do this tour, but couldn't you let Paige come along for part of it? She'd probably get royally bored."

Heavy breathing. As if trying to control her anger.

"I'd love to have her with me. I really would. But the timing isn't right. I haven't been out on the road in some time. I need to get my bearings, especially at the start of the tour." Her divorce had punched holes in her self-confidence in addition to seriously depleting her finances.

Aubrey flipped aimlessly through the travel book until she found a picture of the Parthenon. "Have you told Paige that?"

"Tell her that her father left us almost destitute? That I had to mortgage almost all my personal resources on this tour, so it has to make money? That I'm scared to death of facing an audience again after so many years? She's growing up, but she's not ready to absorb an emotional load like that."

Though her sister was right, Aubrey ached for her young niece. "Okay, I understand. But keep talking to her." She could almost feel the chill coming through the line.

"Of course, I'll keep talking to *my* daughter." Jenna reminded her, yet again, who the parent was. Then her tone changed. "I'm sorry. I'm a little testy. Rehearsals wear me down so."

Aubrey propped the open book between her legs to free one hand to pick up the scarf, draping it over the book. She tried to picture the bright azure blue with the antique white of the Parthenon. "Let's change the subject. Have you heard from Mother lately?"

"Mother? Of course. Almost every day. As if I don't have enough to think about without all her grand ideas."

"She's probably envious."

"Mother just likes to be part of things."

At least Jenna's things. Rarely hers until recently, when her clients had begun to include the Rich and Famous of Beverly Hills. She added the carpet sample to the scarf and book. "Invite her along on the tour. She could watch Paige for you."

Exasperated sigh. "There's no way Mother would agree to come along, even for a few days on *that bus,* as she calls it. Let alone leave her precious country club set in Santa Barbara."

Jenna had that right. But unlike herself, it didn't seem to bother her that their mother could be so distant and self-involved. "Has she . . . asked about me?" Aubrey asked tentatively, dumping book and all on the floor. "Where I am? What I'm doing?"

"I thought you wanted your whereabouts kept secret? You can call her any time, if you want her to know."

"I know," she conceded. "And, no, I don't want her to know anything. She'd only be embarrassed by my problems back in L.A. and feel vindicated that her screw-up daughter had done it yet again."

Jenna didn't reply at once. Eventually, she asked, "What do you want me to say? She's Mother. She's not going to change, and you're going to make yourself crazy hoping she will."

Aubrey continued to stare at the collage of colors she'd thrown on the floor. It wasn't working for her. Something was off.

Jenna could be painfully blunt sometimes, but her assessment of their mother was right on. So why did she keep letting herself believe things could improve? If she could only find some way to make her mother sit up and take notice.

"Aubrey?" Jenna asked in a softer voice. "Look, I didn't mean to sound harsh. But we've been through this so often, it's only going to bring you down if you keep thinking she'll change."

"I know that," Aubrey agreed, stuffing the samples and book back into the portfolio. "It's just that . . . "

"It's just that you're an incurable optimist. Give it up. Live your life, and enjoy it."

Like she hadn't heard that advice from her sister ten—or a hundred—times before.

"My break's almost over. Need to catch my breath first. I'll call again later."

"Sure. Talk to you then."

"Just get the motor coach done on time."

Iris Appleby was like a heat-seeking missile, running after others' talents. She'd sought out Aubrey's father, a studio musician, and when he didn't measure up, she replaced him with her current husband, Billy Appleby, a retired second banana from a popular seventies sitcom. His residuals kept them quite comfortable and allowed her mother to mix with the social set she desired. So she'd turned her attention to her gifted musician daughter.

Jenna's real message had come in that last sentence. *Just get the motor coach done on time.* She wasn't worried . . . yet, but she was hedging her bets by checking in like this.

Fortunately, everything was on schedule with this project. And, unless the critters multiplied overnight and overran things, she had every intention of keeping it that way.

CHAPTER FIVE

On her own, with the guys no longer around, she was able to relax. The images she'd fought to get on paper now found their way there with relative ease. About eleven, she heard movement in the office area. Deciding it was time for a break, she headed over to see what was up.

She tapped lightly on Mitch's office door and then went in.

He sat behind his desk, his listless eyes staring at the desktop, his head cradled between his hands.

"Mitch?" she called softly. "How's Geoff?"

He raised his eyes, taking her in but not actually acknowledging her presence. Then, blinking, he sat back in his chair and sighed. "Don't know for sure. We took him to see his doctor. They ran more tests. Gray took him home and is going to stay there with him."

"I'm . . . sorry. What . . . uh . . . happens now?"

He shrugged. "We wait and see, I guess. By the time we left the doctor's office, he was already showing signs of improvement. We had to talk him into going back home to bed rather than coming in to work."

She edged farther into the room and stood behind one of the desk chairs facing him.

He didn't look at her. It was obvious he was somewhere else.

"Does he need to stay in bed all the time?"

He glanced up at her and blinked, as if just noticing her presence.

She'd gone too far. Gotten too personal.

He didn't close off or become angry, but his voice was a monotone, devoid of any emotion. "No, he can be up and about. Staying in bed is easiest."

"Hmmm." An idea had occurred to her.

He picked up on the cue. "What? You think that's a bad idea?"

Placing her hands against the desk, she leaned forward slightly. "Consider this, the more he can continue his normal routine, the less he'll think about his symptoms and give in to them."

"You think he's giving in to this thing?"

"Not necessarily. But from what you've described, it seems to be getting the better of him. Why not bring him here? To his office, if you think he'll be okay there, or set him up with one of you in your offices?"

He considered her suggestion. She could tell by the way the muscles around his cheeks and neck seemed to relax. "Keep him busy, too occupied to dwell on how he's feeling?"

"You'd have to first check it with his doctor, of course. And one of you would have to pick him up and deliver him home each day." Another idea occurred to her. "Or, move him in here with you guys . . . temporarily."

He looked at her like she'd suggested gravity made things run uphill.

She'd overstepped whatever thin line he'd allowed her near. She started to turn and give him his privacy.

"Don't go. Tell me more."

She pivoted. "I don't want to intrude. Overstep."

One side of his mouth curved slightly upward. "You're way past that, Carpenter, and we both know it. But I still want to hear your idea."

Slightly discombobulated that he was on to her, she managed to keep a smile pasted across her face and retraced her steps to his desk. "What does Geoff do around here? Graham designs, and you're in charge of the actual customizations."

"Sales. And the PR work. Why do you ask?"

"You need a reason to lean on him. Why, despite how he feels physically, you need him here to provide some vital service only he can do."

The curve on his mouth grew wider and his eyes brightened.

"You're right. We haven't gotten that far behind yet, but we will. We'll have to figure out how to get him here. Invent some emergency, maybe?"

She knew exactly how they could do it, but she wasn't sure how Mitch would react to her idea. "How about using me as the reason?" Her question came out in a nervous squeak.

"You?" He raised his brows but didn't laugh. Then, leaning forward, he shook his head, chuckling. "This has got to be good. I gotta hear more."

"Geoff has only seen me once. And I was pretty wired that day. Why not let him think I'm continuing to, uh, be a problem? That he needs to be here to keep me in check."

Only one brow shot up this time. "That's not so far from the truth, you know."

She rolled her eyes. "Gimme a break here, Mitch. I'm the one who came up with the idea, after all. On the spot, no less."

"That's what's so frightening. It's amazing how fast your brain works."

Despite his kidding, the idea seemed to grow on him. "We need to get him here either tonight or tomorrow. Trouble is, today's Friday. Not that we operate on a strict five-day work week, but bringing him in on the weekend seems lame."

It was Friday already? The last few days had flown by. She tried not to think of all the work she still had to do before the motor coach would be done. "What if I insist I need to work through the weekend to keep with the schedule?"

"Then you're going to have to, aren't you?" Amusement crinkled in his eyes. "Painted yourself into a corner, I'd say."

She shrugged. "Like it would impinge on my full social calendar." She pulled a strand of hair back around her ear. "What is there to do around here, anyhow?"

He gave her a wounded look, as if she'd told him his firstborn was one ugly baby.

"What do you do back in the City of Angels on weekends?"

"What do I do?" She tried to think. Actually, her social life for the last several months, while she'd been attempting to build her business, had been almost nonexistent. No need to share that tidbit. "Concerts, clubs, dining at some trendy new restaurant." Pure improvisation.

"There's someone waiting for you back in L.A. you'd be doing that with?"

How had she ever let the conversation get turned on her? "Not at the moment."

Mitch shot her a quick glance and just as suddenly returned his attention to something on his desk. A paperclip?

She turned to leave. Before she'd taken two steps, he spoke again.

"There's no one back home who'll be upset if you attend a picnic with the three of us?" There was a schoolboy quality to his question. A tad shy, the rest bluster.

But it certainly stopped her in her tracks. She'd attributed the pizza last night to being polite and breakfast this morning to being good hosts. This was something else. Intrigued, she replied, "A picnic? Complete with checkered tablecloths, ants, and lemonade?"

He gave a laugh. "Have you ever even been to a picnic in L.A.? I bet if you had, they didn't call it that. Too common."

Now she laughed, because he was absolutely correct. Out there, it would be something *al fresco*. "Who's going to be there?"

His eyes took on a puzzled expression. "Why do you ask? You don't know anyone else in town anyway, do you?"

"No, not really. I have a cousin I've never met." She started to say, the one who recommended them to Jenna, but cut off abruptly. She wasn't ready to reveal that connection yet.

"It's a group of neighbors from the old neighborhood. The second generation still gets together occasionally to reminisce. Even though many of us have moved out."

He stood and pulled on a pair of dark sunglasses. "I need to get over to Geoff's. Try out your idea on Gray." Passing her, he made for the door.

"Wait! Where? When? I need more details."

Hand on the doorknob, he turned back to her. "Picnic's at noon tomorrow. Dankwardt Park. I'll leave you directions for finding it, since Gray and I need to be there early for set up. Wear your most casual clothes."

"Okay," she called to his disappearing back. "Good luck with Geoff."

*

As he drove to his brother's house, Mitch focused on how to convince Geoff they needed him back at work. After all, the idea was the brainchild of Ms. Fix-it, not the doctor. Why was he even considering something coming from her fertile brain? A few days ago, he'd been ready to ship her back to California. Now he was allowing her to advise him on family matters. Geesh!

He'd been listening to a voicemail message from Orville when Aubrey showed up. No pressure, he'd said. Right. This was the second contact this week even though he'd been absolutely clear with Orville about declining his offer. Thanks, but no thanks.

Geoff was napping when he arrived. Mitch and Gray went out to the backyard and leaned back in chaise lounge chairs. Mitch explained Aubrey's idea.

Gray sat forward. "That's brilliant! We convince him Aubrey's driving us crazy."

"Not a huge stretch."

"Yeah, right, bro. I saw how you looked at her this morning."

Mitch ignored the reference to any relationship that might be growing between them. "She has this need to fix things."

"I thought that really bugged you."

"It does, but not when it might work to our advantage." Mitch sat forward as well. "Will you help me convince Geoff to come back?"

"Sure. As long as he's physically ready. We really do need him back. We're barely squeaking by."

They'd brought fried chicken, so when Geoff awoke, the first priority was to get him to eat. Finished, he wiped his hands on several paper napkins, then asked, "What's up?"

"Up?" Gray returned. "We're fine."

"Yeah, fine," Mitch agreed.

They shot expectant looks at each other. Mitch decided the water was about as good as it was going to get for diving in. "We need you back, bro. Work is piling up."

Geoff jerked his head, obviously not anticipating such candor.

Gray quickly cut in with, "We want you healthy first. But if you're starting to feel your old self, we could really use you back in the office."

"Maybe you could bring my work here to me for another few days?"

They hadn't planned for that option. Time to improvise and introduce the problem of Aubrey. "I suppose we could do that," he agreed, "if just the workload was the problem." He looked to Gray for the second verse. His brother was devouring a drumstick. Mitch paused, hoping Geoff would pick up his cue.

Geoff complied. "What is there besides the workload?"

Mitch picked up another piece of chicken and focused on the spot he would soon bite into. *Here goes.* "In a word, Aubrey."

"Aubrey?" Geoff repeated. "You mean that interior decorator from the West Coast? I thought we took care of her earlier in the week?"

"So did we," Mitch answered. "But she's managed to turn the place upside down."

"Like . . . how?"

Gray finally decided to put his oar in. "Remember those stipulations she threw into our agreement?" Geoff nodded. Gray continued. "She's blown them way out of proportion."

"We've gone without clean sheets and towels because she monopolizes the laundry room. Said she couldn't work with the humidity from the washer and dryer," Mitch added.

"Surely you can work out some arrangement with her? Is she there all that much?"

Mitch and Graham exchanged the looks of soldiers under siege. "Actually . . . " Graham said, "she is there all the time now. Or soon will be."

Geoff's eyes widened. "How come?"

"After the first night, she pulled this 'I-have-to-work-late-and-don't-want-to-drive-back-to-my-B&B-alone' routine," Mitch continued. "Then she invented an excuse—June bugs—to move from the air mattress in the laundry room to the sofa in my office."

Geoff turned to Mitch, engrossed. "You've been kicked out of your office?"

Mitch played it up big. "I still get access during the day. But earlier today she was eyeing your office and asking questions about when we thought you'd be back."

He kept his eyes on his piece of chicken. He didn't dare look directly at Geoff.

Geoff actually got to his feet. No cane, no wobbling. "My office? The smallest room?"

"We told her that," Gray chimed in.

"And?" Geoff asked, his voice rising.

"She got this funny female smile on her face. The kind women use to make you think you're some kind of sub-species and couldn't possibly understand their thinking process."

"That's spooky," Geoff said.

"That's not the worst of it," Gray added.

Both brothers turned inquisitive eyes toward him.

Mitch was particularly interested, because they'd already exhausted the repertoire of complaints about Aubrey they'd rehearsed.

Gray paused a moment, adding more drama to their little act. "She's got the hots for Mitch."

"What!" both Mitch and Geoff said at once.

Then Mitch recovered. "It's not unheard of. A few women have found me irresistible."

"Well, yeah," Geoff said, downplaying his amazement, "but they haven't set up quarters underfoot." He turned to their older brother. "What's she done to our boy here, Gray?"

Mitch wanted to hear Graham's reply to this one, too.

But Graham was ready. "For starters, she caught him alone in the middle of the night. Wearing what she'd been sleeping in. With him only in half-zipped pants."

How had Gray become privy to that piece of information? His imagination couldn't be that good.

"Whoa, Mitch. What'd you do? Or should I ask?" Geoff asked in an insinuating tone.

"That's when the bug story came up. So she could use the sofa in my office. I was too tired and too surprised by her audacity to turn her down."

"Did you turn down anything else?" Geoff wanted to know.

"I went to bed . . . alone," Mitch said defensively. Why was this getting to him?

"Then she showed up for breakfast," Gray reported. "Again, in what she'd slept in."

"She also managed to stay late the night before. Hanging around until we took pity on her and shared our pizza." Surprising how easy it was to embroider on the facts.

"So she's invaded the second floor as well?" Geoff asked.

Mitch felt a need to defend Aubrey a little bit. "Only the kitchen and great room."

"Don't forget my bathroom," Gray reminded. "Had to share the last of my clean towels."

Gray started collecting the remains from dinner. He gave Geoff a knowing look. "I saved the best for last." He paused for effect. "She locked herself into the break room with Mitch. For several hours. When I finally sprung them, her hair, and Mitch's too, was messed. Like they'd both been sleeping or . . . "

Mitch grabbed his thighs to retrain himself from jumping up and punching his brother. He didn't like the tone this whole piece was assuming. Aubrey may have given her go-ahead for using her idea to flush out Geoff, but this was taking it too far.

"Nothing happened, Gray!"

Instead of apologizing or even appearing a little chastened, Gray shot a knowing look at Geoff. "See what I mean? She's starting to get to him."

"Gray!" Mitch yelled.

"Look, bro, she's nice enough and darn good looking, but you're still vulnerable. You don't need another woman in your life so soon." It all came out so plausible and earnest.

Before Mitch could think of a response or a way to shut him up, Gray spoke again. This time to Geoff. "That's why you have to come back. We need you to run interference."

Dumbfounded, Geoff said, "You want me lure her away from our baby brother, the hot one?"

"No need to go to such extremes," Gray said. "You need to recover first, remember? What I had in mind was taking over for Mitch in the babysitting department."

"You don't have to spend every waking minute with her in the motor coach," Mitch added. "I already told her I was backing away from that condition. She's convinced me she knows her stuff and can be trusted."

Gray shook his head, then placed a hand on Mitch's shoulder. "See what I mean? It's progressed faster than I thought."

"What do you mean by *babysit*?" Geoff asked.

Mitch said, "We'll tell her you're her contact from now on."

"And how about this?" Gray added, now coming around the table to Geoff. "I think Aubrey has a bit of the nursemaid instinct in her. She'd jump at the chance to check in on you, bring you food and drink, take your temperature, etc., if you want to play along?"

Mitch stared at Gray, trying not to let on to Geoff that their brother had just lost his mind.

"Isn't that . . . sort of . . . taking advantage of her?" Geoff asked. Mitch agreed with him.

"But that's the beauty of it, guys! That's the kind of thing she's shown she likes to do. And if you keep her focused on helping you, she'll forget about Mitch."

"Thanks," Mitch said, having second thoughts about this plan.

"I'll be there Monday morning, barring further complications with my MS."

"Great!" Gray returned. "Only, how about tomorrow instead?"

"Tomorrow?" Geoff asked. "Why so soon?"

Gray looked to Mitch again. "It seems our brother has invited Ms. Carpenter to the neighbors' reunion picnic. He's going to need reinforcements."

Geoff gave Mitch a highly speculative look. "You falling for this woman? Maybe this isn't a good idea after all, Gray?"

"I'm not falling for her," Mitch denied. "She asked what kind of things we did for fun around here, like she expected me to tell her we watched the corn grow. I had to come up with something. The picnic was the first thing that came to mind."

"So, can you join us?" Gray persisted. "You've been standing for the last several minutes without your cane. And you haven't slurred one word."

Geoff smiled. "Is that your not-so-subtle way of telling me to get my carcass out of bed?"

Gray grinned and placed his arm around his brother. "If the sheet fits . . . "

CHAPTER SIX

"Aubrey! Over here," Mitch called out as she walked across the park the next day. As he sprinted toward her, his tan Bermuda shorts showed off powerful, muscular legs. And the white T-shirt, free of grease today, stretched taut over well-defined pecs.

"Hi." She hoped he didn't hear the breathless anticipation in her voice.

He led her toward the shelter house, deliberately sidestepping several people who came up to greet them. Mitch ushered her to one of the food tables. The pungent aromas of grilled brats, sauerkraut and beer greeted her nostrils. Her mouth watered, especially when she spied banana cream and lemon meringue pies on the dessert table.

"Are you the visitor from the West Coast I've been hearing about?" one particularly svelte woman in her late forties asked, taking her hand and favoring her with a huge, genuine smile. "I saw Graham at the cleaners earlier in the week and he told me all about you."

Aubrey held out her hand. The woman looked vaguely familiar. "Guilty. I'm Aubrey Carpenter. And I'm from L.A."

"Graham says you're an interior decorator."

"That's right."

"I'm Debbie Summers." She glanced over her shoulder at three men who were tending the grill. "I need to get back over there before those guys burn all the brats." She winked at Aubrey. "We'll talk later. Nice to meet you, dear."

"Beware of Debbie," Mitch warned. "She was checking you out. She thinks you might be competition for her daughter with Graham."

"Not you?"

He colored slightly. "I . . . uh . . . I've been out of commission.

The vultures circle, but so far, they've given me my space."

"Have no fear, I'm here to protect you from the cloying arms of all these hopeful females." However, she couldn't guarantee that included herself.

"Thanks. But actually, you're also here for another reason. That's why I've been on the lookout for you." He scanned the groups of people already gathered for the event. "To give you a heads up about Geoff."

"Oh? Isn't he feeling well?"

"He's much better. Even walking without his cane. Don't be thrown if he acts strange."

"Strange?"

They were approaching a lone picnic table set away from the shelter house. Mitch motioned for her to sit on the bench.

"Remember your offer to be the fall guy in our scheme to get Geoff back to work?"

She nodded.

"We're going to take you up on it."

"Great! How?"

Mitch shot a look back at his brother. "Geoff thinks he's protecting me from you."

"You gave him the line about my hassling you and making unreal demands?"

"Yeah . . . " He paused, as if there was more.

"And?" Would she have to coax it from him?

He chewed his lip, then sat down next to her. "This next part was Graham's idea, not mine. Remember that, okay?"

She watched him shift in his seat and pull at his shirt. Seeing how ill at ease he was, her suspicions grew. "Go on."

He breathed in deeply. "You've set your sights on me romantically."

It didn't register at first. When it did sink in, she nearly jumped off the bench. "What! That wasn't part of the plan."

"Graham got carried away. It was out of his mouth before I

realized what he was doing."

She attempted to process the idea of Geoff protecting Mitch from her. "What am I supposed to do?" Another thought struck her. "He's not going to offer up himself instead, is he?"

Mitch sat up straighter. "Geoff as Casanova? I suppose he might consider it. He's never been one to retreat from the ladies." With mock seriousness, he said, "You'll be gentle, I hope?"

"Don't kid about this. I don't want to do anything that might hurt him."

"Just play along."

He jumped up and pulled her to her feet. "We'd better join them before they think we're up to something."

"We wouldn't want that," she said, still marveling at the family drama she'd let herself get sucked into.

They joined Graham and Geoff in the line queuing up outside the shelter house. Seeing her, Geoff immediately wedged himself between her and Mitch. "I hear you're our house guest. Hope you won't mind one more male around. I'm moving back temporarily."

He didn't waste time. No wonder he did the PR for the company. How was she supposed to react? She'd had all of two minutes to absorb this change in the script. Should she make it appear like she really was after Mitch? To give Graham's story credence, of course.

He was looking at her, expecting some sort of reaction to his announcement. Why hadn't she accepted those acting lessons when that director back in L.A. had put the moves on her? "That's great news, Geoff. Now I'll get to know all three McKennas."

Geoff edged slightly closer. "How's your project going?"

His smile seemed genuine, interested, his manner less intense and preoccupied than Mitch and not as formal as Graham. But knowing that his assignment was to charm her away from Mitch was disconcerting. She also sensed a certain jockeying for her attention going on amongst the three of them, even though only

Geoff had spoken to her while they'd been in line.

What had she gotten herself into? Finishing the motor coach for Jenna on time, given all of her sister's idiosyncrasies, was challenge enough.

"Things are coming along," she replied tentatively. "I probably should be back at the firehouse right now, finishing my drawings, but the lure of a real live Iowa picnic was too much."

His smile remained in place. "Good! I don't think you'll be disappointed. This is a picnic plus. You play softball? We've got a pick-up game after lunch."

"I'm not much of an athlete." And she planned to say an early adieu after lunch.

"Then you'll be my guest in the stands while we watch these two compete," Geoff said, nodding to Mitch and Graham. "It's an unwritten rule. Only one McKenna per team."

"You make us sound like two overgrown schoolboys," Graham cut in.

"Everyone's afraid of the damage we could do if we teamed up," Mitch joked.

She wondered what that meant.

*

Mitch watched Geoff escort Aubrey to the bleachers before he went to round up the rest of his team. Though it was good to see his brother pretty much back to normal and to see Aubrey somewhat thrown by Geoff's attention, Mitch had a funny feeling about this plan. He couldn't put a name to it, except he found himself resenting Geoff, the very person the plan was designed to help. Go figure.

"Pretty girl."

Mitch turned to see Orville Drummond. He hadn't even known his old friend was at the picnic. He didn't usually take in these things.

"Huh? Oh, you mean the one with my brother. That's our houseguest from L.A."

"I see," Orville said, though he didn't sound convinced.

Though no further explanation was necessary, Mitch continued. "The owner of the coach we're currently working on sent her own interior decorator."

Scratching his head, Orville seemed to stare right through him. "You don't say? Isn't that what you normally do?"

Too late, Mitch saw where this was heading. The attorney in Orville never rested. Mitch attempted to extricate himself from the mire. "I need to be there to . . . uh . . . monitor her work."

"Oh? She doesn't know what she's doing?"

"She's very good at what she does."

"Uh-huh. She needs an assistant, then?"

Mitch felt himself sinking deeper and deeper into the morass. "Well, no, not exactly."

Orville simply looked at him.

"That is," Mitch rushed on to explain, "I . . . uh . . . she . . . uh . . . doesn't know her way around motor coaches. They're built differently than houses."

Orville didn't say anything.

Mitch attempted to escape. "Good to see you again, Orville. I've got to get over to the game." He pulled on his ball glove and cap.

"I'll walk over with you."

They'd hardly gone five yards before Orville launched the topic Mitch knew was coming. "Thought any more about my offer? I left you a message the other day."

Mitch punched his free hand into the glove a few times for fit. "Oh . . . right. Sorry. I heard it but didn't get back to answering it."

"If I didn't know better, Mitch, I'd say you're avoiding the question."

They kept walking, at a slower pace to accommodate Orville, even though Mitch itched to run off. Knowing how persistent Orville could be, Mitch realized he had to say something. "I gave you my answer the other day, Orville. I haven't changed my mind."

Orville stopped, reaching for Mitch's forearm. "You didn't reconsider?"

Mitch took a deep breath and let it out slowly. He didn't want to give the man the least little straw to grasp in hopes he'd change his mind. "I told you. I'm committed to helping my brothers in this business right now. And for some time to come. I can't consider other options."

"Even if you're not needed as much? At least for the time being while this interior decorator is around? Or do you have another project waiting in the wings?"

Attorneys didn't ask questions to which they didn't already know the answers. Orville must be aware of how little business they had lined up at the moment. And he also had to know how tempting the offer was. This was his way of making it more acceptable to Mitch.

He caught sight of Geoff making his way up the rows of bleachers. He wished he'd thought to bring lawn chairs so Geoff could have sat in the shade of a tree rather than directly in the sun. Geoff needed him. He couldn't abandon his brother. "No, Orville. Thanks for thinking of me. And giving me another chance. But I can't."

"But . . . "

"Gotta go. Game's about to start. See you 'round." He took off running for the field, leaving Orville stopped in his tracks, shaking his head.

Mitch joined his team, went through the batting order, punched in his glove again, and attempted to join in the joking to ease pre-game jitters. Throughout, all he could think of was Orville's offer and everything he was leaving behind.

*

From the way Mitch was talking to the players gathered around him, Aubrey surmised he must be captain. Figured. Even though he was the youngest McKenna, he seemed to take the lead whenever the need arose. Which probably accounted for Graham's antics, like stirring the pot with his tale of her *thing* for Mitch. What was with that? Mitch and her? Graham must be the creative one in the family.

Geoff attempted to make conversation. "I got the impression the first day you were here that you weren't too thrilled to be spending your time in the Midwest."

He'd picked up on that, huh? She'd have to remember that Geoff was very astute.

"I thought I'd be spending my summer elsewhere when this project popped up. Ms. DiFranco was very convincing. And, so far, it hasn't been so bad. It's like nothing I've done before."

He put on his sunglasses, since the sun had come out with a vengeance, and pulled his ball cap down so the bill shaded his entire forehead. She wondered if his condition made him burn easily. "What kind of projects have you been doing?"

She wasn't sure how much to reveal. "My clients of late have been the rich and famous of Hollywood. They've been buying up the grand old houses and refurbishing them."

"Sounds interesting. Anyone I'd know?"

"Maybe. But I have to sign confidentiality agreements in order to do the work."

"Oh." He sound disappointed.

Mitch was first at bat and struck out. He dropped the bat and stomped off the field, brushing by the members of his team who rushed out to console him. The next guy landed a single, the next two struck out and the other team was up. Graham brought in the first run.

In the next few innings, both teams managed to score at least one run each time at bat.

"How's it going?" Debbie Summers asked, joining them. "I wanted to get out here sooner, but my kitchen crew had other ideas. Who's ahead?"

"The Green Team, six to four," Geoff answered, his eyes fixed on the action on the field.

"Is that the team your brother's on?" Debbie asked innocently. "Graham, that is."

Debbie's reference to Graham reminded Aubrey of Mitch's comment about Debbie's matchmaking tendencies. She wondered if Debbie had set her sights specifically on Graham or if any McKenna would do. Wouldn't hurt to try. "Graham's on the Red Team," she replied. "Is that the same team your daughter's on?"

Debbie cocked her head, puzzled, but she didn't comment about how Aubrey knew she had a daughter. "Peggy's not playing today. She sprained her ankle last Tuesday."

Oops. "That's too bad. Is she still able to get around?"

"Yes, it's much better. She just can't run on it for a while. That's her over there in the pink halter top. Did you meet her yet?"

"No, I haven't had the pleasure."

Debbie stood and called out, "Peggy! Over here, Peg!"

Though the woman's forcefulness startled Aubrey, no one else seemed to notice.

When the young woman turned around, Aubrey was surprised. She'd expected a real dog, given her mother's intervention in her love life. Peggy Summers was anything but, with long blonde hair, dark blue eyes, and long, lanky legs. Coloring similar to Jenna's, Aubrey realized. Peggy was dressed to show off but not flaunt her figure in her halter top and shorts.

As the young woman climbed the steps of the bleachers, her mother said, "Hon, this is the young woman who's working at the McKennas' for a few weeks."

"Sure, you're . . . "

"She's an interior decorator from Los Angeles," her mother supplied. She turned back to Aubrey. "Aubrey, right? Aubrey Carpenter."

"Good memory." She nodded to Peggy, who momentarily wore a confused look but then settled on the other side of her mother.

"I considered taking an interior decoration course in college," Peggy added, "but never got around to it. Do you like it?"

"It's not the life for everyone, but I like it," Aubrey replied. "Why don't you join me, Peggy, and I'll give you the lowdown." Adroitly, she indicated the spot between herself and Geoff she'd just created by moving over.

Once Peggy was reseated, Aubrey said, "You know Geoff McKenna, don't you?"

Peggy and Geoff exchanged nods. Peggy's neck tinged to almost the same color as her halter top. Geoff fidgeted in his seat, then offered her a water from the cooler at his feet.

"Haven't seen much of you around town lately, Geoff," Peggy said. "Been away?"

Geoff colored slightly himself, but he replied, "Nah. My condition's been kicking up again. Getting a lot of beauty rest, though. You think it helped?"

Although it was light banter, Aubrey heard the undertones of interest in Geoff's reply. She had to hand it to him. He didn't back away from his MS. In fact, he used it. Not to gain Peggy's sympathy, but her attention.

"You don't look too bad," Peggy admitted, a shy smile teasing her lips. "You must have been sleeping around the clock."

Geoff grabbed his chest in jest. "You wound me. Compliment me with one hand and take it all away with the other."

"Not at all," Peggy said, letting it drop there.

Aubrey shifted in her seat to face away from the new couple. The first throes of romance were great for the two parties involved but a bit much for onlookers. "So, Debbie, have you lived in this town long?" she said, searching for a safe topic.

"Forever!" the woman replied without hesitation. "Same neighborhood, almost. When I married Peggy's father, I moved into a split-level three blocks away. Been there ever since."

"I wouldn't know what it's like to live in any one place that long." She offered Debbie a bottle of water from Geoff's cooler, but Debbie refused.

Debbie gave her a knowing look. "Your family moved a lot?"

"More or less. My mother isn't easily satisfied. So we've been around a bit."

Debbie didn't reply. Turning away from Aubrey, she focused her attention straight ahead on the playing field.

Aubrey wondered if she'd inadvertently offended the woman, but let it pass.

By the ninth inning, the score was ten to eight in favor of Graham's team. It was Mitch's last time at bat. He'd struck out twice already and hadn't scored yet.

Even from where she sat, Aubrey read the tension and frustration in his face. He'd not had a productive afternoon compared to his brother, who'd scored three times. Geoff had wondered out loud more than once what was up with his younger brother. His game was off.

Mitch swung and missed. She could see him pucker his lips and pull in his arms. The second pitch resulted in a magnificent foul. Finally, on the third pitch, he connected. She heard the crack of bat hitting ball but couldn't trace its trajectory.

As if shocked to have finally hit the ball, Mitch paused. Then he took off, loping easily around first and second. About halfway between second and third base, he collided with Graham, knocking them both to the ground. Neither moved.

Despite his condition, Geoff barreled down the bleachers like a frightened victim escaping a burning building. He went to his knees, trying to slap Graham to consciousness long before Aubrey and Peggy caught up. "Gray? Can you hear me?"

Mitch was already sitting up, rubbing his head, looking disoriented. "Wha' happened?"

"You and Graham found the same piece of earth at the same time," Aubrey told him. "Are you okay? Anything broken?"

Mitch felt his arms and legs. "I'm okay. How's Gray? Oh!

Woo!" He closed his eyes and his head began to loll.

"Lie back, Mitch," Aubrey ordered, catching his head in her arms just before it hit the dirt. That's when she spied the blood on his arm. "Yes, you are hurt, you Spartan." She raised her head to see if anyone had thought to bring a first aid kit. The teenager who'd been assigned that duty for the day arrived. "Over here," she directed, and immediately took over as nurse.

Meanwhile, Graham had opened his eyes and was attempting to sit up by himself over Geoff's protests. "They didn't count his run, did they? I had him dead to rights."

"Don't worry about that now, guy," Geoff said. "You're in no shape to get up yet. I don't like the way your eyes look. What d'you think, Peggy?"

"He's definitely coming away from this with a shiner," she said. "That bruising around his eye could mean concussion."

"You thinking what I am?" Geoff asked.

"Emergency room," they both said at once.

Geoff turned his attention to Aubrey and Mitch. "How's Mitch doing?"

"I'm fine!" Mitch called back, propping himself up and shaking off both Aubrey's and the teenager's attempts to help him.

Peggy and Geoff got Graham to his feet and helped him hobble to her car.

That left Aubrey and the teenage medic to attend to Mitch, who was already arguing about getting to his feet.

"At least let us get a bandage around that wound," Aubrey pleaded.

"I'm not one of your projects, Aubrey," he bristled. "You don't need to fix me up. It's just a little scratch. Happens all the time at these games."

"Fine!" She backed off and let the kid take over. Maybe she had been acting like a mother hen. The sight of blood had scared her and sent her into first responder overdrive.

She was heading for her car when Debbie Summers caught up with her.

"How are they? Did I see Peggy and Geoff helping Graham off the field?"

"Peggy offered to drive them to the hospital," Aubrey answered, cooling her anger.

"There goes my ride home, then."

That didn't give Aubrey much choice. "I can take you. You'll have to give me directions, though. How soon do you want to leave?"

Debbie looked back toward the field. "Looks like the game's over. Why not now? I'm probably turning red from all that sun anyway."

On the way to Debbie's, Aubrey noted how her rider screwed up her face as if working through a heavy thought. "Did something happen between you and Mitch back there?"

Aubrey didn't want to discuss Mitch with Debbie. Heck, she couldn't even discuss him with herself, because she didn't understand what was happening with him. "Why do you ask?"

"Before you arrived, it was like he'd been patrolling the parking lot waiting for you. Then he stayed glued to your side even when his brothers joined you in the lunch line."

"Well . . ."

"Then you raced to his side when he got hurt."

"Yes, but . . ."

"If you hadn't had me in tow afterwards, you would have run off." Debbie clasped her hands together and rested her case.

"Okay, you wore me down. He snapped at me when I tried to attend to his wound."

"Men do that when they don't want their women to see how vulnerable they are."

"I'm not his woman."

"Whatever you say, dear. But don't go getting your knickers in a knot because he didn't appreciate your nursing skills. It's what men do."

"He hurt my feelings." There she'd said it. Her, the perennial tough cookie.

"He didn't mean to, I'm sure. Well, he probably did mean to come across gruffly so you'd retreat. You've got him scared, Aubrey."

Aubrey almost missed her turn on that one. "Scared? I don't think so, Debbie. Exasperated, yes. And challenged. Maybe even a little bit interested, at least before I turned into Nurse Nellie. But scared? I don't think so."

"Because you're starting to get to him, that's why."

Aubrey scrunched up her nose. "You think?"

"I don't know what's been going on in that firehouse since you've been there, but something's begun to defrost Mitch McKenna."

"Defrost?"

Debbie blinked, as if realizing Aubrey was in the dark. "Six months ago, Mitch's fiancée dumped him in favor of an exciting job in New York. He was devastated and has been acting like a zombie ever since. But that's not who I saw today."

"Really? Do you know the family well?"

"Just casually. Our parents were once neighbors. Though seeing my daughter with Geoff McKenna today, well . . . maybe . . . "

"Mitch told me you were shooting for Graham." She couldn't help herself. Debbie had shared with her. She owed her something.

Debbie returned a sheepish look. "He's sharp. You remember that, Aubrey. You'll have to return the same to keep his interest."

"But after today . . . " Why did she even care? And, as she turned from the tree-lined boulevard, dark from the shade of heavy summer foliage, onto the sun-kissed avenue Debbie lived on, it was like bringing her feelings into the light and recognizing them for what they were. She was not only attracted to Mitch McKenna, she cared for him. More than any male that had graced her horizon in a long time.

"As for me," Debbie continued, oblivious to Aubrey's epiphany, "I can grow to love that Geoff as much as I thought I could love Graham. So Peggy's a year or two older than he is. Geoff's very mature."

"And you're not concerned about the . . . the . . . you know."

"The MS? You can say it out loud, dear. I suppose it will present a bit of a challenge to both of them, but did you see them with their heads together during the game? I'm surprised they got to Graham as quickly as they did for all of the game they were watching."

As Debbie was getting out of the car at her house, she asked, "Would you like to come to dinner sometime while you're here?"

Aubrey tried to think of some excuse to turn down the offer, but her brain was fried from being outdoors all afternoon. "Tight schedule. I'll be working night and day soon."

"You have to eat sometime." Debbie wasn't one to give up easily.

"Well, yes, but . . . "

"I'll call you soon. There's something I'd like to tell you. But not today."

That was strange. Debbie saved that statement until last. Probably something about Hollywood. Everyone always assumed she rubbed elbows with the stars.

When she arrived at the firehouse, an interesting thought struck her. For the first time since her arrival, she'd have the place completely to herself.

CHAPTER SEVEN

"Hi, honey, I'm home!" Aubrey called out as she entered the fire station through the back door. She didn't expect a response and got none. Saturday afternoon in small town Iowa. Alone in this mausoleum of a bus factory. And out of sorts. Mitch's rejection of her help with his wounds still rankled. What was with that guy? It was like he saw accepting help from anyone—well, her—as a sign of weakness.

But he had started to trust her enough to tell her she could work in the motor coach on her own, so she might as well get to it. As Jenna kept reminding her, time was ticking.

She'd been at it about a half hour when she thought she heard a noise outside in the garage area. She wasn't one to let things that go bump in the night get to her, but four in the afternoon was a different matter. Though being alone in the building hadn't bothered her until then, unidentified sounds were disquieting.

Maybe Mitch had returned? And was keeping his distance. She heard another noise, different from the first, but it clearly was a sound. Setting her sketches aside, she rose, opened the door and stepped timidly into the garage. She listened intently for well over a minute. Nothing. Must have imagined it. The place was getting to her. She took a deep breath and willed her heart to stop beating so frantically.

She'd started back to the motor coach when she definitely heard something else. It came from upstairs. It had to be Mitch. She decided to check and give him a chance to apologize.

She made her way to the stairs, taking a moment to listen on each, her heartbeat failing to note her message to slow down. When she got to the top, she hesitated once again before finally getting up the nerve to check out the kitchen. Everything seemed to be in order.

She moved into the living room where they'd watched TV and eaten pizza a few nights earlier. She hadn't heard anything more since coming upstairs. Should she investigate the bedrooms? And if she found something? If it was the guys, she'd royally humiliate herself. And if it was someone . . . or something . . . else, what would she do then?

Her heart banging against her ribcage, for her peace of mind, she had to know.

She helped herself to an iron from a set of golf clubs nestled in a corner of the living room, so she'd at least have something to protect herself with.

She peeked into what must be Graham's room first. A drafting table and chair took up a good quarter of the room. No other sign of life, nor any goblins or other scary apparitions.

She marched herself to what had to be Mitch's door, since it was the only other door in the hallway, and peeked in. The room was clear. She took a deep breath in relief, when Mitch burst into the room from what must have been the bathroom. Her heart paused mid-beat.

He was wrapped in a heavy white Turkish towel. Nothing more. He didn't notice her at first, because he was too intent toweling his hair dry. Then, "What the . . . ?"

"I . . . uh . . . I thought I heard a noise," she managed to get out, gulping for air. "Several. Up here. It must have been," she paused to give him a shaky, sheepish smile, "you."

"You think?" His tone said it all. He was still put out with her.

She tried to think of a smart retort, but her brain was too busy processing the sight before her. God, he was gorgeous! The fact that he was dripping wet didn't hurt any, either. One pec seemed to wink at her. He'd done that deliberately, she decided, when he caught her ogling him.

"This was my first time alone in this place. Wasn't accustomed to the sounds it makes. Just wanted to check it out."

"Yeah, well, thanks. If it had been a burglar, I'm sure you could have beaten him senseless with that club." His words dripped more sarcasm than his body dripped water.

"I'm sorry to have disturbed you." She clutched the golf club to her chest. "The next time I hear sounds overhead, I'll lock myself in the motor coach and let whoever it is steal you blind." She turned, taking whatever dignity remained with her and stomped off.

*

Mitch stood there watching her go, unable to think of something to say but knowing he should. Couldn't very well run after her the way he was dressed. Or not dressed. Though he was reasonably comfortable with his body, encountering a woman he'd known less than a week nearly naked in his own bedroom was unnerving. Damn. She had a way of shaking him up.

He could have called her back, but he doubted she would have listened. Not after the way he'd treated her earlier. He didn't know why he'd done that. She'd looked so scrumptious when she'd first arrived at the park, he found himself finding excuses to be near her. But his collision with Gray had thrown him. Besides that mean cut on his arm, which continued to hurt like hell, the impact had left him winded, like the deflated state of his self-esteem.

He'd snapped with Aubrey's arrival on the field to play nurse. She'd only wanted to help, and he'd dumped on her. Why did he keep sniping at her? Was he that afraid to open up to a woman again? Because that's what it was. She was getting to him. One part of him wanted to give in, and the other was afraid she'd turn out to be another Dianne.

But he wasn't going to find his answers standing here in his bedroom in a growing puddle of shower residue. He needed to dress so he could go repair the damage.

*

Back at the motor coach, Aubrey spent a good five minutes getting her breathing under control. The triple dose of fright, anger, and . . . lust? . . . had taken their toll. She sat slumped against a wall staring at the sketch she'd dropped when she'd gone to play Nancy Drew.

Why had he treated her like that? Sure, she'd startled him. But he'd taken her unawares also, and she hadn't accused him of stupidity. Feminine frailty. Well, fine, if Mitch was going to act like an ass, she'd treat him in kind. No need for hurt feelings.

A gentle rap on the door broke the silence. "Aubrey? You in there?"

Great! Just what she wanted. To go another round with him. "What do you want?"

The door opened. Mitch stuck his head and shoulders through. He was now fully clothed, although his hair still looked damp. "May I come in?"

"It's still technically your property."

He came within a few feet of her, leaned against the wall and paused, as if taking a moment to frame his words. "I came to apologize. For barking at you upstairs. You were frightened, yet brave enough to check it out. That took courage."

She bit her lower lip, holding back harsh words that would undo his statement.

When she didn't say anything, he continued, as if he thought he needed to say more. "I must have scared the . . . whatever . . . out of you when I breezed out of the bathroom."

"That you did."

He slid down the wall and sat on his haunches facing her. "I thought I'd better check on you. For all I knew, you'd be installing a security system before I was dressed."

That again. Why did he keep harping on her initiative?

"I was kidding!"

"I didn't realize."

"Yeah, well, I've been in a pretty sour mood for the last several hours. I can see how you'd think I was still there."

She lifted her chin. "Now you're not?"

"Guess I'd better apologize for that, too," he said, letting his shoulders slump. "I invited you to the picnic and then proceeded to unload on you as soon as you arrived."

"If you had second thoughts about my being there . . . "

"No, it was nothing like that." He shifted position and planted himself beside her. "I . . . uh . . . ran into an old friend just before the game. We had words. I worried all afternoon about having upset him. It affected my game."

"Did you get it resolved?"

"No time. I went right into the game. And then that . . . that collision with Gray. God knows what I did to him. I take it he's not back from the hospital yet?"

"I haven't heard from him or Geoff." Since he was sitting with his left arm facing her, she turned to examine the injury. "How's your arm?"

He shrugged it off. "Just a scratch. Although a pain tablet about now wouldn't be a bad idea."

"Do you want me to get you some?" She'd blurted it out before realizing he probably thought she was overstepping her bounds again.

He put a restraining hand on her forearm. "I'll take care of it. Don't fret yourself."

His touch ignited nerve endings she didn't know existed. She fought to maintain her composure, but she had to keep reminding herself to breathe.

A strange expression came over Mitch, as if he'd been coasting through this conversation in the dark and someone had suddenly turned on the lights. He withdrew his hand, but he continued to stare at her as if just seeing her for the first time.

He looked like a man trapped in front of an oncoming freight train. Then he caught sight of the sketch she'd left on the floor. He reached over to pick it up. "May I?"

The moment was over.

She nodded.

He examined the sketch for quite some time before speaking, even holding it out in front of him in an apparent effort to envision how the interior would look when she got done with it. "Are you going for a theme of some sort?"

"Something like that. Jenna, Ms. DiFranco, puts her entire being into her performances. When they're over, she's completely drained. This is to be her retreat, where she can reenergize before each performance."

"Retreat, huh? How do you do that? There isn't much space."

"I asked her to tell me what takes her mind off her everyday routine. Where in the world she'd go if she wanted to be in her version of Paradise."

"I'm intrigued. What did she say?"

She debated how much of her plans she wanted to divulge. Full disclosure won out. His reaction might help her gauge how well it would go over with her sister. "She said the Greek Isles."

Mitch scoped out the small room. "Not enough room in here for a Parthenon."

She chuckled, despite his making light of her idea. "No Parthenon. But a lot of white. And blue. And maybe a column or two."

"Are you putting me on?"

"No. Too far out?"

"Too stark. Is that her lifestyle?"

Aubrey considered. "Not really. She's down to earth most of the time. Traditional home."

"Wouldn't she want something that was more like home, then? Home on the road?"

She started to thank him for his suggestion, then blow it off, but what he'd said struck a chord. Maybe her idea was a bit far-fetched.

"I know you aren't happy unless you've tweaked something to death, but what if, just this once, you stayed close to the original canvas. Not mess with what works."

She pushed to her feet. "You keep repeating that. Is it so wrong to want to do your best?"

Mitch rose also but stayed out of her path. "Of course not. But you keep trying to change things. Make them better. Maybe all you have to do is maintain. Give her a bit of the familiar."

"The familiar?"

"Yeah. Borrow a couple paintings or photos. Use some of the same colors. And maybe some of her favorite pillows. She'll love it."

"She . . . " She couldn't finish her thought. His words had hit paydirt somewhere inside her brain, and the rest of her body was dancing in the streets. So far, she hadn't been impressed with what she'd seen of his decorating work. But this was brilliant!

"You okay?" Mitch came over to her and placed his hands on her shoulders. "Are the walls closing in on you again? Do you need some water?"

Attempting to catch her breath, she held up a hand for him to give her a minute. "I've been struggling all week trying to come up with a design plan. In five minutes, you laid it in my lap."

A strange gleam came into his eyes. "You like it?"

"How much is it going to cost me if I use it?"

He gave her a puzzled look. "Cost you? You think I won't let you forget it was my idea?"

"Something like that."

He appeared to give her concern some thought. "Can you cook?"

"A little. Why?"

"Pick a night. Fix dinner for all of us." He gave her a smug smile.

No problem. She'd already committed to limited meal prep when she moved in. "Okay. It's a deal."

They stood there, eyeing each other awkwardly, unsure what to do next.

"Well, uh, guess I'll leave you to your drawing," Mitch said at last.

"Oh. All right."

He had his hand on the door when she said, "Wait!" She went to him, but once there, turned shy. What the heck? She rose on tiptoes and kissed him on the cheek.

Though his eyes had gone wide, a hint of a grin told her she'd hit the mark.

"What's that for?" His voice emerged strained and rough.

"Thanks for the idea. I really like it." She backed away slightly, surprised but not overly upset by her brazenness.

He looked her directly in the eyes, glints of something in his own. "Good thing Geoff didn't see that. He'd redouble his efforts to fend you off."

"I took care of that."

"Huh?"

"I got him sidetracked. With Peggy Summers."

"Peggy? I thought she was interested in . . ."

"Graham?" she finished for him. "Perhaps, at the start of the day. But she and Geoff got to talking during the game, and that was that."

"That was what? A couple hours and they're dating?"

"You didn't see them. Once they started talking, no one else existed."

He shook his head in amazement. "That must have been tough on Debbie."

"Actually, Debbie couldn't be happier. She told me so on the way home."

Her comment had him sinking to the door jamb. "She *told* you so? On the way *home?*"

She dropped as well, seating herself on the top of the two steps attached to the motor's coach's outer door. "That's right. She even invited me to dinner sometime while I'm here."

Mitch stared at her. "That was fast. My ex-fiancée didn't get invited for a couple years."

The ex-fiancée again. "How come?"

Mitch didn't reply immediately. "Dianne was a bit of a snob. Debbie's more down-to-earth and readily picked up on Dianne's disdain. She only extended the invitation as a favor to me after we'd gotten engaged."

"How did it go?"

"How do you think? Dianne made a half-hearted attempt to be approachable, but Debbie saw right through her. Thought she was patronizing and condescending. Which she was."

She put a hand over his. "I'm sorry, Mitch." The contact had come naturally, unbidden, but, like before, her response to touching him was anything but. What was with this guy? Was he surrounded with a magnetic field? She withdrew her hand and stuck it in a pocket in her slacks.

"She wasn't all that bad. It just didn't work out. She wanted different things."

"Marriage?" The word was out before she considered why she was asking.

He screwed up his mouth. "Took me a while to reconcile myself to that horrendous wedding she was planning."

"Big?"

"Humongous. She's an only child with older, doting parents. Nothing was too good for their baby. Certainly not me."

She couldn't tell if his tone belied regret or bitterness. "They didn't like you?"

"They liked me. But my occupation didn't thrill them."

"You're kidding. You've got a great thing going here."

He gave her an appreciative look. "Thanks. I didn't realize you knew so much about us."

"A lot of what I know came from Ms. DiFranco. I was going to do my own Internet search before coming here but blew it off to gain an earlier start."

"You were going to check us out?" He tugged at his collar.

"Should I be insulted or impressed?"

"Neither. I do it as a matter of practice with all my clients."

"But we're not your clients."

"Good point." She grinned. "Still, it would have prepared me for the triple threat."

He chuckled. "Is that the way you see us? As a threat?"

She raised her eyebrows. This was going somewhere. Should she be on guard? "Certainly a challenge when I first arrived. But . . . you tend to grow on folks."

Now he raised an eyebrow. "Really? How're we doing?" Keeping his eyes focused directly on her, he retrieved the hand she'd withdrawn and held it gently between his own hands.

Her stomach went into dive bomb mode. And her scalp felt sweaty. "We?" she asked, all brilliant rejoinders fleeing her brain.

He shifted position and moved closer. "Okay. Me. How do you feel about me now?"

Even if she'd known how to reply, her mouth felt as if it had been stuffed with the carpet sample she'd been staring at earlier.

"Aubrey?"

"I, I'm torn, I guess."

He put his arm around her shoulders.

She felt a muscle ripple beneath his shirt. Even though seated, that slight movement had her knees quaking.

"Torn? Between what?"

She turned to look at him. His face was no more than six inches away from hers. "Between throwing you out before I do something foolish and . . . " She could hear his breathing. It was shallow, just like hers. "And . . . "

"Mitch? Aubrey? Where are you?" Geoff's voice cut through the moment like a knife.

"There you are!" Geoff announced, coming around the corner of the coach. "Didn't you hear us calling?" He took in the scene, a brow arched in question. "Did I interrupt something?"

"Aubrey was showing me the drawings she's done so far," Mitch said.

Aubrey smiled broadly. "Want to see?"

Geoff raised a hand. "I'll wait until you're finished. How's it going? On schedule?"

Aubrey and Mitch exchanged glances. "Not as far along as I'd hoped to be by now," she said, "but that's because Mitch gave me a suggestion that blew the wind out of my big idea."

Mitch fixed a bland expression on his face.

"Thanks to his questions, I'm considering this from a new perspective."

"Uh-huh. New perspective," Geoff said, deadpan. "Gray broke his collar bone. It's not as bad as it could've been. Didn't need surgery, just an arm sling for a few days."

"Ouch!" Aubrey said. "How's he feeling?"

"Unlike me, the model patient," Geoff said, "he's uncomfortable and in pain, even though they gave him something for it. With Peggy's help, I was able to get him to bed."

"Peggy?" Mitch asked, seizing the opportunity to turn the tables on his brother.

"Peggy Summers. She drove us to the hospital."

"I took her mom home," Aubrey added. "She invited me to dinner sometime."

"Speaking of dinner . . . " Geoff said. "We're calling out for Chinese. Want to join us?"

Mitch looked at Aubrey. "Chinese? Looks like the party continues upstairs."

CHAPTER EIGHT

It took Aubrey most of the next day, Sunday, to track down her sister, who'd turned off her cell phone. When she finally did connect with Jenna, she described her plans to transform the coach into a home on wheels by including some of Jenna's favorite household goods.

"I like it. It's less dramatic than what you usually do."

"I have to credit Mitch with the initial idea. But I took it and ran with it."

"Mitch? You must be on speaking terms now."

Aubrey remembered the peck on the cheek she'd given him the day before and the aftershocks that assaulted her body. "Yeah, for the most part."

She told her sister about the picnic, baseball game, and Graham's broken collar bone. "We made quite the party of eating Chinese food around his bed, taking turns feeding him."

"He couldn't feed himself?"

"Probably, but with effort. Making a fuss over him seemed to have a recuperative effect. By the time the evening ended, he was sitting up in bed cracking jokes with the rest of us."

"That doesn't sound like the guy I've talked to. He's always so serious."

"Maybe the medication got to him?"

"Have you, uh, moved in yet?"

"Tomorrow. They didn't want me to sleep in the laundry room but really didn't have much else to offer other than their offices. Then Graham, even in his pain, got this bright idea to put me up in the motor coach."

"My motor coach?"

Jenna had never been very good at sharing. She'd become too

comfortable as an only child for nine years before Aubrey showed up. "Just for a few nights. After that, it'll be too torn up. So they're bringing in their next project a week or so early, and I'll move in there once it arrives."

Silence on the other end.

"Jenna? I thought it was a great solution."

"I suppose so. I guess I worry about you getting too wrapped up in their lives. Like you did with Heidi Buxbaum, letting her con you into redecorating that cabin so her husband wouldn't have a thing to do with it."

Aubrey wanted to throw her cell phone. "Jenna. This assignment was your idea."

"It seemed a good idea at the time. You needed a place to escape to, and we thought they'd never find you in Iowa. Besides, with that anti-Midwestern attitude Mother honed in you, I was sure this was one place you could maintain your distance. Looks like I was wrong."

"Don't worry about me. I'm not getting in over my head." She wasn't, was she?

"Okay, I believe you. Besides, it's too late to bring in a replacement."

Ah, Jenna, ever the pragmatist when it came to her own needs. "So, you'll pick out a few items and ship them off tomorrow?"

"Yes. Tomorrow. And Aubrey?"

"I know. Bring it in on time."

"Sooner."

She clicked off without replying to Jenna's last statement. *Yes, Jenna, I'll get it done in time. No, Jenna, I won't get too close to the McKennas.* Besides, if Mitch had been interested, he would have followed up on the kiss on the cheek. And he hadn't.

Why did she keep thinking about that kiss? It was a gesture, no more. He'd solved her dilemma with the design plan and she'd thanked him. And now it was over. Done with.

*

Geoff moved in on Sunday. Since Gray was laid up and sleeping off painkillers, and Peggy had promised to take her little brother to a movie, Mitch was elected to help.

"Guess I sorta fell down on the job yesterday," Geoff commented as they were transporting the first load back to the firehouse.

"What job was that?"

"You know. Serving as buffer between you and Aubrey."

Mitch fiddled with the pickup's CD player, selecting one of his favorite country bands. He didn't want to discuss Aubrey, or her plan to get Geoff to move into the firehouse, and especially not Gray's ludicrous suggestion to Geoff that Aubrey had the hots for him.

Geoff turned to look at him, a curious expression etched on his face. "That find-a-distraction ploy isn't going to work this time, Little Brother. I'm on to you."

"Really? Just what are you on *to*?"

Geoff leaned over and turned off the CD. Settling back in his seat, he said, "Something's going on between you and our house guest. I knew it the minute I came back from the hospital yesterday and found the two of you huddled outside the motor coach. You both looked guilty. If you hadn't been completely dressed, I'd have sworn I'd interrupted some hanky-panky."

Mitch rolled his eyes. "Drop it. Nothing was going on."

"Could've fooled me."

Mitch thumped a palm against the steering wheel. "I'm not ready for another woman."

"Even if the woman in question is ready for you?"

The vehicle jerked as Mitch took a corner a little too fast. "Gray invented that part."

Geoff cracked a knowing smile. "I know. But he was just a little ahead of things. I saw the two of you together. There were more sparks flying between you than you'd find at a welders' convention."

Mitch knew his brother's persistence. It had gotten him through the bad days with his MS. If Mitch didn't find a way to deflect it in the next few minutes, he knew he'd eventually break down and . . . and what? Tell Geoff he was right. That Aubrey was getting under his skin? "Do we have to talk about this now?" he grumbled. "We're almost there."

Geoff studied him, then shook his head. "How much longer are you going to punish yourself? Deny yourself the right to happiness?"

Mitch could forestall Geoff's kidding, and his prodding and probing. But his older brother was deadly serious this time. Surely he hadn't guessed about his yearnings to go back to the law? "What . . . what are you talking about?"

Geoff shifted position, as if about to make a grand pronouncement. "You think you ran Dianne off by going into business with Gray and me. That you disappointed her. Forced her to break things off so she could have the kind of life she craved."

The pickup veered to the right momentarily, until he refocused his attention on the road. "That's crazy!" Mitch shouted, before allowing himself time to think of a better comeback.

"Maybe." Geoff said in a lower tone. "But you never talk about it. What am I supposed to think?"

Mitch swallowed deeply, buying time to think of a plausible reply. "Think that it wasn't meant to be. We were great together in high school and college, but we grew apart."

"Grew apart. Right. Mitch, she dumped you two months before the wedding, went off to New York City and promptly found another guy. If that's too harsh, so be it. You've been brooding over your hurt feelings ever since."

Mitch couldn't blame his brother for going all melodramatic. That's what he wanted others to believe, especially his brothers, so they wouldn't detect his regret about dropping the law. As far as he was concerned, Dianne's dumping him was the best thing she'd ever done for him, even if she did it for less than altruistic reasons.

In the long run, they wouldn't have worked. He knew that now. They wanted different things out of life.

Just as he and Aubrey saw life differently. What had made him include her? The woman kept sneaking unbidden into his thoughts.

"I care about you, guy. Just like you and Gray haven't allowed me to let the MS get to me, I don't want your hurt to get the better of you. It's time for you to move on."

Mitch blew out a long sigh of resignation. Geoff was on a roll. Ignoring him wasn't going to work. Barking at him hadn't helped either. "Move on?"

"You know, find yourself a new lady. And at the moment, Aubrey's the most likely candidate. Why not do something about it?"

"She's only here another few weeks. That's almost the same as a one-night stand."

"It's at least twenty-one nights, bro. That's plenty of time to get over your broken heart, have some fun, and . . . " Here he cocked his head and winked. " . . . not have to worry about any commitments."

*

With the guys occupied elsewhere, Aubrey allowed herself a break, sneaking into Mitch's office to use his exercise equipment. It felt great to be exercising muscles that had been neglected for over a week and cramped inside the motor coach in a variety of uncomfortable positions. Once she got the hang of the apparatus, the workout went smoothly. Time passed quickly.

"Lean into it more. Centers the buttocks."

Startled, Aubrey looked up to see a grizzled older man of about seventy framed in the door. He looked familiar, but she couldn't place him. She swung a leg over the bench, preparing to stand, embarrassed to have been caught.

"Don't get up. You seemed to be enjoying yourself," he said, entering the room.

She stood anyway, not sure who she was addressing. "I was about to finish. I'm Aubrey Carpenter. I'm here on a temporary project finishing the McKennas' latest customization."

He came closer. Dressed in a short-sleeved white shirt and tan slacks, he didn't appear to be a threat. "Orville Drummond. Friend of the family." He extended a hand. "I thought that's who you were. I saw you at the picnic yesterday with the boys."

She accepted his hand. "That's why you look familiar. You were talking to Mitch just before the softball game."

He grimaced. "Ah, you saw that, did you? Not one of my better moments, I'm afraid."

She'd noticed the two men engaged in an intense discussion, but was too far away to discern anything further. "You and Mitch had words?"

Though he continued standing several feet away, he folded his arms in front of him. "I wouldn't exactly call it an argument. Couldn't be that. We both want the same thing. Only Mitch is too thick-headed and proud to admit it."

His candor surprised her, but she also heard frustration in his voice. Not quite sure how to react, she sat down on the bench again. "I'm sorry. I don't know what you're talking about."

He chuckled. "Of course you don't. But I've decided to tell you." He glanced about the room. "Mind if I sit?"

She shook her head.

Settling back on a nearby chair, he placed his hands over his thighs. "There. That's better. Standing gets to me these days."

She waited for him to continue.

"How well do you know Mitch, Ms. Carpenter?"

A week's acquaintance with someone was fairly brief as far as friendships went, but she felt like she knew Mitch McKenna better than most. "I just met him a week ago."

"Oh." His tone conveyed disappointment. Wrinkling his forehead, he seemed to think through what he wanted to say next.

Finally, he asked, "In that time, have you picked up on an attitude? Frustration, disillusionment. That kind of thing."

The man definitely knew Mitch McKenna. But she wasn't so sure she wanted to share her observations. That would be like betraying Mitch.

Orville Drummond must have sensed her dilemma from her hesitation. "You won't be telling tales, Ms. Carpenter. Nothing I don't already know about our guy. In fact, I have something I'd like to share with you."

She blinked. She hadn't been expecting that. "O-kay. But we really don't know each other that well."

He looked at her as if gauging her truthfulness. "Really? Perhaps I misinterpreted what I saw yesterday?"

"Probably."

"Possibly. But I'm a pretty good read of character. Have to be for the courtroom."

"You're an attorney?" His casual appearance suggested otherwise.

"That's right. I run a small practice here in town."

She found herself warming to him. Not because he was a lawyer, which would probably have impressed her mother. But because he didn't look like one. She liked surprises. "What kind of law do you practice?"

"A little bit of everything. Mainly contracts and real estate. Tax law's too complicated. And we don't have enough crime around here, fortunately, to take on very many criminal cases. Sometimes divorces. Don't like that sort of thing, but friends prevail upon me on occasion."

"I see." Although she didn't.

"Mitch clerked for me several years ago."

He was watching her for her response. She didn't disappoint him, because this was news. Mitch a law student? She blinked again and squirmed in her seat. "What did you say?"

"You didn't know?" His gaze was direct and penetrating, again as if he was measuring her. Then he blinked as well, moving on. "Guess that doesn't surprise me. He doesn't mention the law to anyone anymore. Especially not his brothers. That's why I'm confiding in you."

She was intrigued. Enough to rise and take the side chair opposite him. She leaned her chin into a palm. "I'm flattered. Why me?"

He rubbed a hand across his face. "I need an ally, because I want him to rethink his decision to leave the law. He was a damn fine law student, Ms. Carpenter."

She smiled. "Aubrey."

"Orville. I like your willingness to listen."

"That much I can do. So tell me, what happened? Why isn't he practicing law?"

The older man shot a glance at the door. "Where are the guys today?"

Apparently he didn't want them to hear. "Mitch went with Geoff to his house to pick up some clothes and things. Geoff's moving back here temporarily."

He frowned. "Moving back here? He's gotten worse, then?"

He assumed she knew about the MS. Interesting. "He had an episode earlier in the week. He seems fine now, but Mitch and Graham wanted him here for a while, so if anything recurs, they'll be close by."

Orville resettled himself in his chair. "They worry too much about him. Geoff's the most reasonable in the bunch. He can take care of himself." He thought to add, "Most of the time."

"So he told me."

"You don't say?" He gave her a conspiratorial smile. "For being here a week, Aubrey, you've amassed a lot of information."

She laughed. "Don't tell my sister. She thinks I get too involved in other people's lives."

He arched a brow. "Do you?"

"Maybe. But in this case, Geoff volunteered the information.

So are you."

"Touché." He looked toward the door again. "So the guys are gone for a bit?"

"Not Graham. He broke his collar bone in that game yesterday. He's upstairs resting, sleeping off the effects of his painkillers."

He sat up straighter. "Okay, I'd better get on with it then, before they return." He rested his hands on the arms of the chair. "Mitch and Graham changed career paths to go into business with Geoff when his condition worsened. He could no longer travel as a sales rep for a pharmaceutical company. Mitch was just finishing up law school. Didn't even sit for the bar. Walked into my office one day and announced he was quitting. Just like that. No warning. No discussion."

She leaned in. "That sounds like Mitch. He doesn't tend to share his feelings."

"You've got that right. Thing is, even though he doesn't tell you what he's thinking, his mood comes through loud and clear."

She had to smile. "That was certainly the case with me. He didn't want any part of me being here when I first arrived."

"Sure that was about you?" Orville's gaze was once again direct and penetrating.

"I thought so. Why? What else would have accounted for his attitude?"

"You're an interior decorator, right? You're here to finish off the inside of the bus?"

"Motor coach. Yes, so?"

"Mitch usually does that. No training for it, unlike the mechanical part. He worked in my brother's garage in high school. Your arrival should have been a relief for him. One less interior to worry about. But instead, he got miffed."

"How did you know that?"

"Told me so himself one day last week. The day I offered him my business."

"What?" She shot out of the chair and stood facing him.

"I need to cut back. Health reasons. I want Mitch to take over. Incrementally. As little as one day a week at first."

"What did he say?" What a windfall for Mitch. An established practice, a partner who'd let him work back into it gradually.

Orville turned an impassive face to her. "Turned me down cold. Said he couldn't possibly leave his brothers."

"That again."

His eyes widened, taking on a more hopeful expression. "Ah, then, you see my problem."

"Ye-es. I understand what you want, and I think it would be great for Mitch, but neither of us makes his decisions for him. We have to respect that."

He slapped a knee. "Missy! I haven't made it through forty-five years of practicing law respecting other people's decisions." His volume had increased, forcing him to cough slightly. After clearing his throat, he seemed to calm down. "Mitch's been like a son to me. I want him to be happy. I don't think he is in this bus business. That gives me the right to ignore his refusal."

She dropped back into her chair, a little buzzer going off inside her head. She shouldn't be listening to this. She should thank Orville Drummond for his concern and send him on his way before Mitch returned. "What do you want me to do?" Where had that come from? A vein on the side of her forehead began to throb. She ignored it.

Orville gave her a broad smile. "Thank you. I wasn't sure how you'd react. Mitch is going to get around to talking to you." He smiled again at her perplexed expression. "Yes, he will. Don't ask me how I know, except think about it. A week ago he was barking at you, grumbling about your being underfoot. By the end of the week, you're his guest at a picnic."

Orville's comments warmed her. It mattered that he seemed to think Mitch liked her. "So he talks to me. What can I do?"

Chin resting on tented hands, he drew in a deep breath. "Get him to talk about how he feels about his job, why he left the law, or why he feels beholden to his brothers. Take your pick. Any one of those topics will help us discover what's going on inside that head of his."

"And if he does share any of this with me? As much as I want to help you and help him, I don't want to betray his trust."

Now it was Orville's turn to rise. "I haven't visited this office very often. Mitch would have preferred to cut all ties between us, but I wouldn't have it. Look around this room, Miss Interior Decorator. What does it tell you?"

She tried to do as he asked, studying the style of furniture, the colors, the décor. "I draw a blank. Other than he likes his space and to work out. What am I supposed to see?"

Orville nodded. "Exactly. It's a mish mash. He doesn't care." He gazed about the room again. "I don't even see his diploma from law school. What self-respecting attorney, or in his case, attorney-to-be, doesn't display that?"

"Obviously he doesn't want to remember that part of his life."

Orville came over to her and took her hand. "He's hurting, Aubrey. A hurt so deep he doesn't even see it for what it is. Denial. Help him see that. That's all I ask."

He released his hold on her and walked over to the door. "My office is just down the street. Drop by whenever."

"I'll do what I can."

He turned back to her. "And it's our little secret. Okay?"

Secret. Great. Jenna would be delighted with how well she was staying out of the McKennas' lives. On the other hand, Orville's visit had shed light on the secrets Mitch had been keeping. Secrets she meant to crack.

*

"Was that Orville Drummond I saw leaving the building?" Graham asked Aubrey later, as she made him a sandwich.

So much for keeping Orville's visit to herself. "Yes. He stopped by looking for Mitch and found me instead in his office."

Graham put the sandwich back on the plate and sat back in his chair. Scrunching up his eyes, he said, "Did he say what he wanted?"

She thought fast, attempting to find a plausible reply. "Something about continuing a conversation they started at the picnic yesterday." There. That was harmless enough.

Graham relaxed his expression. "That's right! I saw them walking over to the playing field together."

Deliberately neglecting to mention the talk she'd had with the man before his departure, she truthfully answered, "I told him Mitch was at Geoff's and I didn't know when he'd be back. So he left."

Graham examined his sandwich. "Haven't seen Orville for months and now twice in two days. Curious, don't you think?"

Careful, girl. This was dangerous territory. On the other hand, Graham had provided her with an opening. It wouldn't hurt to explore it just a little.

"Who is this Orville?"

He swallowed another bite before replying. "Orville Drummond is the epitome of the folksy country lawyer. For some reason, he and Mitch hit it off when Mitch was in law school."

She feigned surprise. "Mitch was in law school?"

He looked up from the remnants of his meal. "Yes. Hasn't Mitch told you?"

"I guess the subject never came up." She took her hands from the chair and sat down. "What happened? Did he drop out?"

"No. About the time Mitch was finishing his third year, Geoff's MS took him off the road. When he could no longer do his sales job, Mitch and I went into this business with him."

"Oh." She scooted forward in her chair. "Pretty big decision for all of you. Leaving behind promising careers."

A strange expression swept over Graham's face. Like he'd eaten a piece of spoiled lunchmeat. He didn't reply at once.

She tapped her head. "What was it Mitch said you were doing? Engineering?"

"I was an architect." His tone had become quiet.

"Wow! What did you design? Houses? Buildings?"

Graham slumped in his seat. "Nothing so grand. I was lowest man on the totem pole at a large firm in Minneapolis. I ran numbers for other architects, checking their calculations. Sometimes they gave me detail work, but never on anything that would show. Sewage systems. Exciting stuff like that."

She was getting the distinct impression that Graham had been more than willing to leave that job and return home to help Geoff. "Do you still design?"

He emitted something like a chortle, but it held a melancholy tone. "Only bus frames."

"You're happy with the career change?"

He narrowed his eyes, as if trying to decide what to say. "Yeah, I suppose you could say that. Besides, it's warmer here in the winters."

She moved on to the subject she was more interested in. "How about Mitch? Giving up the law seems pretty drastic."

"As soon as he heard what Geoff and I were planning, he insisted he had to be part of it, too."

"Really?" She sat back in her chair. She could readily imagine Mitch pushing his way into the partnership. It seemed to be a birth order thing. As the youngest, he had to be more aggressive than the other two. But she couldn't picture Mitch getting himself through law school and then just putting his training aside. "How did his fiancée take the news?"

"So you know about Dianne? I think she was in shock. She and Mitch had been planning to open their own practice ever since high school. They'd been on the debate team together."

"Is that what broke them up? His decision to give up the law?"

Graham placed his empty milk glass on his plate, which Aubrey shuttled to the sink. He went on, "No. At least not then. She stuck around another two years. But little by little, they started drifting apart."

She was starting to ask what caused the final break, when they heard Mitch calling from downstairs, "Gray, you up there?"

End of topic. Though a little more of the Mitch McKenna puzzle had fallen into place.

"Guess who's back," Graham said.

"You're up!" Mitch framed the doorway. "Those must be some strong pills they gave you. You've been out all day." Then he saw Aubrey seated at the table. Nodding her direction, he asked, "Were you able to contact Ms. DiFranco?"

"Finally. Took a while to track her down."

"How did she, uh, like the plans?"

His question held more than passing curiosity. "Loved 'em." She watched his smile broaden. "You said I could use the fax machine in your office, so I sent them off to her immediately. But she hasn't called back yet."

"Let me know when you hear." Turning back to Graham, he said, "Geoff's arranging the things we brought back in his office. There's still another load at the house. One more trip today. You gonna be okay?"

"I'm fine," Graham replied. "Aubrey made me a sandwich. How's Geoff?"

"The idea of coming here is growing on him, now that he's halfway moved in," Geoff said, coming up behind Mitch. He made for the refrigerator, opened the door and checked out the contents. "Any of that Chinese grub left from last night?"

"You polished that off around one," Mitch reminded him. "Grab some of that lunchmeat. I'll get the bread. A sandwich sounds pretty good."

"I should be getting back to my design plans," she said. "You guys can get back to your bonding."

"Don't go on our account," Geoff interjected, focusing his attention on the sandwich makings he'd removed from the refrigerator. "We're only here long enough to recharge before heading back."

Surprisingly, she didn't want to leave just yet. There was an energy, a dynamic about the brotherhood that intrigued her. Her relationship with Jenna was so different.

Chewing with relish, Geoff sat back in his chair and breathed a sigh of contentment. "Such a simple thing, yet the sandwich gives such pleasure." He was almost purring.

"It's good to see your appetite back," Mitch commented. Then, turning to Graham, he said, "And to see your color back. That was some collision we had yesterday."

"You don't seem to be the worse for wear," Graham responded.

"Oh, yes he is!" Aubrey blurted out. "Ask why he's wearing a long-sleeved T-shirt on a hot June day."

All three men looked at her, surprise and curiosity on two faces. A scowl on Mitch's.

Realizing she'd revealed a piece of information that was news to Graham and Geoff, she felt compelled to explain. "He came away with a mean gash on his arm. It probably should have had stitches, but the kid who patched him up did a pretty good job."

"I'm fine," Mitch cut in, a little too defensively.

"Ri-ight," Geoff said. "We discussed just how right he was on the way back from the house." He seemed to consider what had transpired in the car. Eyes widening, he said, "Why not join us on this next trip, Aubrey? We can show you our parents' old place. Who knows? If this arrangement works and we decide to put it on the market, we might need to fix it up first."

She thought she detected a slight frown on Mitch's face, but he covered it by turning his head away from her. "Uh, thanks, but I need to get back to my drawings."

"Must you?" Graham asked. "Geoff might have something there. Selling the old place could pump money into the business.

Float us until we start seeing a return on our investment."

Mitch shot his head back in the group's direction on that one. "We're not selling the house! If Geoff doesn't want to live there any longer, you or I could move in, Gray. We'll find some other way to keep the business going."

Aubrey edged back in her chair, debating how she could flee this family discussion that was fast becoming more than she wanted to hear.

The brothers appeared to have forgotten about her. Mitch glared. Geoff rolled his eyes. And Graham shook his head in disagreement. What was a self-respecting mediator at heart to do?

"Okay, I'll come along. I could use a break."

CHAPTER NINE

Mitch stewed during the drive back to their parents' place. This wasn't a good idea, showing Aubrey the old homestead. What had possessed Geoff to invite her along? Oh yeah, he'd been harping on how Mitch should get something going with her. Geoff must have thought it was up to him to make sure it happened.

Damn. He didn't need his brothers helping him get a woman. Sure, he was out of practice. He'd been with Dianne for almost seven years. But that didn't mean he was permanently out of commission.

"This is charming." She turned away from him and gazed out the side window at the various landmarks and residences they were passing.

"Got something to record the date, Geoff? Our lady decorator just made history."

Aubrey rolled her eyes. "My first impressions of this place were based on a jaundiced viewpoint."

"Your own?"

"No," she said in a manner he thought a little too forced.

She clamped her mouth shut and occupied herself gazing out the window.

"Whose then?" His curiosity surprised him. It shouldn't matter. But it did.

"It's not important."

Her evasiveness intrigued him. And her interest in the scenery seemed a little too intense. "Then it shouldn't be a problem telling us who."

"Yeah, Aubrey. Who set you against our happy little town?" Geoff asked.

She seemed to hunker down in her corner, deliberately not

facing them. Finally, in a very small voice she said, "My mother."

Geoff leaned farther over the seat. "Your mother?"

"What's she got against us?" Mitch wanted to know.

Aubrey studied her nails.

The subject seemed to make her uncomfortable. Mitch said, "Never mind. No big deal."

"She grew up here."

Aubrey hadn't said anything about having roots in their town. "No kidding? Would we know her?"

She shook her head slightly, as if attempting to come back from somewhere miles away. Still not looking at him, she said, "I doubt it. She left town over thirty years ago."

That wasn't enough to satisfy Geoff. "How come? The grass greener somewhere else? We think it's pretty green here."

Finally, she turned their direction. "Green, yes. But my mother wanted golden. As in California. And, three husbands later, she seems to have found it."

There was a bitterness to her tone. Also what sounded like a note of regret. Idly, Mitch wondered which husband had been Aubrey's father. Or if any of them claimed that distinction.

Straightening her shoulders, she sniffed and sat back against the car seat. "I should have known she was selling me a bill of goods. Burlington is nowhere near as boring and quaint as she portrayed it. She's always been one to exaggerate."

"That's parents for you," Mitch said, attempting to downplay her apparent distress. "For our parents, the rest of the world revolved around this town. Dad changed after Mom died. He started doing and saying things that were totally out of character. Did that happen with your mom? You said your dad had passed away."

Aubrey scrunched up her forehead, apparently thinking through his question. "No, nothing like that. My mother hasn't mellowed with age." She gave him a half-smile. "But then, she divorced my dad and remarried before he died a few years ago."

"Sorry. Didn't realize it was so recent." Mitch regretted having broached the subject. Thankfully, they were about to pull into the driveway of their parents' home. "Here we are. Chez McKenna." Had he really said that?

They entered from the back door. Geoff went in first, flipping on a light and opening the curtains framing the window above the kitchen sink. The room wasn't very large, the house having been built long before large combination kitchen-family rooms became popular.

"What's left to take?" Mitch asked. "I thought we got most of your clothes before."

"Clothes, yes. Shoes and toiletries I still need." Geoff continued on into the dining room they used for both informal and formal dining. Not that they'd done much entertaining since their mom had died. He headed off to his bedroom. Mitch remained with Aubrey, wracking his brain to figure out how to show her the house.

"What do you want us to do?" he called out, flipping through a pile of magazines Geoff had piled on the living room coffee table.

Aubrey had followed him through the house and was now standing a few feet away, gazing at the walls. "Is that you, Mitch?" She stared at a picture of him at age seven. Not his most appealing shot, considering his parents had allowed him to wear a mullet cut and he was missing two teeth.

Why had they continued to leave those photos up? Probably forgot they were there. Leave it to Aubrey to spot them right off. "Would you believe me if I said no?"

She pivoted to face him, an amused look playing across her face. "Not a chance. You may have outgrown the haircut and acquired adult teeth, but that's you. No doubt about it."

"So? What d'you think?" And why did he care?

She continued to study the portrait, even framing her hands around her face to get a better view. "Were Graham and Geoff's pictures taken at the same time?"

He looked up from the travel magazine he'd been scanning.

"Yeah. I remember the day. We drove our mom nuts with the shenanigans we pulled trying to avoid the photographer. See that suit jacket I'm wearing?"

She nodded.

"Hated it. She had to bribe me to keep it on. There was something scratchy around the collar. Spent most of my time trying to pull it away from my neck."

"How old were your brothers?"

He stopped to calculate. "Gray is seven years older than me and Geoff is four. So, I guess they were fourteen and eleven. All of us at the peak of brattiness."

"And that's supposedly ended?"

He groaned. She never missed an opportunity to goad him. "Over the years, the brattiness transformed to cynicism. Shows up especially around California interior decorators who can't seem to stay out of my affairs." He regretted saying it as soon as it was out, although more for the unfortunate use of the word "affairs" than the putdown.

If he'd expected her to wince or cower, he was sadly mistaken. The words had hardly been spoken when she jutted out her chin, her eyes sparkling. "Dream on, my friend. I've been around long enough to know there are no affairs in your life."

Her eyes bored into him and released feelings that had lain dormant for months. Feelings that had only started to come alive in the past few days. He knew the challenge for what it was but still couldn't stop himself from responding. "Really? Does that mean you're volunteering to help me set that straight?"

She didn't move an inch, although her eyes widened and a pink tinge suffused her cheeks. She gulped once. And then twice. "What?" Her voice was barely a whisper.

He knew now how the lemmings drawn to their watery suicides in the sea must feel, inescapably drawn to a fate they knew they should avoid. "You heard me. My brothers think they've seen sparks between us. That it's time for me to forget about being dumped by my fiancée and reenter the dating scene. Or whatever it's called these days."

"Affairs? Dating? Not exactly the same thing, McKenna. Which did you have in mind?" Her eyes continued to glow with a power he didn't know she possessed. She was the general and he a mere private.

"Remind me never to play poker with you. You can bluff with the best of them."

"I'm not bluffing. Were you?" From a whisper just moments before, her voice had grown clear and bold.

And his stomach had grown queasy, reminding him that this was no surreal dream. He'd been flirting, heck, coming on to her. No backing down. His mouth had outrun his brain. And other parts of his body were way ahead of that.

Taking her hand in his, he pulled her into his arms and kissed her. Soundly. Her lips tasted like strawberries. Drawing back, in a raspy murmur, his throat tight as a drum, he said, "Think that's a bluff?"

*

Aubrey held her hands so he couldn't see how they trembled. Trembled? What was going on here? The man had merely kissed her, and the room seemed to be tilting. He'd thrown out the bait and she'd grabbed hold like a wide-mouth bass. Now she was hooked and could either squirm herself silly or play dead. Or . . . ? "Wow. If that kiss was a bluff, remind me never to play poker with you!"

"I . . . uh . . . yeah, okay." Then, the left side of his lip curling up in satisfaction, he added, "I've been wanting to return the favor ever since you kissed me yesterday."

"Oh." That was it? Over so soon? She tried to calm the unsteady beat of her heart, the sensation of a ton of bricks lodged on her chest. This was the last place she'd have thought to begin a romantic entanglement, especially with Geoff so close by in the next room, but so be it. The attraction to Mitch she'd denied all week couldn't be ignored. In an instant of revelation, she realized how much she wanted to give in to it.

Taking his face in her hands, she placed her lips over his with a forcefulness that surprised them both.

The kiss lasted a long time, drawn in as she was by the need for more of him.

He held her tightly against him, so near she could feel his heart beating . . . as erratically as hers. He smelled wonderful, like a pine forest after a deep rain. One part of her brain wondered how long they had before Geoff appeared. The other didn't care.

Almost as soon as she thought it, Geoff burst into the room. "I think that's all . . . uh . . . no, I was wrong. Come to think of it, there are a few more things back there. You two . . . stay here . . . and continue what you were doing."

They broke apart, Aubrey giggling and Mitch rolling his eyes. "That was embarrassing," she said, looking back over her shoulder toward the hallway Geoff had disappeared into.

"Don't mind him," Mitch whispered. "He set this up. I'll bet he's delighted, though a little surprised his efforts weren't in vain."

"Geoff was playing matchmaker? Wasn't it just . . . uh . . . *yesterday* that he was supposed to be heading me off?"

"We're on Midwestern time. Things move fast here."

"Right," she agreed. "Like the corn growing?"

"I thought you'd sworn off those comments?" He pulled her back into his arms.

She snuggled deeper, enjoying the soft whisper of his breath along her hairline, the scent of forests primeval. The moment was brief, too brief. The sounds of Geoff trampling down the hallway interrupted them all too soon.

They separated. Aubrey floated back to once again admire the boys' pictures, Mitch picked up the travel magazine.

Geoff looked from Mitch to Aubrey, a triumphant expression on his face. He heaved two canvas duffel bags onto the floor in front of him. "Can you take these, Mitch?"

Mitch took hold of both bags and hefted them up. "What all are you bringing? These weigh a ton!"

With a sheepish grin, Geoff said, "Sorry. I wanted to show Peggy some of my college scrapbooks."

"And you couldn't just bring her here to view them?" Mitch asked.

Geoff's neck reddened. "I hardly know her. It wouldn't be proper." Then he seemed to remember Aubrey, his head turning her direction, and the inanity of his remark hit him. "It's different bringing you here, Aubrey."

Aubrey and Mitch exchanged confused looks, then turned back to Geoff.

Sensing the absurdity of his last comment, he tried again. "That is, well, you know. You're almost family, having lived with us all week." His expression brightened. "And this was a professional visit, remember? How we can fix the place up if we put it on the market?"

"Right, bro," Mitch said, carrying the bags through the house toward the car.

She made her way through the dining room back to the kitchen. She was reaching for the door when she spotted a small ceramic pot on the ledge above the kitchen sink. African violets. Blooming. On impulse, she grabbed the pot to remind Geoff of home. It needed care, didn't it?

"Got yourself a souvenir?" Mitch asked when she climbed into the cab a minute later.

"Fitting, don't you think. Something to remember the last few minutes. In case that was that?" *Good going, Aubrey. Why not hand him your heart on a silver platter?*

He raised an eyebrow but didn't reply.

Oh, no. I was right! Now he's going to admit that's all there was. Why had she been so flip? Because she'd been caught in an act of kindness. She squirmed in her seat. It felt as if she'd moved two miles when in reality it had probably been no more than two inches.

After what seemed an eternity, Mitch said, "Gimme that thing. Geoff loves it. It's all that's left of our mom's collection. He's tried to keep them alive over the years, but he obviously doesn't have a green thumb." He placed the pot lovingly on the seat between them.

He flashed her a boyish grin. "As for that being that, what do you think? You're here three more weeks. If we can keep it light, I say we go for it and see what happens."

She didn't know whether to be elated or feel like she'd just negotiated a contract. This was what she'd been fantasizing about, wasn't it? Surely she had no illusions of a longer-term relationship growing out of this brief stint in Burlington?

"If I was reading this wrong . . . ?"

Say something, girl. Make up your mind! "No. You were tracking just right." She leaned toward him and took his hand. "I say we . . ."

The thunk of more bundles being loaded into the truck bed cut off the rest of her speech, but from the flicker of interest she'd seen in Mitch's eyes, she knew he'd gotten the message. She quickly retrieved her hand.

The next instant, Geoff opened her door and popped into the back seat. "Whew! Got a little carried away. Found some board games I thought Peggy might like to play." He seemed to realize he'd interrupted something. "Should I come back in a few minutes?"

Mitch checked his watch, then turned the ignition. "Ready and waiting. We've got just enough time to get you back and settled before Aubrey and I head out to dinner."

He favored her with the most good-humored smile he'd bestowed upon her yet. "Have you decided where you want to go?"

Message received, all right. Aubrey watched him check his brother's reaction in the rearview mirror. It must have been what we he was waiting for, because he seemed to chuckle as he put the car in reverse.

"Surprise me."

His eyes glowed lasciviously. "Okay. You asked for it."

*

"Like it?"

It was an hour later. Aubrey and Mitch were seated on the patio of a converted warehouse enjoying the sight of a barge heading downriver.

Aubrey removed her hands from shading her eyes and turned back to her dinner partner, contented. "Very much. I'm used to seeing an endless horizon on the Pacific, except those days when you can actually see Catalina Island. A river, especially the Mississippi, is so different. You can see the other side."

Mitch continued to gaze out on Ol' Man River. "This is one of my favorite parts of living in this town. Did you know it was the first territorial capital of the state back in the 1830s? It was a major port for steamboats traveling between St. Louis and Minneapolis. And then later, a railroad hub for trains going east and west."

"And now?"

He frowned. "And now, not so much, except in architectural legacies left by our ancestors on the town's many hills and bluffs."

"Seems rather flat to me. I'm used to mountains and valleys."

Mitch looked affronted. "Those bluffs behind us don't look flat to me."

She gazed off that direction with a patronizing smile. "Bluffs?" Fearing she'd really insulted him, she quickly added, "Okay, hilly. That okay?"

His shoulders seemed to relax and he, too, smiled, vindicated.

"Have you spent much time in the mountains?"

His gaze seemed to drift over her shoulder to the water beyond. Then he drew his attention back to her. "Once or twice. With Dianne."

"Oh." She'd done it again.

He must have read her mind. "Don't beat yourself up. Her name keeps coming up because she's still recent history. But I'm okay with it." He took her hand in his. "Really."

Though the evening had grown slightly chill, a warm glow washed over her. She liked being here with him at sunset, watching the boaters come in from a day on the sandbars and fishing. She sipped from her glass of wine. Nectar. Perfect.

So why was she about to break the spell? Deliberately. Because for his sake, at least according to Orville, she had to help him get back to what he wanted to do most.

"Isn't your part with the motor coach about over?"

He ran a hand through his hair and put his menu down. "I guess. I'll soon be on to the next coach."

"What will you do with your spare time?"

"Spare time?" He laughed. "You're kidding. Right?"

She picked up her water glass and took a sip. "Alien concept?"

He thought about it for a moment. "What are you getting at, Aubrey? Trying to get rid of me?" He was smiling, but his voice held a note of apprehension.

She'd tried to be so subtle. "No, of course, not! That was just my awkward way of checking out something I learned this weekend."

He lifted a brow. "What was that?"

She forced herself to breathe deeply. She didn't want her level of interest to be too apparent. "That you went to law school but never sat for the bar."

She waited for his response, not knowing what to expect.

He surprised her by sitting back, taking a long sip from his water glass and then presenting her with a knowing smile. "How'd you unearth that piece of information?"

No way was she going to reveal Orville's part in this. She hated ratting out Graham as well, but that she could explain. She related selected parts of her conversation with his brother.

"Leave it to Gray to spill the beans."

"I don't get it. Is it a state secret?"

He studied the menu. "I usually get a rib-eye when I'm here, but that feels heavy tonight. What are you going to have?"

Ignoring the subject. But she wasn't about to give in yet. She set her menu to the side. "Grilled white fish. So what's the story? Why go through three years of law school only to shuck your education and work on motor coaches?"

There. She'd acknowledged the elephant in the room. *Please let this be the right thing to do.*

Mitch closed his menu, carefully placing it to his left and taking great pains to align it with the edge of the table.

He didn't look at her, nor say a word, and his skin color remained the same, yet Aubrey had the distinct impression that she'd just watched him freeze in front of her. She pulled her hands into her lap and rubbed them together to ease the icy chill that had seized them. She leaned into the table. "You didn't answer my question. In fact, you don't seem to be communicating at all. Did I say something to put you off?"

Their waiter arrived to take their orders. Though the interruption cut off her question, she was still grateful for it. At least it got Mitch talking. To the waiter.

She was about to thank him for the dinner invitation and leave (*did this town have taxis?*) when he finally spoke.

"Yes, I studied law. I planned to set up practice here in town. But it wasn't to be." He avoided her eyes.

"What happened?" She knew no discretion.

He stared down at the lone white daisy adorning the table. "The business."

"Couldn't you have done both?"

Silence again. Finally, "Why are you doing this?"

"Asking questions?" Yet another question. She was terrified she'd angered him beyond the brink.

Now he did look her in the eyes. His own eyes vivid green. "Interrogating me. You have to know how difficult it is for me to talk about this. Yet you keep picking away at it."

She sat ramrod-straight, resisting the urge to sit back. "You could tell me it isn't any of my business and to shut up. But you haven't done that."

He released a weighty sigh.

"Instead, you've revealed a few facts at a time. Makes me think you've been wanting to talk about this to someone. But at your own speed."

He gripped the edge of the table so forcefully it shook their water glasses. The action alarmed even him, because he immediately released his grip on the table and glared at her instead. "Don't you ever stop?"

She took great pains to keep her voice low. "I will, if I'm off base. But I don't think I am. Am I?"

He didn't reply. He seemed to be holding his breath.

In his eyes, she saw exasperation with her, embarrassment with this topic. Anguish. She sensed that all she had to do was remain strong a bit longer and he'd break. She hated herself. But this wasn't for Orville. This was for Mitch. And for her.

"Customized motor coaches are high-end. Your average Joe isn't the typical client. It takes a certain type of personality to get along with them and sell them our services. Geoff's got it, Gray doesn't. When the two of them told me about this plan to go into business together, I was sure they'd go under within a year unless I threw in my support."

"Couldn't Geoff have carried the PR end?"

"Under normal circumstances, more than. But three years ago, who knew? He'd been struggling with the MS for months. Trying to keep us from finding out. Did a good job at it too, until the night he blacked out and drove off the road."

"No! Was he hurt?" Neither Geoff nor Graham had mentioned this.

"Bruised. Wrecked the whole front end of the car. Fortunately, it wasn't a heavily traveled road. But it was enough to convince him he couldn't go on like that anymore."

"But even if his PR skills were temporarily impeded by his illness, are they that critical that you had to come on board full time?"

He refrained from speaking while the waiter arranged their salads and breads. "Did Gray tell you why he was willing to get involved in this venture?"

She thought back to her conversation with Graham. "Something about his job in Minneapolis turning out to be less exciting than he hoped."

"That's one way of putting it." Mitch forked a wedge of tomato and sampled it. "He was about to be sacked."

The bread she'd been buttering rested unnoticed in her hand. "He didn't mention that."

"He's never brought it up with me either, or Geoff. Dianne had a sorority sister working in the same firm. When she tried to set the two of them up, her so-called friend backed down, saying she preferred her men to be gainfully employed."

She put the bread back on her plate, uneaten. With her other hand, she reached over to his. "Mitch, I'm so sorry."

"To this day, I don't know what was going on. I suspect he wasn't getting the assignments he wanted and that affected his attitude. He's a good architect. He's done great work on the motor coaches. But at the time, I wasn't sure."

When she started to withdraw her hand from his, he held onto it. "There's more. You want to hear it?"

His eyes pleaded for her attention. Inside her chest cavity, her heart actually hurt. Although some things were falling into place, it was still unclear why Mitch, even if he had gone into business with them, hadn't remained in the law as well. She squeezed his hand. "Yes. Go on."

She sampled her bread, more as a way to digest his information than the food.

He took a couple bites of salad before continuing. "We couldn't have asked for better parents. Mom worked as a secretary in a small insurance office. Dad taught math in the high school. They were planning this blow-out cross country trip as soon as they retired. Then Mom was killed in a car accident. Dad was devastated, absolutely lost without my mother."

"That must have been tough."

He sighed. "Yeah. Grief took its toll on his work. The principal worked out an early retirement for him, put him on disability, and presto, Dad was out of a job living on a pension."

Aubrey winced.

"I was still in school. I couldn't work and handle a heavy schedule of classes. Geoff and Gray came to my rescue, paying the bills for my tuition and room and board."

"How did your dad react to that?"

Mitch finished his salad and set the plate aside. "I don't think he was even aware of what the guys were doing. He wasn't crazy, but he disengaged from reality, focusing on the trip he and Mom had planned. After a while, it wasn't so much the trip as the mode of travel they'd discussed. The next thing I knew, Dad had bought the firehouse and planned to customize RVs."

She finished the last of her salad. "None of you suspected what he was up to?"

"We were too busy reacting to the onset of Geoff's MS and getting through our grief for our mother. Dad caught pneumonia that winter and didn't recover. We discovered the commitments he'd made to several locals to customize their RVs when we went through his effects that spring. Second year of law school, and I thought I could litigate us out of the mess."

He stopped at that point. As if this next part was going to be even more difficult.

She waited.

Before he began again, their dinners arrived. They each took a few bites of their respective entrees before he continued. "I had a swelled head in law school."

"No!"

"Top-notch grades, the profs loved me. And Dianne boosted my ego. When Dad's business problems cropped up, I was sure I could make short shrift of them. And I could have, if I'd bothered to check out a few legal facts. I thought I knew it all. Went to court unprepared."

"What happened?"

He took another bite of swordfish. "We couldn't get out of Dad's commitments. So I spent the summer before my last year of law school working on RVs. Geoff helped when he could, and Gray came down every weekend. We managed to finish up by the end of summer."

In her head, she ran through the timeline he'd laid out. He'd brought her up to about six or eight months prior to the three of them going into business. "So the stage was set?"

"More or less. We had the firehouse. We'd successfully completed a few RVs. And we'd discovered we were a pretty good team."

"And you doubted the two of them couldn't make it on their own."

He made a face. "I owed them so much. I couldn't let them down."

She watched him start to say something else, then return instead to his swordfish. There was more. There had to be, because none of this explained why he'd completely left the law.

She turned to her own dinner. The white fish was delicious. Not too dry, not too mushy. She looked up to find him watching her. "What? Is there broccoli on my teeth?"

He shook his head. "You're holding back, trying not to ask me something else."

"What makes you think that?"

"You're eating around your fish, clockwise."

Despite the serious nature of their conversation, she laughed. "And that says I'm holding back?"

"You're concentrating too much on eating your fish so you won't inadvertently pop another question."

He was right, but his theory was crazy. She always ate like this, didn't she? "Why didn't you become a lawyer?" There, it was out. So much for his theory.

"I told you. Because I was too smug, I made a mess of dealing with my father's affairs. I finished school and went into business with the guys. The rest you know."

He turned his attention back to his meal. He didn't appear to be upset with her, but his body language indicated he didn't want to talk about it further.

She placed her fork on her plate. "Do you miss it?"

"I feel like dessert tonight. How 'bout you? Ice cream? Strawberry shortcake?"

"I asked you a question." She took special pains to keep her voice level.

He took another sip of water. "I've answered as many as I plan to. At least on that topic."

His tone rang with steel. He'd definitely had enough. Her question would have to wait for another day. "Strawberry shortcake. Sounds good."

He motioned to the waiter, who'd been hovering hopefully, and ordered.

Once the shortcake arrived, her nose detected an unknown, unpleasant odor. Her first thought was of a fish-kill on the nearby river, because the smell reminded her of a seafood market. She'd just lifted her spoon to her mouth, her nose wrinkling, when a woman two tables away jumped out of her chair and pushed away from the table, shrieking.

A second later, two children at another table started beating their heads with their hands.

Aubrey looked to Mitch, confused. What was going on?

Before he could answer, something dark, about an inch and a half long, landed squarely in the whipped cream covering the shortcake. Then two more plopped on the white linen tablecloth. Then more. When one found her bare arm, she was out of her seat, screeching also. She batted the creature away, but another found her hair. "Mitch! Help me."

Instantly, he flicked one from her hair, then brushed three more off her back. Grabbing her hand, they dashed inside the restaurant along with all the other diners vacating the patio.

"What is this?" Aubrey finally got out.

"Mayflies. They swarm like this maybe once or twice a summer, usually out over the river or along the shoreline. They moved in a little closer tonight."

"The other night it was those creepy-crawly bugs. This place is a virtual jungle."

Mitch chuckled. "Seems like that, doesn't it? This should be over soon, an hour tops."

Aubrey couldn't believe his nonchalant attitude. "What about the rest of the town? Is this a state of emergency?"

"Only if they left the top down on their convertibles."

"I'm sorry, sir," their waiter interrupted. "Some of those pests made it through an open window in the kitchen, so we're closing for the night. You're welcome to stay in the bar until the commotion dies down outside."

A few minutes later, seated at a small table in the bar, Mitch leaned in to touch her hair. "I thought I saw another one in that do of yours, but it was just the light playing across your curls."

"Thanks." The evening had been going so well, even with Mitch's reluctance to answer her questions. That was over. All she wanted to do was get to his car without being attacked by those indescribably icky flying creatures.

Mitch watched her, a look of concern in his eyes. He snagged a waiter and ordered a glass of wine for them both. "Drink this slowly. Savor it," he directed when it arrived.

She did as ordered, since it was easier to sip than to make sense of the last few minutes. The wine was cool and dry, slipping effortlessly down her throat.

"How're you doing?"

"Just one more question. Now that I've experienced mayflies and June bugs, are July spiders on the way?"

CHAPTER TEN

After the events of the weekend, Monday turned out to be pretty run of the mill. The only item of note was the email from Jenna greenlighting the design plans. She loved them. She would select the pieces she wanted to surround herself with and ship them the next day.

Once Aubrey had emailed her orders to her vendors and set up visits from local painting and carpeting subcontractors, her work came to a standstill. The guys had taken off to pick up the next coach they'd be working on and wouldn't be back in town for hours. With time on her hands, she found herself wandering down the street to Orville Drummond's office.

Orville was finishing a brief due later in the day, but he came out to the reception area to greet her within ten minutes. "Well, well, missy. I was hoping you'd take me up on my offer. Didn't expect you quite so soon, but I should've known. You work fast."

"Perhaps too fast," she said, settling into the leather visitor's chair he offered her.

He took a minute to loosen his tie before he replied. "Why's that?"

She replayed her dinner conversation of the night before. "Mitch revealed more than I thought he would, but he clammed up before I could find out why he didn't stay with the law, at least on a part-time basis, once he started working on the motor coaches. Once he decided he'd said enough, he changed the subject and wouldn't budge."

Orville picked up a blank business envelope and began tapping it against his desktop. "He does that well. That's why he'd make a superb attorney. But don't let that deter you."

She related how the evening had ended early with the arrival of the mayflies.

"I heard talk at the coffee shop this morning about those buggers. Stay away from the riverfront today. There'll be heaps of dead ones littering the street. They smell to high heaven."

"They leave them there like that?" She was incredulous.

"Not as long as I'm on the city council. They'll be gone before the day's out. But it'll take a good rain or a few more days before that awful smell dissipates."

He dropped the envelope. "Enough of that. Spent more time talking about them than they're worth." He sat back and rubbed his chin. "Maybe that wasn't such a bad thing. Not the mayflies. Ending your cross-examination there."

"Why do you say that?"

"Mitch and I used to have lengthy discussions when he worked for me. He'd argue long and hard for his side, rarely backing down. Then he'd go off and think about it some more, and later, he'd say, 'I've been considering our debate. I still don't agree, but I see your point.'"

She ran back over the last few days in her head. Had she observed the same characteristic? He certainly had backed away from his original reaction to her. "But that was with you, Orville. You were his mentor. I'm the interloper. You really think he'll let me revisit the topic?"

He pursed his lips, considering her question. "Where did you say you had this talk?"

"At dinner last night. At a restaurant near the riverfront."

He gave her a knowing smile, like she'd said something very profound. "And did you both just happen to wind up at that eating place or was it an arranged appointment?"

"The latter." She still didn't see the point.

"In other words, a *date*?"

"I don't see what that . . . " Oh, wait. Yes, she did. Now.

Orville nodded his head. "Something's happened, hasn't it?"

She looked away. "I guess you could say we're an item."

"Uh-huh. Well, however you want to put it, he likes you. He's going to cogitate on whatever comments you made, and, one of these days, out of the blue, he'll tell you more."

"You think so?"

"Can't guarantee it, but don't be surprised if he does." He picked up the envelope and started tapping it again. "Keep your distance from him for a day or two. Or if you do go out again, don't mention this. Let him stew. See if my theory works."

Doing nothing for a day or two suited her fine. She had work to do. That decided, she said good-bye, promising to keep him posted.

Making her way along the street to the firehouse, she wondered how she'd occupy her time the rest of the day. Her stomach growled. Two o'clock. She'd missed lunch. No wonder.

On the way to the nearest fast food establishment, inspiration hit. She'd prepare dinner for her hosts. She could do spaghetti, if she purchased the sauce. That was the extent of her culinary skills. She'd augment the menu with take-out items from the deli. Her steps became lighter. She was going to pay Mitch back for that great idea sooner than he expected.

*

The guys were doing a little cooking on their own about then. They'd picked up the new coach from the distributor in Davenport and were now on their way back to town. Today was one of those late June days when the weather was perfect. The sun glowed on the cornfields and soybean patches where the growth was about a foot high and healthy. The humidity was low. It was comfortable to be outside without sweating and getting a parched throat after fifteen minutes.

Mitch drove. Gray, with his broken collar bone, rode shotgun with a cushion behind him, and Geoff sat behind them, enumerating every wonderful quality of Peggy Summers he'd discovered in the last forty-eight hours. Finishing the frame-by-frame description of an old movie they'd watched the night before, he thought to ask, "How was your evening, Mitch? Did Aubrey like the restaurant?"

Since they hadn't mentioned anything about his date with Aubrey on the way to pick up the coach, Mitch thought he was off the hook. No such luck. "Fine."

Gray shot him a look. "Uh-huh? Surely there's more?"

"C'mon, Mitch. Spill," Geoff ordered.

You'd think they were a pair of fishwives the way they wanted all the sordid details. *Okay, guys. For once, I've got something to tell.* "She liked the place just fine . . . until dessert."

"Dessert?" Graham asked. "She didn't like the offerings?"

"On the contrary. She wanted to eat on the patio, so she could enjoy the river at sunset. Unfortunately, the river at sunset put her right in the path of marauding mayflies. They dive-bombed her shortcake, then got friendly with her."

"Mayflies! It's that time of year again, isn't it?" Geoff observed.

"That would unnerve anyone," Graham added. Thanks to his sling, he struggled to open the bottle of water he'd brought along and took a few sips. "Has she ever seen the pests?"

"I don't think so," Mitch replied. "And if she never sees them again, she'll be delighted. It took two glasses of wine to calm her nerves."

"Poor Aubrey," Geoff bemoaned. "She's certainly experienced her share of Midwestern culture in the short time she's been here."

"Has it only been a week?" Gray asked. "Seems longer. She really grows on you."

Mitch didn't care for his brother's sudden interest in Aubrey. "How do you mean?"

"Uh, you know."

"Yeah, I know," Mitch replied, "but what do you know?"

"Uh, well, she's easy to talk to."

Mitch took a long swig from his own bottle of water. His mouth had gone dry. "True. Although I hadn't noticed the two of you talking all that much."

Gray swiveled and made a show of gazing at the passing landscape.

"Have you?" Mitch pushed.

"Have I what?"

"Been talking to her a lot."

Gray turned back and started checking the various gauges on the motor coach, flipping the air conditioning buttons one way then another. "You saw us," he finally said, a bit too defensively. "When you and Geoff came back from your first trip to the house yesterday."

"Oh, yeah," Geoff threw in. "You were snarfing down a sandwich she'd made you."

"That's right," Gray answered. "She was asking me about how the three of us decided to go into business together."

"Really?" Mitch said, raising a brow.

"She asked what I'd done before and if I ever missed it."

Geoff stuck his head into the conversation. "What did you say? I thought you were itching to get out of that dead-end design job. You didn't say that for my sake, I hope?"

Gray threw a quick glance over his shoulder. "I told you, Geoff. I know I complain about finances, but I've had the time of my life starting this business."

Geoff didn't say anything but nodded his head.

That tied a bow on the discussion. For the next few minutes, each sat in silence.

Mitch had suspected there was more to Aubrey's conversation with Graham but apparently not. She'd been making small talk while Gray ate. To keep him company.

She'd been so determined to play detective about his legal career the evening before. Attempting to appear so disinterested, and yet there'd been a glow in her eyes, as if she was solving some big math problem. A captivating combination of adorable and seductive.

"You know," Gray said, breaking through Mitch's thoughts, "I recall she asked me a question I wasn't sure how to answer."

The palms of Mitch's hands began to itch. "Oh? What was that?" he asked nonchalantly.

Gray twisted his lips in an effort to remember her words. "After I told her about me, she made a comment about you, Mitch. Something about how it must have been difficult for you to make the switch from the law to this company."

"Uh-huh," Mitch said, trying to keep his response noncommittal.

"How did she put it?" Gray scratched his head with his free hand. "I know. I told her that the career change had come easily for you too. Then she said, 'Oh, did you ask him?' I started to say, 'Yes, of course,' but I got to wondering how it had come up. I couldn't remember. But we must have talked about it. Right?"

Mitch's palms now prickled. And his stomach was rumbling from more than all the water he'd been consuming. Aubrey had admitted that Gray told her he'd gone to law school. But she hadn't bothered to mention this part of her chat. At dinner, she'd been trolling for information about the same thing. Why was she so interested in why he wasn't practicing law?

He gripped the steering wheel with more pressure than necessary and stared straight ahead at the road, willing his brothers to drop the subject. Why couldn't Aubrey leave things alone? But then, if she did, she wouldn't be Aubrey.

"We did talk about it, didn't we Mitch?" Gray wanted to know.

"Hmmm?" He pretended to be distracted.

Geoff picked up the theme. "Not sitting for the bar. Not going into the law. You didn't feel pressured into this business, did you?"

Mitch didn't answer. Damn her! It had never occurred to his brothers to ask him that question, the one he wanted more than anything to avoid, until she started her probing.

*

Though Aubrey returned to the firehouse anxious to give Emeril a run for his money, she entered the kitchen somewhat intimidated. Except for the brief hide-and-go-seek episode on Saturday when she'd been chasing down a prowler and wound up ogling Mitch in his towel, she hadn't been alone in their living quarters. But they'd told her more than once to make herself at home. It had even been Mitch's idea for her to cook them dinner.

She estimated she had about two hours before the guys returned. Plenty of time. No sweat. She could take her time setting the table, find some background music, and give the wine she'd purchased as a last-minute thought time to cool.

The time went by swiftly. When she was down to forty-five minutes, it was time to brown the ground sirloin. Opening a few cabinet doors, she found a heavy skillet on the third try.

She'd just turned on the burner under the skillet when she thought she heard the buzz of her cell phone. It was in her purse, which she'd set on one of the kitchen chairs when she unloaded the groceries.

"Aunt Aubrey?"

Paige. Her voice sounded tight and strained.

"I've got to talk to you."

Now what had Jenna done? "Hi, cookie. What's up?"

"What's that crackling sound?"

"Crackling? Oh, that. I'm cooking. Me. Can you believe it?"

"That's . . . great. What kind of cooking makes that sound?"

"Hamburger. I'm browning it to go into spaghetti sauce."

"Uh, you might want to turn down the heat," her niece suggested. Paige was well aware of Aubrey's limited cooking skills. She'd tried to grill her a steak a while back and wound up with a charred mess even Jenna's dog wouldn't touch

Aubrey shot a glance at the skillet. It did seem to be popping and sizzling more than warranted. She turned it down a notch. "Hint taken, kid. But just so the sound doesn't compete with our conversation, I'll go in the next room." She wandered into the living room and settled a hip against the sofa. "Now, tell me why you called."

"It's Mom," Paige cried. "She's still set on taking this concert tour without me."

"Weren't you going to lay off her for a few days, give her some time to reconsider?"

"I was, until Mom invited more people on the trip. She did that just so there wouldn't be room for me, Aunt Aubrey." Her voice had taken on a whiney quality, but she was also hurt.

What did Jenna think she was doing? Didn't she realize how sensitive Paige's feelings were these days? "Are you sure she asked these people on the tour, Paige? Maybe they're just riding out on the first day as some kind of going-away party?" She moved around to the front of the sofa and sat down. This was going to take a while.

"I heard her on the phone. She said to plan on at least a week, maybe two, if they were having a good time."

"Oh," was about all Aubrey could muster.

"What should I do?" Paige's voice was a plea. "The tour starts in a few more weeks."

I'm well aware of that, Paige. "How about I call your mom and talk to her?"

"Would you?"

"Don't get your hopes up. I'm not promising I can do anything to help you, other than find out what your mom's plans are."

Heavy sigh. Of resignation. "Okay. I understand."

"What's your mom's schedule these days, Hon? Is she still rehearsing heavy?"

"I, I'm not sure. Let me check the calendar she keeps on her desk."

Aubrey listened as Paige apparently moved from whatever room she'd been calling from, probably her own, and made her way to Jenna's office.

After a bit, Paige came back on. "Here it is. It says she's at the rehearsal hall today until six and tomorrow from nine to three. Aunt Aubrey? Are you in Iowa? Someplace called Burlington?"

Had Jenna told Paige her whereabouts? She thought she'd made it quite clear to her sister that no one, not even Paige, could know where she was.

"Aunt Aubrey? Are you still there?"

Aubrey's throat constricted. She tried to speak but couldn't. Her hand gripping the end table, she made herself take several deep breaths. "Ye-es. Sorry, dear. I was, uh, writing down your mother's hours."

"Are you okay?" The concern in Paige's voice came through loud and clear.

"Yes. Yes, I'm fine." She struggled to absorb the shock of Paige knowing where she was while at the same time deciding how to deal with it. "What made you ask . . . if I was in . . . " She deliberately made it sound like she couldn't remember the name of the town.

"Burlington. That's what this note says, anyhow." Paige repeated the address.

Why would Jenna have written down her location and left it out for anyone to see? Then she remembered. The shipment of Jenna's household items. Jenna had sent them off today. She must have been in a hurry to get to rehearsal and forgotten to put the address away.

Aubrey tried to think of a reason to explain the information. *Think, Aubrey.* "I . . . uh . . . I'm here visiting a friend," she blurted out. Well, she was, wasn't she? Sort of.

"A friend?"

Why did Paige sound so incredulous? She had friends. Like Heidi Buxbaum? Aubrey might not be visiting Heidi, but she was definitely the reason why Aubrey was holing up here.

"My friend is having a tough time right now. Career problems." *Thank you, Mitch.* She selected details from her recent experience to make her story ring true. The rest she invented as she went. "And a family member has a serious medical condition. I'm here for support."

Paige seemed to be thinking through Aubrey's story. She didn't reply at first. "Is your friend doing better? You've been away over a week. When are you coming home?"

"It looks like I'll be here a few more weeks, cookie."

"Oh, Aunt Aubrey! I'm sorry for your friend, but I need you, too. You've got to come back and help me with Mom."

Precious Paige. Aubrey loved her like her own daughter, but fourteen-year-olds were naturally egocentric. "You're going to be fine, Paige. I need to talk to your mom." She looked at her watch. "I can't do that for at least another four hours, so why don't you . . . " She coughed. Something irritated her nostrils. Something acrid, like smoke. Smoke! The ground sirloin she'd left browning while she calmed Paige.

"Gotta go. The meat is burning."

She didn't wait for a response. She ran into the kitchen, coughing more with each step. The room had disappeared behind billowing gray-black smoke. Covering her mouth with the apron she'd had around her waist, she made her way to where she'd left the skillet. She couldn't see any fire, but she couldn't see much of anything.

She'd just reached the stove and turned off the burner when a shrill blare sounded. The smoke alarm. She needed to get out of there. Get the smoking skillet out of there too.

With the last vestige of the wits she had about her, she remembered to bring her cell phone so she could call 911.

*

Mitch and the guys were a block away from the fire house when they spied the two fire trucks and emergency services vehicle in front of the building. The irony escaped them as fear for their home and business took hold. The motor coach! Was it on fire?

Braking in the middle of the street behind the fire equipment, Mitch, with the other two close behind, scrambled out of the motor coach they'd been returning and ran for the building.

Two police officers stood in their path. Gray brought up the rear, traveling slower.

"Sorry, folks. No one gets past this line," one of the officers told them.

"This is our building," Mitch explained. "What happened?" Then he remembered Aubrey. His heart plummeted into the pit of his stomach. "Was there a woman in there?"

The two officers exchanged looks, then appeared to glance over his shoulders to someone across the street. "You're the owner, huh?" the other officer responded.

"Yes, yes! I'm Mitch McKenna and these are my brothers. And also my partners. Tell me what's happened."

"You need to talk to the chief. He's over there near the EMT." The officer pointed to a spot behind them. "I'll take you over."

On their way to the chief, they passed firefighters emerging from the building, shedding their coats and hats. Others were headed back into the building with large fans. The significance didn't register. Right now, all he cared about was finding Aubrey safe and sound.

"Chief, these are the building owners. Want to know why we're here and how the lady's doing."

The chief was standing near the cab of one fire truck. When he glanced up, he looked familiar to Mitch. "Are you the McKennas?"

They nodded in unison.

"I'm Jason Smalley," the chief said, extending his hand. "You're Mitch McKenna, right? We've played in softball tournaments against each other. Sorry we have to renew acquaintances under these circumstances."

"What circumstances?" Gray asked, taking over. "We just arrived."

Jason Smalley eyed Gray. "Sorry. I thought you knew. Unattended hamburger in the kitchen upstairs created a general smokestorm throughout the building. Luckily, nothing caught fire. You shouldn't have any smoke damage, except the residual odor for a few days."

"Hamburger? Unattended?" Geoff looked from Mitch to Gray,

a perplexed expression on his face. "I haven't been in the kitchen all day. How about you guys?"

As the other two shook their heads, the chief cut in. "Uh, well, it appears that honor goes to your houseguest." He checked his notepad briefly. "A Ms. Aubrey Carpenter?"

"Aubrey!" all three shouted.

"Is she okay?" Mitch asked, his stomach continuing to churn.

Jason Smalley cracked his first smile. "More than. We wanted her to get checked out at the hospital for smoke inhalation. But she was too busy ordering smoke extinction services. I finally talked her into being examined by the EMT guys. She's in the ambulance now."

All three of them started off that direction, until the chief called them back. "I need some information for insurance purposes. One of you needs to stay behind and help me out."

Gray volunteered. Mitch and Geoff dashed to the ambulance. Mitch got there first.

"They told me Aubrey Carpenter's here. Can we see her?"

The EMT, who'd been guarding the ambulance door, shook his head in disbelief. "Yeah. Doc's about finished with her. Maybe you can talk some sense into her. She won't listen to us."

At that moment, the door opened, and another EMT stepped out, giving an exasperated sigh. "You guys here for Ms. Carpenter?"

Mitch stepped forward. "That's right. How is she?"

"Stubborn. Didn't seem to suffer from all that smoke, although I'd prefer to do more tests at the hospital. She tells me she's fine. You deal with her."

Mitch shot a glance at Geoff to see if he was just as confused. Geoff shrugged back.

Mitch knocked on the door. "Aubrey? It's Mitch and Geoff. Can we come in?"

A muffled "Come in," greeted them.

Aubrey sat at the bottom of the narrow stretcher that ran

through the center of the vehicle, head down, her hair a jumble. Dark streaks smudged her light green knit top and pants.

"Aubrey? How are you?" Mitch asked, stepping into the van. Without thinking, he reached out and touched an errant curl. "You had us worried. We saw the emergency vehicles and thought the place had gone up in smoke."

Aubrey lifted her head so he could see her eyes for the first time. They were red-rimmed and filled with tears. "Oh, Mitch, Geoff. I'm so sorry! I was just trying to help."

That last phrase sent a wave of panic coursing through him. How many times had she said that since landing on their doorstep? Still, she looked pathetic. "What happened?"

He looked to Geoff for support, help dealing with this newly repentant Aubrey, but Geoff appeared to be tongue-tied, at a loss how to react to this pitiful version of their houseguest.

"I . . . I was making dinner for us. Remember, you told me I should do that to repay you for your decorating idea?"

"Yeah," he said, not really remembering but afraid to tell her otherwise.

"I decided to do it today. I had time on my hands that I probably won't have from here on . . . well, who knows after this stunt what my schedule will be."

Geoff leaned into the doorway. "That explains the hamburger. What caused the smoke?"

Her eyes moved from Geoff to Mitch, then to the floor. Her response was a quiet, "Me."

"We sorta suspected that," Mitch said as tactfully as possible. "But . . . how?"

"My niece called. She was upset about a problem she's having with her mother. I guess I . . . got distracted." Having gotten that out was like breaking up a logjam. The next several sentences rolled out in a flurry. "I wasn't gone more than a few minutes. I never would have walked away like that, but she was so upset, and

I couldn't hear her with the meat browning, and I turned it down, it wasn't high heat at all. Did it do much damage? They wouldn't tell me anything. All they wanted to do was run instruments down my throat. I'm fine. I haven't coughed in a few minutes. Do you see a water bottle around here? I am a little parched. They said I could drink some water, if I take small sips. I ran out with the skillet, but I didn't burn my hands. They said . . . "

"Aubrey!" Mitch interrupted. He couldn't take the rambling any longer. Was she in shock? "Stop. We'll talk later. We shouldn't have hit you with all our questions."

Geoff patted one of her hands. "Yeah, we'll find out later. Relax. Take deep breaths."

Aubrey attempted to catch her breath, as instructed. But she no more than tried that than she was spewing out more. "Did they find the skillet? I know I brought it out with me, but I can't remember what happened to it. It looked like a good one. You don't want to lose it. Maybe your insurance will cover it. You do have insurance on the place? I don't know if mine will . . . "

"Stop! You're giving me a headache. We'll talk about all this later, Aubrey. I'm going to get the truck, then I'm taking you to the hospital."

"No! I'm fine, really. I already told the EMTs that."

Mitch took her hand. "Please. Do this for me. I need to know you're all right."

"Do I have to?"

She was like a child. He wondered if she had some desperate fear of hospitals. Too bad. He couldn't afford to placate her. Smoke inhalation was nothing to slough off. "I'll stay with you the whole time, if you want. You need to do this. I don't want you keeling over in a day or two. You . . . and we . . . won't be able to finish the coach."

That did it. He could see the possibility register in her eyes.

He didn't give her time to change her mind. Indicating Geoff should get the coach they'd just driven back from Davenport off the street, he motioned for the EMTs to rejoin them so they could be on their way.

*

"I've got good news and bad news," Graham informed them when he joined them later, after accompanying the fire chief through of the building to identify damage. "The good news is that there's no structural damage. No water damage either, since they didn't use the hoses."

Ever the optimist, Mitch asked, "So what's the bad news?"

"It will take a few days to get the smoke smell out. During that time," Graham paused and eyeballed his brothers, "we have to vacate the premises."

Geoff put down the drumstick he'd just bitten into. "Great! I just got moved in!"

"Looks like we'll be heading back to the old homestead for a few days," Graham replied.

A miserable Aubrey asked no one in particular, "What have I done?"

Graham turned to her. "Don't worry about it, Aubrey. Our insurance covers the smoke extinction process, and there's plenty of room for you at the house, too."

Geoff slapped a hand over his mouth as if he'd just remembered something. "Uh. Hotel McKenna isn't available. When I decided to move into the firehouse, I called an exterminator. Given Aubrey's experience here with the June bugs, I thought I'd take precautions at home."

Mitch leaned in. "Call them and postpone it."

"Can't. They started today while we were out of town. I'm not supposed to go back in the house for a couple days."

Holding his hands up in surrender, Graham said, "So now what do we do?"

Aubrey wanted to sink into a hole in the floor. She'd been frightened more than she wanted to admit when she'd seen all that smoke swirling in every direction around her. Once the firefighters and emergency equipment had arrived, she'd been worried out of her mind that the building would be destroyed. And now, sitting here with the guys, she was embarrassed and humiliated by her stupidity and thoughtlessness. She was a fixer, not a destroyer, and she wanted desperately to make things right.

"Will the insurance cover a few nights at a motel?" Mitch asked.

"I suppose," Graham said. "But I doubt if we can get rooms. There's a regional church meeting here this week."

She seemed to be trading one bed for another. The B&B, the laundry room, Jenna's coach . . . .Jenna's coach! "You've got two motor coaches on site. How about using them? I was supposed to be in the DiFranco coach anyhow."

Geoff cuffed her shoulder. "Great idea!" Turning to Graham, he asked, "Did the smoke get into the coach? If the doors were shut, the seals should have prevented that."

Graham tilted his head and rubbed his chin. "The chief and I discussed that. He thought it should be fine, although he didn't test it. Might be a challenge getting in there to drive it out, though. The chief didn't leave behind the oxygen masks we wore during our inspection."

"I don't know that we'll need the other coach," Mitch said.

All three heads turned his direction. "Why not?" Geoff asked. "We'll park both around back. Put Aubrey in one and the three of us in the other."

"You don't mind being by yourself, do you, Aubrey? You were going to do it inside the firehouse. You'll be just as safe out in back, if you lock the door," Graham reassured her.

Even with the guys nearby in the other coach, she wasn't real crazy about the idea, but after the havoc she'd created, she couldn't object. "No, I . . . "

"She can't," Mitch announced. "That's what I was starting to say. She needs to be under observation for the next twenty-four hours, just in case they missed something at the hospital."

News to her. "You, you don't have to do that, Mitch. I'm fine."

Mitch shook his head. "Sorry, Aubrey. You don't have any say in this. We're liable for your well-being. To get our insurance paid, we have to take these precautions."

So much for tenderness and caring. She was a liability. Which, when she thought about it, was pretty much what Mitch had been telling her all along.

"Why don't you stay in her coach then, Mitch, and Gray and I'll camp out in the other one," Geoff proposed.

That drew a scowl from Graham and Mitch rolled his eyes.

Seeing their reaction, Geoff quickly added, "The two of you are seeing each other, aren't you? What's so bad with that?"

Aubrey asked herself the same question, although she immediately rejected the idea. Things hadn't reached that point yet. And probably never would, now that she'd nearly burned down his business and his home. Guys didn't take well to pyromaniac girlfriends. They wanted to make the heat themselves.

Mitch's expression froze. "No, Geoff. That won't work. Besides, I'm dead on my feet from driving. I need you two to back me up."

Scratching his head, Geoff asked, "How often do we have to check her? Is this going to turn into a slumber party?"

"It's not like she has a concussion, where we'd have to check her eyes every so often," Mitch explained. "We just have to be nearby so in case she starts coughing, she doesn't gag."

"What about beds?" Graham asked. "Our bedrolls are back in the firehouse."

Mitch eyed him tolerantly. "Creature comfort first thing on your mind, huh, bro? What about food and clothes?"

The other three exchanged surprised looks.

"Hadn't thought of that," Geoff said.

It just kept getting better. "Look, guys, I don't know what my insurance will cover, but give me the bills. It's the least I can do." She'd worry later about how she'd pay.

Graham peeked at his watch. "It's getting late. We'd better get going, if we're going to hit the stores."

By the time they returned to the motor coach, they were all beat. No one wanted to stay up talking or playing cards or even snacking. Instead, they each set about settling in for the night.

They gave Aubrey the bed, but since there was no linen on it yet, she got a sleeping bag as well. She nestled into her bedroll, keeping her flashlight and a bottle of water handy. She could probably serve as her own nursemaid, because she doubted she could sleep in these new surroundings. On the other hand, her eyes drooped and her entire body throbbed. The unfamiliar sounds of the night around her, both in the coach and outside, kept her conscious for all of ten minutes. Then she was out.

*

Sometime in the wee hours, what must have been a train whistle, sharp and cacophonous, drilled into her semiconscious state, bringing her out of a deep slumber. She blinked her eyes open, only to be greeted with a heavy veil of black nothingness. Thunder ripped through her chest. What was this? Where was she?

Disoriented, she started to hyperventilate, her heart crashing against her chest wall. She had to escape, but when she tried to run, she couldn't move her legs. She was trapped, caught up in some unknown web, bound tightly, like a mummy.

Sound came from her mouth, but it wasn't words. "Mmmmn," was all she could get out.

"Aubrey?"

Someone was calling her name. Who?

"Aubrey? Can you hear me?"

She felt the shroud being peeled away from her. Now she could move her legs, and when she discovered they were no longer pinned down, she began kicking.

"Easy," someone told her in a gentle whisper. "You're okay. Take a deep breath."

She attempted to do so and fell into a coughing fit. Strong, safe arms went around her, propping her up against a cool, steely chest.

Where was she? And who was holding her? "What?" Wherever she was, she felt secure. Fear drained out of her, easing her breathing.

"It's me, Aubrey. Mitch."

"Mitch?" That meant something, she was sure of it. But she didn't know what.

"Mitch McKenna. Can you breathe now?"

"Breathe?" She must be breathing. She was still alive. Wasn't she? "Yes, I guess so. What . . . what happened?"

She still couldn't see him, though her eyes were wide open. But she could feel him. His arms stayed wrapped around her in a viselike hold. Comforting. Out of instinct, she snuggled deeper, attempting to take in more of his essence, not knowing why, only that it was the one thing keeping her from the abyss right then.

Bright light bombarded her eyes, forcing her to blink several times to shut it out.

"Aubrey? Mitch? What's up?"

"Aim that light away from us, Gray. Aubrey woke up and didn't know where she was," the presence who'd called himself Mitch said.

The light shifted to a spot near them but no longer fell directly on her.

"It wasn't the smoke inhalation?"

Smoke inhalation? What were they talking about? She hadn't smelled smoke. She'd smelled deep forest.

"Nah, I don't think so," the voice next to her called back in a stage whisper.

"What don't you think?" another voice asked in the dark.

"Guys, go back to sleep. Everything's okay."

Three male voices? And all had apparently been nearby. While she slept?

"I heard moaning and screaming," the second voice said. "What was that?"

"Was that me?" She vaguely remembered struggling to say something. But screaming?

"She's claustrophobic, okay?" the voice named Mitch pronounced, sounding peeved. "I'm guessing something woke her up and she didn't remember where she was."

Claustrophobic? That's right. That happened every so often. That went a long way toward explaining why she'd been so frightened and disoriented. "Trapped," she mumbled. "Couldn't move."

"You were sleeping in a bedroll. You must not have been able to unzip it."

Another light came on, and she could see one of the men moving away from what appeared to be the wall. Graham? Right, Graham. It was coming back to her. And Geoff sat cross-legged a few feet away, concern etched in his face. And Mitch was holding her in his arms. In his arms? The realization caused her to turn suddenly, and she bumped heads with him.

"Sorry," he said, backing off slightly.

She rubbed her forehead. It hurt, not from her head butting Mitch's, but from the confusion swirling around inside. She wanted more than anything to settle back into his arms, but she sensed more than knew that the moment was over. For now.

"You're prone to claustrophobia?" Graham asked. "Why didn't you tell us before we settled into these tight quarters?"

"I . . . I . . . ." Few people knew about her claustrophobia. It wasn't something she liked to share about herself. Now all three McKennas knew. It made her feel more vulnerable than ever.

"It hasn't bothered her much since she's been here," Mitch said, as if that explained it all.

Both Geoff and Graham looked to Mitch. "You knew?"

"It showed up when we got locked in the break room."

"Oh, well, that says it all," Geoff said, sounding unconvinced. Moving in closer, he took her hand and said, "Do you think you can get back to sleep, Aubrey? Or do we need to find you someplace less confining?"

She didn't know how to answer. She was certainly tired enough. But what if she woke again while it was still dark?

"We'll leave a light on near you," Mitch offered.

"I guess that's okay." She could hear her doubts coming through in her response.

Mitch studied her. "Here. You lie down and I'll arrange your sleeping bag around you." He pulled a blanket from his shoulders. "Put this over you, so you won't need to zip up again."

She let him guide her back into her bedroll. He fussed a bit, straightening the blanket, checking the light. His ministrations did little to calm her. Instead, every touch, every pull of the blanket sent sensations through her that would do little to help her sleep. When she was settled in, he remained by her side, watchful.

"Close your eyes. You'll surprise yourself with how fast you can get back to sleep."

And, despite his proximity, she did. She slept through the rest of the night and didn't stir until a beam of sunlight urged her awake the next morning.

She moved her head to the side and saw Mitch lying there on the floor, only a few feet away. No bedroll, and only a sheet covering him. Snoring softly.

She liked the sound. It was reassuring. Mitch had played guard and nursemaid through the night. He didn't have to do that. But she was glad he did.

The gentle rise and fall of his chest fascinated her. So natural. Unfettered. He was relaxed. During his waking hours, he was always focused on something. Problem solving. Working on the coach. Arguing with her. But right now, none of that mattered. His mind was elsewhere, dreaming of something. Mitch, dreaming?

The idea intrigued her. Of course, everyone dreamed. But Mitch letting himself go. Relinquishing his earthly bounds. Delicious!

What was he dreaming about? Her? She quickly checked his expression. Was that a hint of a smile, or was she fooling herself? Did she matter at all to him?

As if he'd heard her thoughts, he began to stir. He came awake almost immediately. Then he spied her watching him. A contented smile crept onto his face. "You're awake. How did you sleep?"

He sat up quickly, scratched his head, rubbed his arms and chest and came closer. "Feel better this morning?"

She nodded.

"That's great." He took her hand in his, and waves of heat rushed up her arm. "You had us worried. I never would've told the guys about . . . about . . . "

"My claustrophobia. You can say it." After the embarrassment of hearing them discuss it ad nauseam the night before, this morning, it didn't bother her.

"Yeah, that." He turned toward the two lumps across the room that were his sleeping brothers, then returned his gaze to her. In a lowered voice, he said, "Have you ever seen anyone about this condition?"

"I talked to my doctor after the first episode a few years ago."

He raised an eyebrow. "And?"

"She said it could be founded in some deep emotional problem I hadn't been able to deal with. But, since I didn't want to get psychological help, she recommended some books that would help me avoid it as much as possible and cope with it during onsets."

He studied her again, crinkling his brow as if considering his next statement. "Time to review a few chapters."

CHAPTER ELEVEN

"Sure you don't want to go fishing with us?" Geoff asked as he and Gray prepared to take off for the state park twenty-five miles away.

Mitch put down the pad he'd been jotting on. "Too much to do as we get started on this coach."

"If that's what you prefer," Gray said with resignation. Turning to Geoff, he said, "Glad you thought of this idea, bro. We haven't taken a weekday off in ages."

They headed for the door. "See ya later, Mitch," they both called on their way out.

"Where'd the guys go?" Aubrey asked, returning from the bathroom. She was clad in an oversized red T-shirt and black shorts. Her freshly washed hair hung straight, and her face bore the sheen of a recent scrub. His hormones were in overdrive.

"Fishing. Geoff's been on the phone with Peggy, enlightening her about the events of yesterday. When she heard he couldn't get back in the firehouse, she suggested they take the day off and enjoy her family's outboard."

She walked over to the refrigerator and pulled out a bottle of orange juice. "Sounds like fun. I'm glad my exploits benefited someone."

"I doubt they'll catch anything, but the idea was to relax. Neither has taken a day off in a long time." He grabbed the bag of bagels and offered her one.

She accepted a cinnamon-topped roll. "Neither have you, from what I hear. Why didn't you go?" She shot him a quizzical look.

"Me? I would've been a fifth wheel. Too many for Peggy's boat, because her younger brother was going along, also." He dropped down near where she sat, close enough to breathe in the intoxicating perfume of soap.

She finished her bite of bagel, then stared him down. "This isn't more of your keep-an-eye-on-Aubrey mission, is it? I'm fine. Last night, er, this morning, was a fluke."

"I know that. But unlike Geoff and Gray, I've got work to do. This coach needs to be gone over with an eagle eye. Wanna take notes for me?"

In answer, she reached in her purse and pulled out a small notepad. "Longhand okay?"

"Sure. But remember, this could've been your day to go shopping or sightseeing." He waited for the inevitable comment about the state of shopping or sightseeing in this little burg.

It didn't come. Instead, she smiled sweetly. "That's okay. I spent enough on clothes last night and saw the sights, at least the animal life, at the restaurant the night before." She fiddled around in her purse and pulled out a ballpoint pen. "Ready?"

*

It only took her twenty minutes to realize she'd made a huge mistake. Going over the new coach with Mitch was a snore. Was this how he spent his days? Measuring (well, to be fair, she did that too), feeling surfaces, locating screws and bolts, undoing screws and bolts, tightening screws and bolts. Fishing, even if all she caught were a deeper tan, would have been more productive.

"I'm thirsty. Did we get bottled water last night?" She already knew the answer.

Mitch looked up from the hubcap he was checking. "Don't think so."

"I'll go get some. Maybe get sandwich makings for lunch while I'm at it."

Mitch returned his attention to the hubcap. "Told you it'd be boring."

She left him chuckling. It was unnerving how he was picking

up on her foibles so quickly. She just hoped that he wasn't on to her real mission.

In the parking lot of the supermarket, she grabbed her cell phone. "Orville?" she said, when a male voice came on the line. "It's Aubrey Carpenter. I think today's our lucky day."

She filled him in on the smoke incident, which, of course, he'd already heard about.

"So Mitch has the day free."

"You got it. He sees it differently, of course, but a little sweet talk and encouragement from you, and you might convince him to do some legal work."

"Hmmm. Let me think a minute. I'm sure I can come up with something."

"Just not too obvious."

"Aubrey, dear, remember who the attorney is here. I'll be the soul of discretion."

She clicked off, wondering if she should keep her distance while Orville worked his wonders, or if he'd need her there for support. In the end, prudence won out. Well, okay, cowardice. She took her time buying groceries.

*

"What are you doing out in this hot sun at high noon?"

Mitch twisted his neck slightly to see Orville Drummond standing a few feet behind him at the open hood to the coach's engine. Withdrawing the wrench he'd been using to screw a bolt tighter, he stood, wiping his hands on a rag he pulled from his shorts pocket.

"Orville! Nice to see you. This is getting to be a habit." Not again. There was only one reason why his older friend would leave his cool, cozy office and trek down the block in this blazing sun. At least, for once, he wasn't wearing his customary summer wool suit. Matlock had nothing on Orville.

Orville's face assumed a sheepish expression. Although, he also looked hopeful. "Far as I'm concerned, we don't see each other often enough."

Mitch considered his words, then decided to let his response ride.

"But this isn't a social visit, boy. I need your help."

Mitch started to remind him of the offer he'd turned down the week before, but Orville held up a hand. "No, I'm not here about that, although I haven't given up yet, no matter what you said. I'm here now because I need help with a thorny problem that's popped up."

Orville yanked a white handkerchief from his pants pocket and dabbed at the perspiration dotting his forehead. "How about taking a break? Got any water inside this thing?"

Mitch kicked himself mentally for keeping the old guy out in the heat of the day. "Sure," he said, placing a hand on Orville's shoulder and steering him toward the door of the coach. "It'll have to be from the tap. Aubrey's out getting the bottled stuff."

"Aubrey? That the California decorator?"

"Yeah."

"How's that going?"

"Don't ask."

Mitch retrieved a paper cup, filled it, then handed it to Orville.

Orville took a sip and visibly seemed to relax, as the water cooled his insides and the air conditioning helped the outside. He settled into the living room sofa. "Remember the Donnelly case?"

Mitch poured a cup of water for himself. "Children contesting a will where the mom had left it all to the stepfather?" He hadn't thought of that fiasco in a long time. He was in the middle of preparing a brief when a huge argument broke out among the four offspring. Something about two of them having received money from their mother just months before her death. The other two had gone ballistic at the revelation.

He nodded. "It's coming back to me. What's up? The kids are suing each other now?"

Orville gave him a rueful smile. "That's about the size of it. The stepfather passed away about six months ago. Left everything to two of the four. The only thing the other two received was a letter condemning them for challenging his inheritance."

"Sounds like the Donnellys are singlehandedly paying for your retirement, Orville. Which ones are your clients this time?"

"Ironically, the two named in the will. I need to know the strength of the arguments you gathered to support them five years ago so I can refute them now."

Mitch poured another cup of water. It really was hot today. "I left you volumes of notes."

Orville pulled at his shirt collar. "That you did. Thing is, the filing date was moved up and I need to act on this tomorrow. When I heard you've been smoked out of the firehouse, it was like a miracle, for me anyhow, so I could make it through this crazy family free-for-all."

The old guy didn't give up. But then, he'd always liked that about Orville.

"I only need a few hours of your time. Today, while you're *homeless*. You can set up shop in my office."

It was enticing. Hell, Orville's original offer had been haunting him for days. That particular temptation he had to avoid. But this was short-term. And it was stiflingly hot outside. And humid.

Nah, he couldn't, could he? There was Aubrey to think about. She was still embarrassed about turning them out of their home. She'd soon be returning. He couldn't desert her.

His cell phone, clipped to his waist, buzzed.

"Mitch? It's Aubrey. I found this darling tearoom. Can you scare up lunch on your own? I know I said I'd bring back sandwich fixings, so if you want me to still do that, I will."

Mitch stared at the phone. Was she psychic? At the very

least, her timing left him wondering. "Don't worry about me. Something's come up that will take me most of the afternoon."

*

Aubrey put her cell phone down on the small round table where she sat in the tearoom. She'd done her part. The rest was up to Orville.

Here she was at a place called To a Tea, ready to order. Surprisingly, the room was almost full for a Tuesday in early summer. Two waitresses dressed in light blue pinafores, à la Alice in Wonderland, were busy taking orders and delivering lunches and beverages. She wondered if the Mad Hatter was the owner or the chef. It could affect her choice of entrée.

She studied the menu. The place seemed to specialize in tea and ambience, not a wide variety of menu offerings. Five. Chicken Florentine. That would do. She was about to put her phone away when it chirped.

"Aubrey! It's Geoff."

"I thought you were out on a lake fishing."

"I am. Brought my cell with me. Habit. Peggy wanted me to call you. She's inviting you to stay at their house tonight and until it's okay to go back in the firehouse."

That was neighborly. On second thought, she wondered how Peggy had reacted to her sleeping in the same room with the three men. The same room as Geoff.

"Even if you pass, she invited us all to dinner. Thought you'd like that. Down-home cooking. No fast food. No mayflies."

She chuckled. "The last part alone is enough to get me there. But it's not necessary to put me up. I'm starting to get the hang of the sleeping bag."

"Are you sure?" he asked. "Wouldn't you like to get in a full night's sleep?"

Great, had he shared the information about her claustrophobia with Peggy, too?

"Aubrey? She says to tell you they have a hot tub."

"And the guest room has its own private bath," she heard Peggy say in the background.

What the heck? Sleeping on an actual bed again did have its merits. "Okay, okay, you've convinced me."

She was about to take her first bite of an apple tart when she heard her phone burring again. Now what? They'd landed a fish? "Hi again."

"Again?" the caller asked. A female voice. An older female voice. Her mother.

"Mother? Hi. This is a surprise."

"What have you done to Heidi Buxbaum?" No "hello," no "how are you doing, dear?"

"Heidi? What are you talking about, Mother? I haven't seen Heidi in a couple weeks."

"Well, I have. The woman's beside herself because you left her high and dry with an incomplete decorating project."

Thank you, Heidi. You not only neglected to tell me your husband still owned the cabin, but now you're dragging Mother into this.

"I . . . I did complete it. At least I took it as far as I could until I found out she didn't have clear claim to it."

"That's not what she says. Something about furniture not being delivered. Draperies not hung. What you do with your business is your affair, Aubrey. Not mine. I don't need your clients interrupting my luncheon with dear friends to rant and rave about your lack of responsibility."

"I'm . . . I'm sorry, Mother. I had no idea she'd drive up to Santa Barbara to disturb you."

"She's looking for you. Apparently you haven't answered her calls in over two weeks."

Damn! She should've sent something legal-looking to Heidi telling her there'd been a breach of contract. At the time, she'd been too frightened by Heidi's brute of a husband's threats of running her out of business. Instead, she'd gotten out of Dodge. "I did call her."

She could almost hear her mother fuming. Clicking her manicured nails on the tabletop, no doubt. Tapping her Ferragamos on the carpeting.

"Heidi Buxbaum's affairs do not concern me. None of your clients concern me."

Not true. If Heidi's ties with Hollywood had been stronger, if her former husband, Cyril, had been a director or producer instead of a caterer, even a highly successful caterer, her mother would have claimed blood kinship.

"I'm sorry she got you involved in this, Mother. I'll contact her and get this worked out."

"I certainly hope so. Good-bye."

Just like that, the inquisition—no, the indictment—was over. At least she said good-bye.

*

"How's it going?" Orville asked, sticking his head into the small office he'd given Mitch.

Mitch jotted down one more case citation from the law book he'd been perusing and began massaging the back of his neck. Déjà vu. How many times before had he labored for hours in this office, losing himself in tracking down information?

"Got the goods to win the case. Just need to write up my findings."

A satisfied smile spread over the older man's face. "No kidding? I knew you could do it!"

"Yeah, well, your expectations probably exceed my capabilities, since it's taken most of the afternoon just to find what I was looking for. I used to be much quicker with a search."

Pulling on his eyeglasses, Orville glanced over Mitch's shoulder.

"Looks good to me."

"Thanks. But you're prejudiced, especially since now you don't have to do this."

Orville chuckled. "Got me there. I really do appreciate your doing this for me."

Mitch leaned into the chair, satisfaction coursing through his body as if he'd just finished a mile run. It felt fantastic to stretch his mental muscles again. "I know what you're up to, Orville. It worked today because I had the time, and this beat out sunstroke. But this was a one-time deal. Don't think you can tempt me to come back to the law with part-time jobs."

Orville raised his hands in surrender. "You got me, Mitch. Red-handed."

Mitch's mind went on alert. Orville didn't ordinarily back down or admit when he'd been caught. "Is that all you have to say for yourself?"

Orville gave him a bland look. Mr. Innocence. "What more do you want me to say? You don't think I set up that fire at your place so you'd have a day off?"

"Of course not! And it wasn't a fire. Aubrey left hamburger browning on the burner too long and the smoke overtook the place."

"Pretty defensive of someone you could barely tolerate a week ago."

Mitch shrugged. It was bad enough his brothers were starting to suspect he had feelings for Aubrey. He didn't need Orville's commentary. He checked his watch. "I've got another hour or so to complete this report. Can't stay beyond that. My brother's invited me to his new girlfriend's house for dinner."

"Peggy Summers? Nice girl. Gonna eat the fish they caught today?"

"How did you know that?" Orville's sources of information continued to amaze him.

"You should know better than most, it's my business to know everyone else's business." He patted Mitch on the back as he shuffled out of the room. "Pull the door behind you when you leave and the place will be sealed tight as a drum." At the door, he turned. "Thanks again. I enjoyed having you back."

"I enjoyed it too, Orville. Just don't get any further ideas."

Hearing the outside door close, Mitch returned to his work. He'd heavily padded the amount of time it would take him to complete the task so Orville wouldn't hang around to continue to promote his joining the practice. And he wanted to be alone with his thoughts before heading out for the night.

He may have told Orville that further legal work was out of the question, but the message hadn't reached his own brain yet. He couldn't lock out the temptation, the possibility of someday getting back to this. What he loved. He hadn't needed this afternoon working for Orville to know that. Yet, Orville's little ploy had hit the target—gotten his adrenalin flowing, made his heart pump faster. It had been great.

He made short work of the summation. Finished, he flicked off the lights and allowed himself one last glance around the room. Computer, desk, shelves of time-worn law books. Heaven on earth. All he needed to make life meaningful, at least career-wise, was in this room. He'd never see it again.

CHAPTER TWELVE

"More rhubarb, Aubrey?" Debbie Summers asked, offering her the bowl.

Aubrey held up a hand. "No, thanks. It was delicious, but I'm stuffed."

"I'll have some more, Mrs. Summers," Geoff said from the other side of the table.

Playing up to Peggy's mother already. The guy must have it bad.

Debbie looked his direction. "Of course, Geoff. You worked up quite an appetite today."

"You should have seen him, Mom," Peggy cut in, her hand resting on Geoff's arm like that was its permanent perch. "He insisted I take credit for that big boy, the twenty-three-inch one, but he's the one responsible for hauling him in. That fish fought us for almost ten minutes."

"I wasn't going to let him get the better of me," Geoff replied. "Didn't know when I'd get back out there to finish him off, if I didn't get it done today."

Peggy beamed back at him. "It was our pleasure, wasn't it, Tommy?" Her younger brother paused long enough from eating to give a high sign.

Where was Mitch? Hopefully, his late arrival meant he'd gotten so engrossed in whatever Orville had given him to do that he'd lost track of time. That would be the best result she could imagine.

Geoff must have read her mind, because after eyeballing his watch, he said, "Wonder what's keeping Mitch."

Peggy cut off speculation. "I'm glad you said yes to staying with us, Aubrey. It'll be fun to have another woman around here besides Mom and me."

"I appreciate the offer," Aubrey said.

"I should've said something Saturday," Debbie added, reentering the room with another platter of fish. "After all, you *are* family."

"What?" Aubrey almost dropped her glass of lemonade.

Debbie watched her reaction from where she stood across the table. "I didn't think you knew. Or you would've said something. I almost told you Saturday."

Everyone stopped eating, taking in this exchange.

"I don't understand, Debbie. We're related?"

"Your mother's my cousin."

"My mother?"

Debbie fixed her with a tolerant smile. "That's right. Iris Bolger DiFranco Carpenter. I forget her latest husband's name. She grew up here in town. Not too far from here, actually."

Aubrey's temples pulsed frenetically. She supposed she should have expected to run into someone who knew her mother in the old days, but it never occurred to her it would be the Summers family.

Surprise and curiosity blended to make her a little giddy. "Did . . . did you know each other well?" Her mother never said much about the family and friends she left behind.

Debbie lowered her eyes and gave her a wry smile. "Then, yes. It wasn't like we were best buddies. She was a few years older. But we had great times when our families got together."

"Wow," was about all Aubrey could say. She'd never heard much, anything, about her Iowa cousins. Her mother denied that she even had a childhood, let alone lived here at one time.

"I saw her less frequently once we got older," Debbie added. "Got invited to her wedding to Stan DiFranco but lost touch after that. Didn't even get to see their little girl when she was born. That's why I was so delighted when I met Jenna through the Internet."

"Jenna?" Graham asked, his voice rising.

"DiFranco?" Geoff echoed.

Debbie's perplexed expression went from Aubrey to the two

McKenna brothers and back again to Aubrey. "Why, yes. Jenna DiFranco, Aubrey's half-sister."

So much for keeping that quiet.

Both Graham and Geoff, their faces mottled in astonishment, turned her direction.

She was about to respond when, over her shoulder, she heard, "Jenna DiFranco is your half-sister?" Mitch stood just inside the doorway. He wasn't smiling.

Inhaling deeply, she released her breath, knowing it was time to come clean. Past time. She attempted a weak smile. "That's right. We thought if you knew, it would put more pressure on you than you needed."

Though still appearing confused, Debbie regained her hostess persona enough to usher Mitch to an empty chair at the table.

Mitch gave her a curt, polite nod of appreciation, then turned his full attention on Aubrey, who was seated next to him. "So you thought you'd spare us the additional tension?"

She nodded. It sounded pretty lame when he put it that way. But she couldn't tell them how Jenna had come to her rescue with this make-work project.

"Uh, Aubrey. I hope you know that any comments we made about your sister weren't intended as slams," Graham said, a sheepish expression on his face.

Good old Graham. Always the diplomat. And fearful of losing their client.

She shot him a reassuring smile. "Don't worry, Graham. She gets to me sometimes, too."

Geoff stared at her, brows furrowed, as if debating whether to say something.

"Yes, Geoff?" she said, sensing he needed an invitation to spill.

"Is that why . . . why you were so . . . negative about the place when you first arrived?" He had the grace to blush and actually looked away from her, but he'd still asked the question.

Surprised by his candor, she gave an embarrassed little chuckle in response. But then, she supposed she owed them some explanation. "My mother has very few good memories of this town. I grew up exposed to that *attitude*. I guess I brought some of it with me."

Aubrey sensed the tension that permeated the room. Mitch turned away from her and continued to eat his dinner without speaking. Geoff and Graham silently watched Mitch's reaction, then dropped their eyes to their own plates. Debbie swiped at the perspiration on her forehead. And Peggy wore a look of bewilderment.

Aubrey realized she needed to say something more to cut through the drama. "Jenna hinted for weeks that she'd like me to do the interior of the coach. I turned her down. My business was thriving, and I didn't feel I could spare the time away from it, even for her."

Peggy, the only one who faced her directly, folded her hands in her lap and tilted her head. "What made you change your mind?"

Ugh. Why had she opened that door? "I . . . uh . . . had an unexpected break in the project I was working on," she said, searching for where she'd go from there.

"Oh? What?"

Bless Peggy's inquiring little heart! Why couldn't she leave it alone? The guys knew enough to refrain from asking further questions. And this was her cousin?

Aubrey pasted a smile across her face. "The furn . . . uh, no, the draperies . . . uh, actually the interior painting . . . ." *Oh, heck!* She'd run out of excuses. "The truth is, Peggy, I decorated a mountain hideway for my client, only to learn she no longer owned it. Her former husband did. And Louis XIV wasn't exactly what he had in mind for his fishing cabin."

Graham's mouth exploded, expelling the sip of water he'd just taken. Geoff nearly choked on his dessert. Debbie, who'd been handing Mitch a piece of apple pie, dropped the plate on the table and stood motionless, her mouth agape, watching the pie slide away.

Mitch turned to face Aubrey, his eyes crinkling in amusement. "Louis XIV, huh? That's what I would've chosen if I redid my cabin in the woods."

"Stop it!" she cried. "You're reducing this to a joke! This is serious stuff. The husband didn't find it funny. At all."

Mitch put down his forkful of pie. "Can you blame him? Sounds pretty frou-frou to me."

Aubrey made a face, attempting to get her temper under control.

"Sorry, no offense intended," Mitch said.

"I put a lot of time and heart into fixing up that cabin."

Mitch shrugged. "I'm sure you did, but didn't it ever seem . . . uh, how should I put this . . . uh, *frivolous*, to doll up a shack like that?"

"Frivolous!" How dare he reduce all her hard work to that one-word description? "That project could have won me an article in 'House Beautiful.'" That said, she discovered everyone was eying her as if she was speaking in tongues. "What?" she asked, lowering her voice.

They exchanged glances, all of them averting her eyes.

Mitch leaned back in his chair and ran his hands through his hair.

Peggy lifted her brows Geoff's direction. He, in turn, focused his attention on his pie. Graham busied himself with his lemonade.

"I . . . uh . . . guess none of us has enough experience with your line of work to fully appreciate your predicament," Peggy said. She busied herself collecting plates and silver.

Geoff joined her, grabbing glasses and bowls.

Aubrey continued to sit there, wondering what it was she'd said that had put such a damper on the party. She'd had to defend herself, hadn't she? She couldn't let Mitch's *frivolous* comment go unchallenged. She'd had to whitewash the interior woodwork in order to make the delicate pastels of the furniture look right. She'd lost sleep coming up with a way to cover the plank floors.

And in the end? It was rather frivolous. Not that she'd let Mitch know that.

While Debbie cleaned up in the kitchen, the others slipped off to a backyard game of badminton. She kept her distance.

"Want to give it a try?" Mitch stood a few feet away, in his hand, the funny-looking white thing they'd been batting over the net.

"I . . . I don't think so."

He offered her the birdie. "You could take out some of that frustration on this little fella."

"You think I'm frustrated?"

He attempted a smile. "You weren't too thrilled with my comments a little while ago."

She blew out a breath, fanning her bangs. "You called my work frivolous. That bites."

She wasn't getting his drift. "And your constant questions about why I'm not an attorney. How should they make me feel about my job?"

She flinched, as if he'd slapped her. Rather than reply, though, she drew up one of the lawn chairs Debbie had set out and dropped into it.

Mitch did the same.

She made a thing about not looking at him. "Don't feel you have to keep me company."

"I didn't want to play. That game never appealed to me."

"Badminton, right? Never played it." She gave him a quick side glance, then clutched her hands in her lap.

*

Why was he making her so uncomfortable? He debated whether it was safe yet to broach the topic that had brought him over to her. Swiveling, he moved in to face her. "Are you like your sister?"

"Huh?"

"Jenna DiFranco. I've only talked to her on the phone. Would I have seen the resemblance if I'd ever met her?"

"I doubt it. Except maybe the fact that we're both female. Jenna's delicate. Sophisticated. Even ethereal when she's playing. I'm . . . "

"Something else entirely," he finished for her, his voice catching on the last word. His eyes held hers. He'd not noticed until now the flecks of green among the blue.

Her eyes widened, as if taken aback by his gaze. She let out a deep sigh. "Why do you bring up my sister?"

One moment he wanted to throttle her for keeping mum on the family ties, and the next, he found himself wanting to . . . to . . . God! He couldn't do this. He jerked back in his chair, nearly toppling it. "I feel like a fool for missing the connection."

She tilted her head away from him, apparently surprised by his revelation. "How would you have known?"

How would he? "As you've pointed out more than once, I've been trained to question situations that don't add up. And you haven't from the moment you arrived."

She drew back. "I've been up front with you."

He thought back to their experience in the locked break room and how she'd freaked out. Why would someone submit herself to a situation so contradictory to her own well-being? The same someone who would fail to verify the rightful owner of a mountain cabin before transforming it into a chi-chi chalet.

Talk about seeing associations.

Somewhere in the recesses of his brain, an alarm sounded. It started as a dull tolling, but it grew by the second until his head throbbed with the pounding realization. He jumped from the chair to stand facing her, his finger pointing. "What was that about being *up front*?"

Her eyes blinked several times.

He no longer sought to track the errant flecks of color within them. "I have been."

"Even when you've run out of cover stories and have been caught red-handed?" He stared at her incredulously, still not quite taking in what his brain had just put together.

She stood too, placing hands on hips. "What's with you?"

He ground his lips together until he could almost bite through them. "What's with me? You've run away from that fiasco back in L.A., haven't you?"

She thrust a hand forward, as if to push him away.

Towering over her, he held his position, willing her to admit the truth.

She backed into her lawn chair and knocked it over before she stalked off.

He'd expected tears, more cover-up, continued denial. Or an argument. Not temper. Shoulders squared, she stomped away, as if the fact that he'd finally seen through her was an affront. Go figure.

Let her cool her jets. He needed time to absorb what he'd just figured out. She hadn't denied it, and she would have, had he been the least bit off.

He watched the badminton game for a while and watched her watching the game, though she really wasn't. She was fuming. She'd lied to them all about her reason for being there, and she was angered by his calling her on it. Thing was, from the way she'd described the situation out in California, it didn't strike him as reason enough to pick up stakes and flee.

And, despite the way she irritated him, he wanted to help her. Bur first, he had to get her talking to him.

After a few minutes, he made his way over to her. He grasped her hand. "We have some unfinished business to discuss." He didn't give her a chance to demur. He pulled her across the yard and out to the front porch and relative privacy.

She attempted to drag her feet. "Ow! My arm's coming out of its socket."

"Don't give me any grief, Aubrey. You've had ample time to regroup your thoughts. Now it's time to spill them. To me."

At the porch, he pivoted suddenly and stopped. She didn't and plowed right into him.

"Oof! Hey! Signal or something."

"Sorry." He reached for her hands. They were warm and smooth and felt like they were made to be held by his. "I guessed right, didn't I?"

She studied the plank floor, not answering.

"Didn't I?"

She lifted an obstinate chin, her blues now focused directly on him. Scowling, she blew out a puff of air. "Yes! Okay. Yes, you were correct." She narrowed her eyes, as if daring him to say more. "Happy?"

He felt her heart. "Still ticking, I see. Admitting your big secret wasn't heart-stopping." On the other hand, mere contact with her almost stopped his own ticker. Or had it revved up?

She continued to stare him down, seething.

He pulled her over to the glider just outside the front door. "Tell me about it."

She bit her lip, as if fighting to keep from saying anything. Finally, she said, "You don't want to hear this, Mitch. It's not a pretty story."

"Try me."

She settled into the cushion and studied her nails.

Mitch waited as long as he could tolerate the silence. Then, he said, "Spill."

"Okay, McKenna. You've run me to ground. Here goes." She stared straight ahead. "I own a modest but growing business in L.A. restoring deteriorating homes to their former Hollywood glory. My mother has this thing about anything connected to the Business. For the first time in my life, she noticed me."

"Okay?"

"Eager for her additional approval, I made a deal with an antique dealer to take some Louise XIV off his hands in order to gain entrée to other offerings in his inventory for future projects." She stopped. She'd arrived at the not-so-pretty part. "I was so damned determined to use them as soon as possible, I guess I didn't think through the ramifications of filling the rustic mountain cabin with furnishings so blatantly wrong for it."

God, that sounded terrible, even to her. She wanted to stop there.

"Go on."

"Although I considered my client, Heidi Buxbaum, a friend, I was sure she'd tell me where to get off if I mentioned the antiques. Then I could at least tell the dealer I'd tried. I pitched her a preposterous scheme to whitewash every wall—exposed oak, mind you—then sponge them with gilt so the Louis XIV would fit in. I expected her to laugh in my face, then I'd back off, come up with something more orthodox, and we'd both be happy."

"But instead, she liked it."

She rolled her eyes. "Can you believe it? I know I should have suspected something right then and run for the hills. Well, away from them, since that's where the cabin was."

"Why didn't you?"

"Suspect something? Or run?" She actually cracked a smile. "For starters, my ego had begun to outdistance my talents."

He restrained a snicker.

"I thought I'd done such a brilliant job describing my plans that I could actually pull it off. And if I did, not only would I have found an owner for the Louis XIV, I would have also racked up a decorating coup I could use to gain more clients."

"So what's the deal about her not owning the place?"

"Heidi collects men . . . and husbands . . . like I accumulate ballpoint pens in the bottom of my purse. I knew that, but it never occurred to me that she was in the midst of shedding her current spouse because he'd been doing a little collecting of his own. So I didn't question her motives. I went merrily on my way painting, sponging, decoupaging, and blithely overlooked the due diligence to check ownership."

He leaned forward. "You simply assumed she owned it?"

She looked heavenward, closing her eyes. "Pathetic, right? I told you it wasn't pretty."

He considered her story. "Did she move out when you started attacking the walls?"

"No. She had at least one house in town."

"How far away?"

"Maybe twenty miles. This place was up in the hills northwest of town."

"Did she ever go with you?"

Aubrey closed her eyes, trying to remember. "I'm not sure. She must have, although now that I think about it, I don't recall her actually giving me a key." She thought some more on it. "I know. She was going to give it to me the day she signed the contract in my office, but then she remembered she'd loaned it to a friend for a few days. We met for lunch a few days later, and that's when she turned it over."

"But she definitely handed you the key?"

"Yeah. Why?"

"*De facto* evidence of ownership. Although the fact that she made you wait for it could mean she needed time to finesse it away from her husband."

Aubrey sat forward. "*De facto*? That's legal terminology. What are you getting at?"

He wasn't sure, except he felt himself being pulled into her dilemma, and he couldn't stop it. He didn't want to. He turned to her, once again taking her hands in his. "How did the husband get involved?"

"She gave a party to celebrate the end of the project. He showed up and started ranting about how she had no right to mess with *his* property. Then he turned to me and told me point blank he was going to sue me for unlawful destruction of property *and* breaking and entering. Which would mean criminal charges."

"Is that when you fled town?"

"I sought out Heidi first. She was hiding in her room. All

she wanted to know was about Cyril, her husband. Had he been angry or hurt? Had he brought anyone with him? Then it dawned on me. She'd set the whole thing up for his benefit, including parading me in front of him."

"That was your first inkling that she'd used you?" He was pretty sure, but not absolutely.

"It hit me with the force of a speeding freight train. I was dumbfounded. My professional reputation was on the line, and all she could think about was whether she'd made her husband miserable enough. With my decorating."

She sprang from her seat and started for the porch railing.

"Don't go yet."

She looked back over her shoulder. "I'm not. I just can't sit there rethinking the whole catastrophe without it still riling me."

"Why didn't you fight back?" He rose and joined her, putting his arm around her shoulder. He wanted to crush her to him, reassure her that he was on her side, even though her wisdom might have been somewhat impaired.

She turned to face him. "I did. At least at first. I confronted Heidi with my speculation and told her in no uncertain terms that I wasn't going to suffer for this disaster. Not when she'd deliberately misled me and misrepresented the facts."

"And?"

"She pulled out my bill. Started going down it, item by item, tsk-tsking the so-called inflated price of each piece. She said it would be a shame if my clientele were to learn how I'd fleeced her."

Aubrey wasn't a dupe. She was intelligent and reputable, if just a tad bit impetuous. He continued to hold her, rubbing her shoulder, whispering soothing nothings into her ear. "It's okay, honey. You've been holding that in too long."

"I should have found an attorney right away, but my sister came up with this idea as an alternative. She knows Heidi's husband. He works with her former husband. Another jerk. She was afraid he'd use the opportunity to hurt her further, through me, following their extremely acrimonious divorce."

Pieces were starting to fit into place. Especially why Aubrey would run. If it had just been herself, she probably would have fought back. But with the possibility of it spilling over onto her sister, she was vulnerable to her sister's fears.

"Jenna thought Heidi's husband would cool down. With time. As long as I was out of the picture, not around to remind him of how his former wife had duped him."

"So she sent you here to hide out while you waited."

He felt her head nodding against his chest. It tickled the hairs beneath his knit shirt and made him want to pull her tighter.

She lifted her head. Whether she was expecting a kiss or not, he complied. Twice. Three times. Several more, until it all blended into one long, mind-bending exchange.

All the control he'd so carefully built up against reacting to her since her arrival evaporated. He groaned into her lips, knowingly succumbing to the attraction pulling at him.

She moaned back, nuzzling his neck. "Oh, Mitch."

No turning back now. Not that he wanted to. A light from inside the house flickered in his eyes. No good. Too public. He maneuvered them into a dark corner of the porch where he let his hands roam freely over her.

She gulped, although she continued to hold tight. "We . . . should . . . stop."

He slid his lips away from hers briefly and breathed into her ear, "Yeah, I know. Easier said than done."

She tore her eyes from his long enough to peek over his shoulder toward the house. "It's dark. They'll be coming in soon from the game. And they'll be looking for us."

Had he not had something else to tell her, it might have been all but impossible to break it off. "You realize what you've done, don't you?" His voice was husky.

"Kissed your socks off?"

"That, too." He stood back just enough to see her reaction to his next words. "You finally followed through and found yourself an attorney."

*

"You're going to represent me?" Incredulous, she had to grasp the railing to keep her balance. "After all your denials about wanting to practice the law again?"

Though it was one of the longest days of the year, twilight had finally descended. She could barely see his face to discern how serious he was.

He pulled away from her slightly and tugged at his shirt. "I can't be your attorney of record, since I haven't sat for the bar, but I can check into some things."

"Things? Like what?"

Backing into the railing, he leaned against it, lowering himself so she could see his expression from the light pouring onto the porch from the living room inside. Concern showed through in his narrowed eyes and firm-set jaw.

"Like how this woman—Heidi?—represented the project to you. And how she made the place available to you. And publicly acknowledged, at her party, that she'd asked you to redecorate the place."

"Then I can't be sued?" She was almost afraid to say the word aloud.

He put his hand on her shoulder and squeezed it. "Didn't say that. Anyone can sue."

"Oh." She tried to keep the disappointment out of her voice, but it was there.

He squeezed again. "That doesn't mean they have a leg to stand on, though. And that's what I want to look into. What's this husband like?"

"Cyril?"

"Cyril? People still stick their kids with names like that?"

"Hollywood loves unusual names. Easier to remember. He was

probably a Charley or Carl before his catering business took off."

He put an arm around her and pulled her to his side. "What do you know about him?"

She thought about it. How many times had she even seen him? "For a guy named Cyril, he's pretty scary. Looks like a weight lifter. Tall. Shoulder-length bleached blond hair. And even though Heidi brought her own fortune to the marriage, he was already a successful caterer. Used to do craft service for television productions, but he branched off to celebrity parties years ago and made a fortune all over again."

"And he was running around on his wife? Which is why she divorced him?"

She tried to recall just how Heidi had put it. She hadn't referred to her estranged spouse directly when they'd discussed renovation plans. Thinking back, Heidi had probably avoided the subject so that Aubrey wouldn't put two and two together, that the project was her own sweet vengeance on her philandering husband. "She never really said. I think I learned about the end of their marriage from other acquaintances."

He was staring at her, a heart-stopping, penetrating look that told her he was struggling to keep from resuming what they'd been engaged in a minute ago. "I should go." He didn't sound convinced, but he kept his distance. "Stay here another day. Call me tomorrow with the names of the vendors and contractors you used on the project. And anyone else who might have information about this Heidi."

He was removing temptation. She wasn't prepared for the intense letdown the thought of being away from him, even for a day, was already having on her.

"Okay. But can't I help some other way?" There wasn't much to do around the Summers's place. Debbie wouldn't allow her in the kitchen. And Peggy would either be at work or off with Geoff.

He started to touch her, then withdrew his hand as if it had been burned. "Just . . . stay here. Make lists. I've got to go." He turned and raced to his car.

CHAPTER THIRTEEN

"Mornin', Orville," Mitch said, dropping onto the empty seat on the other side of the booth. Two could play this game of staged encounter, and it was his turn. He needed help.

The older man's eyes brightened as he took in his visitor. "Mornin' yourself. I didn't think you drank coffee."

"I don't. But this icy mocha latte stuff is growing on me. And I wanted to pick your brain. Got a minute?"

Orville fixed him with a curious gaze. "For you, at least ten. What's up?"

Mitch filled him in on Aubrey's situation. When he finished, he took a few swigs of the mocha concoction he'd purchased on a lark, just to be a good patron. Not bad.

Orville leaned against the back of his seat and rubbed his chin. "I don't get it. Why'd she run? The client misrepresented the job. Aubrey—Ms. Carpenter—was the victim. Not the other way around."

Mitch breathed a deep sigh of relief. He hadn't realized he'd been holding his breath until Orville confirmed his own take on the case. "The way I see it," he began, adopting his most authoritative tone, "she's got three problems. First, she needs to get paid. I'm thinking her friend may have the bucks, but she's cheap and is using her ex's wrath as a way to get out of paying."

"I agree." Orville stirred his coffee. "What else?"

"Next, we need to nip in the bud any lawsuit the ex might be planning. He doesn't have a case, but he's intimidating. I suspect his temper was a major factor prompting Aubrey to hit the road. That and Problem Number Three, fear for her professional reputation. In her business, that's everything."

Nodding his head, Orville continued to sip his coffee. "Pretty good summation. You don't think the woman and her ex-spouse were in cahoots, do you?"

"I considered that. But from the way Aubrey described this big coming-out party the wife threw, the whole idea was to shove the frou-frou furnishings down the ex's throat."

"Still, it wouldn't hurt to check into the possibility and eliminate it." He asked Mitch for the names of the client and her ex-husband. "The guy's some big shot caterer in Hollywood?"

"That's what Aubrey says. Catering's like the third hottest industry out there. Following making movies and making clients."

Orville sniffed. "You sound like a real fan of the place. I don't get the impression it's a place you'd like to visit, let alone live."

Mitch narrowed his eyes. "Why would I even consider it?"

Orville raised his brows and just sat there looking back at him.

"What are you getting at, Orville?" Then it hit him. "You think I might join Aubrey out there?" He could hear his voice rise.

Orville's brows shot even higher.

Mitch shook his head vociferously. "No, no, no, no! No way. I'm a Midwestern guy, born and bred. I have no desire to live on the Coast."

"And Aubrey?"

Mitch held up his hands in surrender. "I'm looking into this fiasco as a favor to her. She's been a big help to me, to all three of us McKennas, in the brief time she's been here. And yes, I like her." Thoughts of the scene on the Summers' porch the night before raced unbidden through his brain. That had been happening a lot since last night. To ward them off, he said, "But I'm not ready to pick up stakes here."

Orville continued to eye him but let the subject drop. After a bit, he said, "I have some contacts out there. I'll give them a call and see what they can dig up on this . . . " he picked up his notepad and tried to read his own scribbling, " . . . Cyril Buxbaum."

"I was hoping you'd offer to do just that."

"And, since I owe you for helping out me out of a jam yesterday, I'll do some research for you today. Unless you'd like to do it yourself?"

Orville averted his eyes, but the subtlety wasn't lost on Mitch. Orville's tone was a little too hopeful.

"Good try, my friend. But I've got a motor coach calling my name. I'm moonlighting on this as a favor to Aubrey."

"Give me a day or so. I'll let you know what I find out."

The two men strolled out the door together, Orville turning one direction and Mitch heading the other, toward the firehouse. Before he'd gone ten feet, Orville called out to him. "You know, Aubrey might like it here. Did you consider that?"

Mitch started to answer, then simply shook his head at his friend. Orville just didn't know when to give up.

*

"What would you like for dinner?" Debbie asked, swooping into the kitchen, where Aubrey had been hammering away on her lists all afternoon. "It's just you and me tonight. Peggy and Geoff are out on the town doing dinner and a movie away from the other two brothers. Something about the motor coach being a little close for four people. And Tommy is spending the night at a friend's."

"Don't feel you have to stay here and keep me entertained. You probably don't get too many nights off yourself." Although with everyone away all day, she'd had her fill of alone time. Even Debbie's chattiness seemed welcome at the moment.

Debbie placed a hand over Aubrey's. "I wouldn't dream of leaving you alone. Not when we've only got you with us another day or so. You're family, dear."

Aubrey forced a smile. Debbie's words, simply spoken, were heartfelt, and meant more to Aubrey than she would have thought possible a day ago. She squeezed Debbie's hand. "Okay. You're on. Want to order out or give a hopeless novice a cooking lesson?"

Debbie chose the latter, though she kept the menu simple. The humidity had subsided, so they chose to eat on the deck, but only after Debbie reassured her, twice, that mayflies didn't come in this far from the river.

After they cleared up, Debbie returned to the kitchen carrying a yellowed ten-pound candy box. "Got a few things in here I wanted to show you." She opened the lid and rooted through the contents. "There it is." She pulled out a dog-eared black and white photo and placed it in front of Aubrey.

Out of politeness, tinged with just a bit of curiosity, Aubrey scanned the subjects, a teenage girl and a younger girl. They were outdoors, seated at a picnic table with several people around them, smiling faces. She turned to Debbie. "Is this you?"

"I wasn't sure you'd see the likeness. Do you recognize the older one?"

Aubrey studied the teenager. She looked vaguely familiar. "That's my mother!" she said, surprised. She'd rarely seen pictures of her mother as a young girl, but the teenager reminded her of herself. She hadn't seen it at first, because she hadn't been looking for it. But now that she realized who it was, the similarity in looks pelted her.

"Hasn't she ever shown you these pictures?" Debbie almost looked offended.

"Actually, no. The only time Mother has talked about her early years has been to badmouth this town. I'm embarrassed to admit her feelings about this place influenced me when I first arrived."

Debbie pulled out the chair next to her and sank into it. "I'm not surprised. Iris left here with a chip on her shoulder a mile wide."

"Do you know why?"

Debbie scrunched up her brows and busied herself straightening the contents of the napkin holder in the middle of the table. She glanced back at the photo Aubrey still held. "She must have been about fifteen in that picture. The summer I was twelve. I'd just gotten my hair cut short so I'd be more comfortable when I was walking beans for my grandfather."

Aubrey held the photo out, continuing to gaze upon the woman she barely recognized. "Fifteen. It's hard to think of her any way than the way she is now. She looks so warm and open in this."

"I take it she's a little more demanding these days?"

Aubrey turned to Debbie, about to confirm the statement, but at the last moment, feeling somewhat disloyal, she tempered what she'd been about to say. "A tad, yes."

"That's understandable. Her life changed so much the year after that picture was taken."

"How? I don't remember Mother saying anything about the year she was sixteen."

Debbie arched a brow. "You're kidding? She almost became a movie star."

Aubrey jerked in her seat. "Movie star? No! Tell me about it."

Debbie pulled the dilapidated candy box toward her. "I can do better than that. If I can find what I'm looking for, that is." She riffled through the odds and ends in the box, which were considerable. Finally, she whipped out a yellowed newspaper clipping. "Here, read this."

A movie company had come to town, apparently the fall after the picture of her mother and Debbie had been taken. In appreciation for the town's allowing them to film scenes in several public spots, the movie folks had offered to fill a bit part with a local actress. The part was for a teenage girl, and after several hundred had shown up to audition, Iris Bolger won the role.

"Mother in a movie?" She couldn't get used to the concept. "She's never said anything about this, Debbie. What film was it?"

Debbie told her the name.

"I've seen that film, but I didn't see my mother in it. Did they cut the part?"

Debbie settled back in her chair and placed her hands on the table, folding them. "Two days before shooting was to take place, your grandfather had a heart attack. Though he hung on several more days, my aunt thought Iris's place was at his side, not making movies."

Her mother had actually landed a part in a film, what had to have been the most glorious moment in her life, and it had been taken away from her. No wonder there was little love lost between her mother and her grandmother, who had passed away when Aubrey was a small child.

Debbie leaned forward and took Aubrey's hand in her own. "The trauma of losing her beloved father and the part in the movie affected your mother tremendously. After months of grieving, she was a hollow shell of her former self, saddened and greatly disappointed."

"I knew my grandfather died when Mother was still in high school."

"The bitterness didn't show up until she learned she had to go to work to help support the family. Working after school and on weekends left little time for the drama lessons she dreamed about. Her mother couldn't afford them, anyway."

Aubrey sat back, releasing Debbie's hand. "I knew about her having to work, even in high school. But I didn't know . . . she never talked about . . . the whole story."

Debbie returned her attention to the box of mementoes. "There's one more clipping I thought you'd like to see. It's somewhere here. Give me a minute."

Aubrey rose and paced in front of the kitchen sink while Debbie searched. It was so much to take in. All this information about a young girl she hardly knew.

"Ah ha! Success. Come here, Aubrey. You need to see this part of your mother's story as well." Debbie placed the newspaper piece in her hands. It included a faded picture of her mother and a young Jenna, maybe five years old, and a man who Aubrey assumed was Stanley DiFranco, Jenna's father. Jenna resembled him around the eyes and had the same fair hair.

The story recounted how DiFranco had been named salesman of the year by a local department store. She skimmed it at first, trying to determine why Debbie thought it important. It was the second time through that the quote stood out. "DiFranco said he owes his success in the sales world to the support of his loving wife, who willingly stays at home raising their daughter so he can devote his attention to selling women's shoes."

The general reader would have gone right past this statement, pausing only long enough to surmise that all was well in the DiFranco household. But Aubrey read between the lines. DiFranco received kudos, his wife stayed at home. Neither his wife nor his daughter was even named in the article. And, though there was nothing wrong with selling women's shoes, she knew it would have frustrated her mother no end to have that held up as the family's big success.

"Stanley was a strange fish," Debbie said, once Aubrey looked up from reading the article. "A good father and provider, but your mother was never in love with him."

She said it with such authority, Aubrey had to blink. Had everyone known except him? "She told you?"

"No, not in so many words. But I could tell. I was in my early twenties by then, married and starting my own family. A woman in love, like I was, knows these things. I couldn't see any sparks, except when Stanley would say something about the good life they led. Your mother would turn her head and start doing something else. She was miserable."

"Did you see them much in those days?"

Debbie studied her nails. "No, not that often. He made my husband and me feel uncomfortable. He seemed so . . . smug. Self-important. And it was obvious how wrong he was. His family was about to self-destruct and he didn't have a clue."

Aubrey needed to think this through. Debbie's box of goodies was like the revelation of whodunit in a mystery. Things that she'd barely heard about as she was growing up were coming back to her in a rush of memory. It made her dizzy.

"Would you mind if I go outside by myself for a bit? I need time to absorb this."

Debbie watched her pace. "Of course not, dear. I hope I didn't upset you."

"No, not at all. But all of this back story about my mother is making my head throb." She started for the door. "Thank you. This has been helpful."

"Good. I'm glad you think so." As Aubrey reached the door, Debbie asked, "Would you like them? They're more meaningful to you than they are to me."

"I . . . I . . . " Though tempted, the idea of having so much information about her mother in her possession overwhelmed her. "That's very thoughtful. All right."

Debbie beamed. "That offer about using our hot tub still goes, if you're interested?"

Hot tub on a hot night? Maybe that would help her sort through this new information.

"You can use one of Peggy's bathing suits, if you don't have one. Peggy collects 'em. She won't miss one."

What the heck? Peggy was about her size. Well, maybe a little thinner, but not much. "Okay, I'll take you up on it."

*

Aubrey hunkered down in the roiling hot water so that only her head and neck were above the surface. Behind her, a jet spray pummeled her backside with zillions of tiny bubbles. Across the tub, her toes touched two other jets shooting off their own watery ammunition. The steady hum of the motor was hypnotic, lulling her into a soporific stupor.

This was a good idea. She hadn't enjoyed the soothing miracles of a hot tub in some time. And she needed time to think . . . time to take in the new image of her mother that Debbie's mementoes suggested. Here, in the evening twilight, away from Debbie's solicitousness, she attempted to clear her brain of the new data rattling around inside it.

"That's some grimace you're wearing. Did you get into it with Debbie?"

She blinked her eyes open to find Mitch standing on the other side of the tub, a strange look in his eyes.

"Grimace? I was trying to relax. Must have been straining too hard."

"Tough day?" He settled a hip on the wooden platform surrounding the tub.

"Not really. I spent most of my time working on that list you wanted. It's in my room. I'll go get it if . . . " She started to pull herself out of the water, but he put out a restraining hand.

"No need to hurry. I stopped by to give you some news."

Even though the light was fast dissipating, she noticed how cloudy his eyes had grown. If she didn't know better, she'd say that intense look was meant for her. Duh! She'd forgotten about the bathing suit when she'd risen. He was ogling her. Imagine that.

She scooted down under the water, watching him watch every disappearing inch of her body. Was he here to pick up where he left off the night before? And if he did, how was she going to react? So much for telling him she was open to a short-term fling. That didn't appeal to her now. She was still very much attracted to him, she could tell that by the erratic throbbing in the lower parts of her body. But if she gave in to her desires, would she ever be able to turn off her feelings for him when it was time to return to California?

While her better judgment debated what her actions for the remainder of the evening should be, her libido took over. "Want to join me?" *Where had that raspy voice come from?*

His eyes widened, like a little boy offered a chance to raid the candy store. For a moment, he seemed about to take her up on it, then, abruptly, he backed off. "Appealing idea, but since I didn't know about the pool party, I'm here without swim trunks."

Her libido continued to control her speaking parts. Slowly, she said, "No need for those."

She watched him absorb the shock wave her invitation produced. It definitely took him by surprise. He fisted his hands, then releasing the tension, continued to roll his fingers. Meanwhile, he bit his lower lip and attempted to focus on some spot above her, but his eyes kept coming back to her. She enjoyed the heady feeling that gave her. It made her feel powerful, and for once, with this fantastic piece of male architecture, in control.

When his gaze returned to hers, their eyes dueled, hers daring him to take her up on her suggestion, his daring her to retract it before he did.

"Aubrey?" Debbie's call broke the spell.

They both looked toward the house. God, what if Debbie had come out there and found them together in the tub, Mitch sans clothing?

"Yes, Debbie, I'm out here. Mitch is here too."

Debbie's head popped around the trellis that sheltered the hot tub. "I know. I sent him. Since he's here to keep you company, I'm going to a movie. Be back in a couple hours." She didn't give Aubrey or Mitch time to respond. She just turned and flitted off.

In the ensuing quiet, augmented only by the shush of the hot tub's motor, Aubrey turned back to Mitch and he continued to stare her down. Shortly, they heard the sound of Debbie's car backing down the driveway and into the street.

"Well?" She didn't recognize this brazen creature. Nor could she stop her.

"Okay, lady. You talked me into it." In one swift movement, he shucked his knit shirt. In the next, he'd unzipped his shorts and stripped down to nothing but his briefs. A full-grown erection strained against the front.

Aubrey couldn't take her eyes from the region. She knew she was gawking, but that didn't stop her. Fortunately, Mitch bounded into the water about that time, easing himself onto the bench a third of the way around the circumference from her.

"Whoo, this is hot!"

"You were expecting a cold shower?"

At that, he arched a brow and slid a little closer. "I probably could use one, as I'm sure you've noticed." He moved even closer, reaching under the water to find her hand, pulling it into his own. He brought it to his mouth and caressed it with his lips.

"Mitch . . . I . . . " She had no idea what she would say. He cut her off before she found out.

"You turned my day into hell, you know. All I could think of was finishing what we started last night."

"Uh . . . "

"Even when I was playing amateur detective, all I could think of was how that was helping you."

He slipped an arm behind her shoulders and drew her into his embrace. Tipping her chin up with his index finger, he kissed her as if they'd been apart twenty-four years instead of twenty-four hours. Long, deep, and hungrily. When he finally broke away, he kept his lips near her, whispering in her ear, "Oh, baby, I've missed you."

She draped her arms around his neck, so he wouldn't move away. "Me, too." Her voice was a hoarse whisper.

He pulled back slightly, just enough to take in the skimpy two-piece bathing suit beneath the water line. "You look great, by the way. When did you get the suit?"

"It's Peggy's. Thinking we're about the same size, Debbie told me to help myself. I must be two sizes larger. It's barely hanging onto me."

"You don't say?" He actually leered at her. "I think it fits fine." He cocked his head. "Although . . . " he reached behind her neck and cradled the knotted shoulder straps, " . . . you really don't need this."

He moved his fingers—a technique surely acquired from twiddling all those nuts and bolts over the years—and within seconds, the knot was undone. The top fell forward, barely covering her breasts, like a scanty wet washcloth. He ducked a hand under her armpit and performed the same magic on the knot keeping the remaining part of the top on her.

Keeping his eyes on her chest, he flicked the tiny garment over his shoulder. It floated briefly on the turbulent water, then sank to the bottom. Neither seemed to notice.

"You're more gorgeous than I imagined."

Aubrey fought the initial reaction to cross her arms over her naked breasts. Mitch's lascivious smile of appreciation kept her arms down. As she grew bolder under his gaze, she draped her arms over the back of the tub, letting her breasts protrude further.

Inside her, every atom of her being slammed into each other more chaotically than the waves lapping against her pebbly nipples. Though already surrounded by water, she could feel the moisture of her growing passion pool in the bikini panties. Every nerve ending was on fire, despite the water that should have been extinguishing the conflagration.

She tried to remember something she'd been thinking about just prior to going topless for Mitch. It had been important. But now it was difficult to think. Her brain must have disengaged about the same time her top disembarked the Good Ship Aubrey.

All she could do at the moment was feel, not think. Feel the sensation of warm water splashing her breasts. Feel the wantonness of basking in Mitch's attention. Feel the war being fought inside her as her body begged her to take the next step, bring Mitch to it.

Mitch bowed before her, his head almost disappearing under the water. He took a breast in each hand.

She felt his intake of breath. A shudder ran through him.

At first, he simply held each breast, lifting it slightly, squeezing.

His touch nearly knocked her off her perch. Did the man realize what that small act of possession did to her?

Ever so subtly, his thumbs circumnavigated the nipples. Restrained, gentle, masterful. She thought she'd melt away into the agitated water if he kept at it much longer. *Please, please, please take one in your mouth.*

As if reading her mind, he brought his mouth to one breast, covering the entire rosy area. His tongue flicked teasingly over the nipple, making it grow even more taut.

She heard herself make small mewling sounds, whimpering from the agony of it.

Her response made him work harder at his ministrations, drawing the breast further into his mouth and sucking. In her crotch and her toes, she experienced a neural shower, sending her senses into overload.

About the time she thought she was going to implode from the sensations pounding her body, he stopped long enough to pant out, "Do you know what you're doing to me? You're . . . amazing."

She could barely breathe. She was turning him on. Her. Aubrey Carpenter, the accidentally celibate interior decorator who hadn't had a date in six months.

He moved his attention to the other breast, and the earthquake inside her began all over again. She arched her back so he could take even more into his mouth. Exquisite torture. *Don't stop, Mitch. Don't ever stop.*

Playfully, he'd submerge, then take hold of her under the water with his mouth, like a school of fish kissing the shoreline.

Each time he'd emerge, the water clung to his dark eyelashes like liquid diamonds. As if he needed to look any better to her. His hair plastered to his head accentuated his cat eyes— Neptune claiming his trophy.

He kissed her again, folding her once more into his chest. The awareness of skin on skin had her molding herself tighter to him, wanting to be even closer. The scent of man mixing with the chlorine in the water titillated her nostrils.

*

Mitch paused long enough to catch his breath. He'd been going at it fast and furious. He was out of practice, although it was incredible how it came back to him so readily. While he breathed deeply, he had a moment of lucidity, the first since he'd arrived on the scene to witness Aubrey stretched across the hot tub like a ripe flower ready to be plucked.

Intuitively, he knew this period of awareness would be brief, because he was a man possessed. A man aroused beyond the point of no return. He was going to have her, here and now. She was so luscious. He wanted to feel and taste and explore every inch of her.

He twisted his head to nuzzle her neck. The same neck that had been stuck out more than once since this creature had graced his door, but rather than break it, as he might have fantasized the first day, all he wanted now was to sniff the wonderful floral fragrance emanating from it and plant tiny kisses along the silken column.

"Umm . . . " Eyes closed, she seemed to float without benefit of the water supporting her.

He reached down to feel her backside. Her buttocks were firm and rounded, made for cradling in his hands. He let one hand wander farther down the back of her leg and felt a muscle twitch. He let it roam back up, probing under the bikini bottom to cup her warm, soft skin.

"You've got too many clothes on," he said into her ear in a jagged breath. In the time it took a wave to ripple across the water's surface, he'd pulled the bikini bottom down and off, throwing it over his shoulder onto the platform.

She moaned and rubbed her abdomen against his enlarged penis.

He nearly shot out of the water like a missile fired into space. The heat she generated could have produced enough propulsion.

"Mitch." It came in a whisper, like a siren song urging him to move along.

He shoved a hand inside the elastic band of his briefs and made short work of pulling them off. Then he pretty much lost it, giving in to the pure ecstasy of being naked next to her. The warm water formed a bond, sealing their bodies together, and for several heartbeats, he simply lived in the sensation.

"Ever made love in a hot tub, California Girl?" His question emerged as a gasp.

She pulled far enough away from him to scan his face, her eyes dark and wide. "No. How about you?"

In response, he grabbed her ass and pressed her tightly against him, wanting to ram himself into her, inside her and simultaneously trying to hold off, to extend this fantastic interlude. It may not happen again, but he wanted this time to be right. Immersed as he was in his own fervor, he wanted this to be good for her too.

"Never. This is like the first time." God, why did he say that?

She stared into his eyes, her own smoldering. "Yes. It is." Her voice barely a whisper.

"I can't hold back much longer. Are you ready?"

"Oh yes, yes!"

"Wait a second!" He leaned over and grasped the shorts he'd discarded along the side of the tub. Pulling out his wallet, he quickly retrieved the small package holding protection.

"Let me," she offered, her eyes glowing. "The water will be a challenge." She deftly removed the condom from the wrapper and slid it onto him.

That accomplished, he pulled her back into his embrace and leaned into the side of the tub. His lips sought hers once again while his hand sought her mound. He pushed his hand back further to locate her sex. It was puffy and ripe for the taking. He guided himself to her opening and thrust.

"Ah," she sighed, moving her hips to the same rhythm, her hands clutching his shoulders tightly. She broke away from the kiss to move her lips to his neck and began nuzzling him.

As if his sensory system wasn't already in overdrive, what she did to his neck drove him over the edge. He'd meant to take his time, keep at it as long as he could endure the tension, but he couldn't help himself. He gave in to the absolute pleasure, letting go.

When he'd spent himself, he expelled a breath, remaining inside her, savoring the warmth. Her muscles tightened around him, as if trying to hold him there forever. Fine with him. He didn't have any immediate plans to vacate the spot.

Her grip on his shoulders loosened enough for her to move her hands into his hair. "That . . . that was so good. I don't want it to end."

He breathed into her hair. "Me neither."

They stayed like that, huddled in each other's arms, relishing the intimacy, the afterglow.

When his back rebelled on him, he finally had to leave her, but not by much. He dropped onto the bench, bringing her with him onto his lap.

She drew her hands away from his hair and draped them around his neck, continuing to plant feather kisses around his ear.

"You think Debbie will mind that we made ourselves at home in her hot tub?" he finally asked, breaking the companionable silence.

"She wouldn't have sent you out here if she felt that way. Nor would she have so conveniently decided to go to the movies."

"Good point." He knew they were saying things now to ease away from the passion. But he didn't feel the least bit awkward. Just comfortable and satiated. Boy, was he satiated! Thank goodness for the water. It helped buoy him, since his body needed rest.

Aubrey seemed to sense that. "Want to towel off and go in the house? Debbie isn't due back for at least another hour."

"You're not suggesting . . . " He let his question end there, but arched a brow so she'd know what he meant.

She lowered her lids. "Who knows? The night's still young."

He helped her out of the tub, marveling at the fantastic twists and turns of her body as she emerged from the water. Water bubbles clung to her like tiny glistening jewels. He grew hard again just looking at her. He grabbed for his shorts and sought his briefs, to shield himself.

She retrieved her bikini, pulled a towel off a nearby chair. "Here, I'll get another inside."

"Leave the jets on for now. I'll turn them off later," he said.

They dried their feet, so they wouldn't track water through the house. Then, hand in hand, they went inside, and Aubrey showed him to the room she was occupying.

She dug inside the bathroom closet and returned with two giant bath towels that she laid over the bedspread.

They didn't dress. They crawled into the center of the bed and went into each other's arms. He couldn't believe how comfortable he felt cuddling her in his embrace. Like they belonged that way.

"This is nice," she said, her eyes barely open. "I forgot how sleepy I get after a hot tub."

"Me, too. But I shouldn't get too comfortable. Wouldn't want to wear out my welcome with Debbie, especially if she were to come home and find us like this fast asleep."

She sighed, and ran a hand through his hair. "You're right. But, stay a little longer. I don't expect her home for a while."

He jiggled his arm underneath her back. "You're twisting my arm."

"Keep it there a little longer."

"Okay." He held up his other arm. "What should I do about this one?"

"I bet you can think of some inventive way to keep it occupied."

So he did, spending the next several minutes proving her correct.

CHAPTER FOURTEEN

It was almost ten when Mitch let himself out of the house. He'd allowed himself a brief though much-needed nap after he and Aubrey made love a second time. When the alarm sounded thirty minutes later, he reluctantly dragged himself from the bed, dressed, and said goodnight to a still-drowsy Aubrey. She pressed him to stay longer, but he begged off. He was pretty sure Debbie would suspect what had happened in the hot tub, even though he drained it, but there was no need to flaunt this time with Aubrey.

He drove back to the firehouse in a daze. Only habit kept him on track, because his mind was elsewhere. Reliving the night with Aubrey. Already wondering what she was doing, if she'd immediately fallen back asleep or was having as much difficulty concentrating as he was. Telling himself that, as great as the evening had been, this had to be the end of it, he couldn't let down his defenses again. Knowing the likelihood of keeping that pact with himself was negligible.

The car approached the turn in the road where Mosquito Park overlooked the river a hundred feet below. He slowed to a stop and took in the view. There was a full moon tonight. High in the clear summer sky, it threw its silvery beams across the dark, murky water like a luminous fan. He didn't usually notice such things, but tonight . . . tonight was different . . . magical. He wasn't ready for the spell he'd been under to come to an end.

What had he done tonight? Given in to his physical urges, for sure. But he'd also shared a part of himself with Aubrey that he'd never shared with Dianne. For an hour or so, he'd thrown caution to the wind and simply enjoyed the pure physical sensations of making love to a beautiful, willing woman. When it was over, he felt complete, sated.

It was like it had been with Dianne and yet a whole new dimension had been added to it. With Dianne, he'd been content and relaxed after he climaxed, and he could have very easily rolled over and slept away the night had she not insisted they cuddle and continue to talk.

But tonight? Tonight he'd been the one to wrap his arms around Aubrey and whisper sweet nothings. Old-fashioned phrase, but it summed up his desires pretty well. Of course, it hadn't come out as flowery as he would have wished. All his knowledge of poetry had flown out the window the day he passed his English Lit final in college. Whatever he'd said, which he barely remembered, had been the utterings of a man bereft of fancy talk.

What he did remember was the look in her eyes when he whispered those sentiments. Her eyes had grown wide, as if surprised. But they'd sparkled too, apparently pleased with the attention. And something more. Wonder. Yes, that was it. Wonder. Like she wasn't accustomed to receiving such accolades.

But that couldn't be the case. Aubrey was a sophisticated, beautiful, intelligent woman. She must have had a never-ending line of men seeking her favors back in L.A. Unless her mother's influence had affected her self-confidence in that department as well? Boy, if it had, he was going to do his best to undo that.

Good grief! Was this him, Mitch McKenna, Mr. "Leave-Things-Alone-That-Aren't-Broke," contemplating an intervention in someone else's life? Aubrey's Ms. Fix-it tendencies were definitely wearing off on him.

Was this why she'd been pushing him to get back into the law? Because she'd been overcome with this need he was feeling now to protect her from herself, from her fears and self-doubts? Sometimes a person had to step up to the plate and make things happen.

He rubbed his eyes. So much for taking in the view. The nap had merely postponed the lethargy produced by the hot tub. He needed to get back to the firehouse before his mounting fatigue affected his driving.

*

Aubrey lay in bed, begging her fatigue to get the better of her. But it was no use. Despite the lingering drowsiness caused by the hot tub, she couldn't relax, couldn't drift off to needed sleep. Her mind was too active replaying the scenes with Mitch. To say it had been great sex was an understatement. It had been phenomenal sex. Earth-moving sex. The kind she'd only read about and hardly believed existed.

But something else had happened. She tried to analyze what she felt, name it, but it eluded her. All she knew was that it had taken her to new ground, a place she'd never gone before.

She couldn't let herself get carried away with whatever this was with Mitch. They'd agreed to enjoy each other's company during her brief stay, and when the project was finished in a few weeks, she'd walk away with no regrets. Why was she getting so concerned about that now?

She'd known him little more than a week. This was a fling. A great mind-popping sex fling that she'd remember fondly when she was back in California, but nonetheless a fling, a short-term, going-nowhere fling. But after this evening, it no longer felt like a fling. It felt like something more. And that scared her, because she had no idea how to deal with it.

This wasn't supposed to happen. It was supposed to be casual and light, just like all her other *interludes* in L.A. She could deal with those. You went into them with no expectations, except maybe to have a good time for a bit, and then it ended. Generally, if you were lucky, you walked away friends. You survived without losing your balance.

But this time? She felt off-balance and her sense of well-being was shot.

Though Debbie kept her house fully air-conditioned, Aubrey barely felt the effects. Her pillowcase was damp from perspiration collaring her neck. She kicked off the sheet that covered her. That wasn't enough, so she dragged herself from bed to turn up the ceiling fan.

He hadn't wanted to stay the night. Said he didn't want to run into Debbie in the morning. Had he been anxious to escape her? A "wham-bam-thank-you-ma'am" kind of evening? No, surely not. He'd been so . . . so . . . caring . . . and sensitive to her needs. Almost like he was falling for her.

Falling for her? No, no way. She didn't want to think about it. If she did, she'd have to deal with the idea of being in love. Was he having the same thoughts?

She smashed her pillows into submission, willing herself to sleep. All these thoughts about making love with Mitch were devouring the energy she needed for the next few days of remodeling. She needed to be in top form.

Think of something else, Aubrey. Her mother's early life here in this town. Paige. Heidi Buxbaum. *No, don't go there.* Let Mitch and Orville handle that one. Just thinking about it made her crazy. Whether she'd do it again if tempted, she didn't know. She thought she'd learned her lesson, but her experiences of the last few days had taught her that things often were not as they seemed.

Things like thinking you were falling in love with a guy when it was only hot, hot, hot mutual attraction.

Before she could dissect that one, though, sleep finally . . . mercifully . . . overcame her.

*

Back at the motor coach, Mitch slipped soundlessly into his bedroll, trying not to wake his brothers. He awoke refreshed and abnormally optimistic. Incredibly, nothing seemed impossible today, even the thought of returning to the law. Of course, he'd have to phase into it, actually out of his commitments to his brothers. But his experience helping Orville and Aubrey during the last few days had lifted the veil of doubt he'd been carrying around like a shroud for some time. The intimacies he'd shared with Aubrey last night hadn't hurt either.

He lay there watching beams of light grow into brilliant shards of sunshine cutting through the blinds. His thoughts returned again to the night before. And Aubrey. It had been great sex, no question about that. But when it was over, he felt more than satisfied. He felt content.

Who would have thought Ms. Fix-it could fix him? But that's what she'd managed to do. Not just physically. She'd pushed and prodded him into thinking there might be a way he could practice law and still help his brothers. Have the best of both worlds.

"What's on your mind, bro?" Gray said, still in his own bedroll a few feet away.

"Shhh. Don't wake Geoff."

"Geoff's already awake," his other brother said, rolling over. "What's up?"

"Probably us," Mitch said. "What is this? It's barely five-thirty."

"Floor's hard," Gray said.

"You got that right," Geoff agreed.

Gray added, "You should've taken the bed, since Aubrey's no longer using it."

"Thought I was up to it," Geoff returned. "But hope this was our last night camping out."

Sitting up, Gray ran both hands through his hair. "Should be. The chief is coming over around eight to check out the building. Cross your fingers his little meter is going to say yes."

Geoff switched his attention to Mitch. "You turned in rather late."

Mitch busied himself fluffing up his pillow, so he wouldn't have to look at his brothers. One glance at him, and they'd both know what he'd been up to. "You were asleep when I got in."

Gray kicked out of his bedroll and rose, scratching his back. He made his way over to the fridge and pulled out a bottle of water. "What about you, Geoff?"

"I was in early. But I have plans for that lady."

Gray and Mitch, eyebrows raised, exchanged looks. Before the onset of the MS, Geoff had been quite the ladies' man. There was always at least one woman in his life, if not more. But Peggy was the first woman he'd paid attention to since discovering he had the condition. Even though they'd been seeing each other less than a week, it had all the earmarks of being serious.

"Just keep your private life private, if you know what I mean," Gray said. "I seem to be the only one without a woman in my life right now, and I don't need to be reminded of the fact."

Geoff glanced Mitch's way. "How about you?"

Mitch knew where this was going and didn't want to make the trip. "Me?"

"You and Aubrey," Geoff pushed. "Something's going on. You were wound tighter than a drum the other night at Debbie's. Within hours, your expression and whole attitude changed. We haven't seen you in such a good mood in a long time."

"And your point is?"

"His point is," Gray interjected, "we may not have to work out the logistics of where to put our houseguest much longer if she's spending her time in your room."

"Don't jump to conclusions, guys. Yeah, things have changed between Aubrey and me. But she's got a job to complete on an even tighter schedule than we originally thought. Neither one of us needs the distraction of an aff . . . of a dalli . . . "

"Give it up, Mitch," Geoff said, thumping him on the back. "We've got you figured out. But if you want to play this low key, we'll play along."

*

Within an hour of the fire chief pronouncing the *all clear*, Aubrey moved out of Debbie's place. To her surprise, she wasn't anxious to return to the firehouse. She didn't want to run into Mitch. The same man whose ear she'd licked only hours before. But it was time to get back to work. Past time, considering the various obstacles that had delayed her.

What was making her back away from Mitch like this? Just a few hours ago she was pleading with him to stay the night. It must be all that head talk before she finally nodded off. Thoughts about how her feelings for Mitch might be growing more serious than she'd bargained for. She couldn't face him this morning.

And then there was all the business about her mother. She was supposed to have been working through that new information in the hot tub. And then Mitch had showed up. All thoughts of her mother had fled without her having had time to process them.

"You want these boxes in the living room or back here, lady?" The arrival of Jenna's things had interrupted her finger pleating of the drapes in the bedroom.

"If there's room, stack them along one wall out there," she said, preferring to leave the bedroom clear.

The delivery completed, she dragged herself away from the window treatment long enough to inspect the shipment. Just the right amount. For once, her sister had not overcompensated and sent half her house.

"There you are." Mitch draped himself in the doorway to the back bedroom. He looked relieved. "Thought you'd still be at Debbie's but couldn't get through on your cell."

Damn. She'd hoped he'd be too busy this morning to discover her hiding out in the coach. Inexplicably, her heart beat faster and her palms began to sweat.

"I, uh, turned it off so I could get some work done. After Geoff called to say I could move back in."

Mitch surveyed the boxes now taking up half the coach's living room. "Looks like you returned in the nick of time."

She glanced at the stack of assorted furnishings. "The delivery guy was here early." She wished he'd leave. She wasn't ready to sit and chat with him in broad daylight after giving her body to him in the dark the night before.

It was downright awkward. With other lovers, she'd leave after the lovemaking, or the guy would depart in the middle of the night. Seeing each other a few hours later? It was . . . unheard of.

Just the sight of him this morning had her heart thundering in her ears.

"Mind if I join you?" he asked, not waiting for an invitation to settle into one of the room's chairs.

"I . . . uh . . . was just finishing this window treatment." *Go away, Mitch. Give me my space, Mitch.* Turning away from him, she reached for the fabric and started folding it again.

"I want to talk about last night."

"Regrets already?" Damn. She hadn't meant to sound so flip.

He winced, as if she'd slapped him. "You were okay with my leaving when I did?"

She didn't know how to reply, so she attempted to slough it off, keep it casual. "Yeah, sure. We were in someone else's house. It wouldn't have been proper for you to stick around for breakfast."

He eyed her warily. "You angry?"

She shook her head but didn't look him in the eyes. "I'm fine. Except for lack of sleep."

He came closer, though he didn't touch her. "Oh? I slept like a baby."

Obviously he hadn't suffered from the second thoughts that had plagued her. Men. He probably would have rolled over and slept the night away if he hadn't been concerned about running into Debbie. "That makes one of us with a clear head this morning."

Now he did touch her, laying his fingertips on her forehead. "Headache?"

The contact nearly fried her brain. She jerked away, bristling at the show of familiarity and her body's reaction to it. "A little. Mainly lack of energy. I've got a lot to do."

He continued to eye her, concern written in his narrowed eyes. "Did you get breakfast? I know how you feel about caffeine, but maybe some juice?"

She backed up a step, nearly tripping over the bolt of fabric. "I had cereal at Debbie's."

"Good. But remember there's juice in the break room, if you want some. Just don't . . . "

"Close the door," she finished for him, unable to keep the half-smile generated by that memory from showing. "I remember."

He smiled back, continuing to watch her as if waiting for her to make the next move. Finally, after she'd remained silent several beats, he said, "About last night . . . "

She couldn't do this, couldn't replay their lovemaking like two film critics reviewing the latest flick. "Don't worry about my reading too much into it. I enjoyed it, you were great, but . . . it's . . . " She started to say "over" but changed it at the last second to "morning now. The light of day makes things look different."

"But . . . "

"I really don't have time to chat, Mitch."

"Oh."

She could hear the disappointment in his voice. She'd hurt him, deliberately. She hated that, but she didn't know what else to do. She needed time to examine these new feelings bombarding her, thoughts about Mitch, about her mother, about herself. Maybe when she figured out how she felt about it all, she could jump back into the sexual banter. Not today.

"It's just that I've gotten so far behind on this job. It's overwhelming." That was the most humane letdown she could summon.

He rose, having finally read her mood. "Sorry. I didn't realize you'd started to work already." He backed toward the door. "I'll leave. I'm in the other coach, if you need me." He raised his eyes, apparently hoping she'd ask him to stay. When she didn't, he left.

She'd been intentionally rude to him. She hardly recognized the person who'd driven him away.

*

Mitch stomped off to the other coach, his anger mounting in the same proportion to his growing perplexity with Aubrey. He hoped she hadn't seen him flinch when her actions had made it so clear that she didn't want him there. What was with her this morning?

Get over it, McKenna. She offered herself to you, you complied, it was fantastic, and now it's over. That's all there was to it.

Still, it grated that all she'd wanted was the physical part. They'd shared some pretty deep moments during the last few days. Even though he'd been more than willing to follow through when he saw that remarkable body shimmering in the water, somewhere in the back of his brain, or a little further down in the area of his heart, he'd been motivated by more caring feelings when he made love to her. He thought those feelings were mutual.

He'd read her wrong. Was he disappointed she didn't feel the same? On the other hand, maybe she'd expected him to pull her into his arms as soon as he arrived. Fat chance. She'd built a fortress with all that fabric and huddled behind it as soon as she saw him.

He had to find something else to occupy his time. Something like . . . the California pizza king. He drew out his cell phone and punched in Orville's number, catching his friend on the second ring. "Any news from the West Coast yet?"

"What's with you this morning?"

Mitch released a heavy, audible sigh for his friend's benefit. "Sorry. I just had another run-in with Aubrey. I thought the sooner we took care of her situation in California, the sooner she would be able to return home."

"Uh-huh. And that's what you want? To get rid of her?"

"I don't know, Orville. One minute . . . I . . . she . . . and then the next . . . "

"Sounds like a lover's quarrel to me. You run across someone who knocks your socks off, and your emotions fall all over themselves attempting to deal with it. The inability to finish sentences is a sure sign."

Orville was a pretty wise old coot. But Mitch wasn't inclined to tell him so at the moment. "Okay. I've calmed down. Do you have any news?"

"We just started looking into this yesterday. I'm good, and I've got good contacts, but don't expect miracles."

Mitch blew out a breath. "Sorry. Didn't mean to push. Well, okay, I did, but not to suggest you aren't doing your best. Have you learned anything at all?"

No immediate reply. He must have really irritated his friend.

Finally, Orville said, "Well . . . I did learn something, but I wanted a little more time to play around with it, dislodge it without disturbing all the roots so we can follow where it leads."

Mitch scowled. "If I say pretty please?"

"Cool your jets, boy. It seems the Buxbaum divorce is off and they're back together."

Letting out a whistle, Mitch moved into the coach so he could hear more clearly. "Interesting. Since when? What happened to reunite the happy couple?"

"I've only got the main headline. My sources are checking out the rest."

Something major had happened out on the Coast. What it meant, he couldn't be sure yet. If Heidi and Cyril were indeed back together, had Heidi's plan succeeded? Or Cyril's?

"Still there?"

"Yeah. I'm thinking through what your news means for Aubrey's case." Her case? Had he really thought of it that way? Yesterday, it had been nothing more than doing a friend a favor. Ah, well, as long as he continued to think of it in the singular, one case, no more than that, he could deal with it and resist being pulled back into Orville's orbit. To hell with the optimism earlier this morning where he'd actually begun to think about some sort of part-time arrangement with Orville.

"I'd say it means something pretty big. The divorce papers had already been served. Something compelling must have turned that train around."

"That's the way I see it, too." Mitch settled on the floor of the coach.

"Give me another day, Mitch. Maybe two."

Disappointed, there wasn't much other choice. "Keep at it, Orville. My gut says we're on a very short timeline here."

Clicking off, he settled his back against a wall and surveyed the interior of the coach. A lot to do yet, but he couldn't focus on the task at hand. Too full of other thoughts—making love to Aubrey, her apparent lack of interest the day after, and how he was going to help her rescue her professional reputation. Sighing, he set about unbolting armchairs and the dining room table.

*

The window treatment occupied the rest of the morning. She'd finished the pleating, tacked it in place, and was in the process of hanging it from the cornice when someone behind her said, "You Aubrey Carpenter?"

"Um-hum," she managed to get out, her lips clamped down on screws.

"If that's a yes, I've got a delivery for you."

Thinking it another shipment from Jenna, she held up a hand, to signal for him to give her a minute to finish with the screw she was putting in.

"Uh, lady, could you hurry. I've got several more deliveries to make before noon."

"Okay. What have you got for me now? I thought you unloaded the full shipment be . . . oh, you're not that guy."

Sweating profusely, the burly deliveryman mopped his forehead and face while he waited for her to sign. He tucked his handkerchief in a shorts pocket, then handed her a legal-size manila envelope followed by a clipboard and pencil. "Sign right there by your name, ma'am."

Assuming the packet held more directions from her sister, she quickly scribbled her name and handed back the clipboard. Once he left, she flipped the envelope onto the counter, retrieved her screws and returned to the window hanging. Several minutes passed before it hit her. The name of the sender! She'd been so sure the item was from Jenna, she'd barely given the sender's name much attention. But it hadn't read Jenna DiFranco.

She dropped the unhung fabric and swooped up the envelope. The return address was that of a law firm in Santa Monica, California. Oh, no! It couldn't be? With foreboding, her stomach reeled like it did on turbulent air flights. Hands shaking, she ripped open the envelope and pulled out a very official-looking document. She scanned the contents to get the general gist. Heidi and Cyril Buxbaum, complainants. Aubrey Carpenter, defendant. Misrepresentation of business. Heidi and her supposed ex-husband, were suing her?

This wasn't supposed to happen. Mitch and Orville were taking care of it. They'd told her Heidi didn't have a case. What had happened?

She flung herself from the coach and dashed across the garage floor to the other coach screaming for Mitch before she remembered she was trying to avoid him. So much for playing it cool. She needed him. She couldn't hide any longer.

"Mitch! Mitch, are you here?" She raced up the two steps of the other coach and burst through the door.

He was on the floor, several tools spread around him, surrounded by the cabinets that had previously hung in the coach's kitchen area. The minute he saw her, his expression changed from one of concentration to one of concern. He jerked to his feet and came over to her. "What's up?"

"This was just delivered." She held out the document. "Is it what I think it is? Is Heidi really suing me?"

He flipped through the package. As he read on, his expression hardened, his brows furrowing. Then he began shaking his head as if finding it difficult to believe what he'd just taken in. "Did you say this woman was a friend of yours?"

"*Was* being the operative word. Or, at least I thought she was."
Mitch held the document in front of him, flicking it back and
forth as if it was a piece of evidence. "I only skimmed this complaint
but from what I read, I'd say your entanglement with this Heidi
person is more than a simple misunderstanding. She's out for blood."

Aubrey collapsed in a heap on the floor, reaching for the complaint.
"That's the way it looked to me too. I hoped you'd tell me otherwise."

He settled himself next to her. "This changes things."

Her stomach plunged, like she'd fallen down an elevator shaft.
"I sensed that was the case, but I still hoped I was wrong."

Mitch took a deep breath, pursing his lips. Bad news was on
the way. "She says she only asked you to redo one room in the
cabin and stipulated that it had to fit in with the rest of the décor.
Moreover, although she authorized an expenditure of up to five
thousand dollars for new furniture, you paid triple that amount."

"That is such a lie!"

He patted her hand. "I don't doubt it, but she makes it sound pretty
credible. And . . . she's got Cyril backing her up, along with another
friend, a Carol Casswell, and her personal assistant, Jeremy Walters."

Aubrey ripped the pages open. "Where does it say that? Carol
has had it in for me ever since an incident last year with a certain
studio exec. I . . . uh . . . started seeing him before she thought her
time with him was up. And Jeremy? Heidi's little puppy dog. He'd
say anything to please her and keep his job."

Mitch wrapped a comforting arm around her. "You don't
have to convince me, sweetheart." He pushed a stray lock of hair
behind her ears. "But I have to warn you, she's got at least these
three supposedly credible witnesses on her side. We have to rebut
every single thing she's claimed."

Despite her earlier hesitation, the feel of his arm around her
was reassuring. "Can we do that?"

"We have to, or they might win. We can't let that happen. They
want half a million to restore the cabin to its *prior grandeur*, I'm
quoting now, and another half mil for punitive damages, since you

allegedly jeopardized their recovering marriage."

She checked his eyes to see if he was serious. "I'd say you're kidding, but I know better."

He nodded.

All she could think of was how her mother was going to react to this news. She'd be embarrassed, of course. Actually, mortified. She would very likely disassociate herself from her younger daughter forever.

Mitch watched her. Probably reading her thoughts. "So much for this coach today. I have work to do." He rose, offering her a hand. "I need to review this complaint more closely. I'll make you a copy so you can do the same. Jot down your thoughts in the margins. Anything that occurs to you, no matter how insignificant it may seem."

She could only nod. This couldn't be happening to her.

He guided her to the door, climbed down the steps first, then gave her a hand. She started to turn toward Jenna's coach, when another thought hit her. "The design project! I can't handle two priorities."

"Then don't," he said, placing a hand on her shoulder. "You have to protect yourself from this suit right now."

"But . . . ."

"I know, your sister's coach is important. We'll figure out a way to get it done, the way she wants it, on time. But for today . . . go read."

Back at Jenna's coach, Aubrey retrieved the fabric and started on the second window while she waited for her copy of the complaint. She didn't get far. Her hands shook too much. What had she ever done to Heidi Buxbaum to warrant this horrible reaction?

She sniffed, suspending her introspection. What was that smell? Or fragrance? She sniffed again. Cologne. A sweet floral fragrance, like lily of the valley. Not what she wore. More like . . . Paige? She sniffed a third time. Hardly discernible now. Must have been her imagination. Stress did that to people. And if there was anything she had in spades right now, it was stress.

CHAPTER FIFTEEN

"Think harder, Aubrey. What you've given me so far is good but not enough to refute her claims." Mitch held a ballpoint pen over his legal pad, poised to write down anything new.

Orville hovered in a corner, leaning against Mitch's exercise equipment. "Patience, man. Don't you see she's doing her best to reconstruct this business deal?"

After investing two days claiming she had to dissect the complaint and attempting to recall every minor detail that had gone into redoing the Buxbaum cabin, Aubrey was anxious to get back to Jenna's motor coach. She was at least four days behind her already ambitious schedule.

"I've told you every little tidbit I can remember," she said yet again.

Mitch rose, slid around the front of his desk and leaned against it. He scooped up her hand in his. "I know you think you have. But trust me, the first several times through, most witnesses generally remember only a small percent of what their brains have tucked away."

He was touching her again. Didn't he realize what that did to her? Her body temperature must have shot up ten degrees. For the last forty-eight hours, she'd managed to evade him, claiming she had to dissect the brief. She had to get away from him now before he realized his effect on her.

She heard a muffled noise, like a refrigerator closing, in the break room next door. Probably Geoff or Graham. "How about a break? Lemonade?"

Mitch let go of her hand, his expression toughening slightly. "Of course, if you must. But we really need for you to continue with this for a little while yet." He shot a glance at Orville over his shoulder. "Should we tell her?"

"Tell me what?"

Orville joined Mitch by the desk, a wary look on his face as he studied Aubrey. "My contacts in California have reported in."

"Yes?" Her voice raised in apprehension, Mitch's effect on her momentarily forgotten.

Mitch and Orville exchanged looks, then Orville said, "All the named witnesses corroborate Mrs. Buxbaum's story."

Aubrey shot to her feet. "They're lying! Either intentionally, or as her dupes."

Orville put out a hand, trying to calm her. "Of course they are. We know that. But how do we prove it? Without more to go on from you, they have a pretty solid case."

She shook her head in disbelief. "How, when there's no truth in it?"

"Enough truth to hold water, Aubrey, unless we can punch holes in it," Mitch said.

Orville added, "It would help if you had more documentation, Aubrey."

"I've given you all that was on my laptop. That's the same as my office."

Mitch rose and returned to his chair. He flipped through a hefty file folder. "I've printed every document and gone through each at least three times. There's nothing here, especially a signed contract." He eyed her pointedly.

"I can explain that."

Mitch settled back into his chair. "That I'd like to hear."

"It's not like I usually do business that way." She could hear the defensiveness in her voice. "It's just that, well, Heidi was afraid Cyril would use our project against her when their case went before a judge. Property settlement, you know. And so . . . "

"And so . . . ?" Both men probed.

"And so we did it on a handshake."

They stared at her as if she didn't know any better.

"Don't give me that poor, pathetic female look. I don't do business like that every day. In fact, I've never done it before, and obviously will never do it again. If I even get a chance."

Mitch started to say something, stopped, then started again. "Think back to the first time you talked to Heidi about the job."

Aubrey sat back in her chair and closed her eyes, trying to recall those events. A creaking sound broke into her thoughts. "What was that?"

"What was what?" Orville replied.

"It sounded like a door closing nearby. Didn't you hear it?"

Mitch looked up from the files he'd been perusing. "Sound? No, I was reading the complaint."

"Never mind. Nerves, I guess." It was the second unexplained sound she'd heard within the hour.

Think back, Aubrey. She went back to the day Heidi had offered her the job. "We met over lunch at Santera's. That's a restaurant in Santa Monica. Very trendy."

They established the approximate date as well as who paid for lunch. Heidi. In cash.

"In other words, there's no record you were there," Orville surmised. "Unless you spoke to someone at the restaurant?" His voice rose hopefully.

"We did see someone." A woman, though the name didn't immediately come to mind. It was a friend of Heidi's. "Uh-oh." Scowl. "You don't want to hear this."

Mitch came out of his chair again. "Why not?" His tone carried an ominous note.

Her stomach lurched, like the floor had suddenly disappeared from beneath her. No, they weren't going to like this. "A friend of Heidi's stopped by the table. Heidi hugged me and made this big deal about my treating her to lunch on her birthday. I thought it odd at the time but didn't say anything. But later, after the woman left, Heidi sloughed it off as a running joke between them."

Orville scratched his chin in thought. "Doesn't sound so bad to me."
"There's more."

Both men inhaled deep breaths, waiting for the other shoe to fall.

"Heidi introduced me as her interior decorator from hell and then laughingly told her friend I'd been pitching this mad scheme to turn her hunting lodge into a lover's retreat."

Both men groaned.

"That's bad, isn't it?"

Mitch rubbed behind an ear. "Depends. What did you say? Did you agree?"

"I don't recall my exact words, or if I said anything at all," she began, "but I wanted the job. It seemed harmless to play along. I must have smirked or made some expression to make it look like we were conspiring."

More groans, this time accompanied by the gnashing of teeth and the wringing of hands.

Her lower lip started to tremble. Then her hands began to shake. She felt like she was about to throw up. "Is . . . is that the end of the line?" She sat there, holding her stomach, placing one hand over the other to stifle the tremors. Her eyes burned with unshed tears.

Orville gave her a weak but hopeful smile. "You're doing great, Aubrey."

That unleashed the waterworks. She pursed her lips to fight off the deluge.

Orville squeezed her hand. "If we're going to fight off this woman's claim, Mitch and I need to know every single weapon she has in her arsenal. We're good lawyers, sweetie. Well, I am. Mitch hasn't decided yet that he is, too. We can do this."

Eyelids fluttering, she nodded her thanks. She tried to speak but could only gasp.

"We're not going to kid you," Mitch said. "The case they've put together is looking more and more brutal. But we're both behind you. And you've got the best defense—the truth."

She sniffed, then finally gave in to the urge and wiped away the tears streaming down her cheeks. Orville handed her a tissue, even dabbing her eyes himself with another tissue when her shaking hands dropped the first.

When she'd calmed, Orville said, "Why did you go along with this Buxbaum woman's unorthodox request?"

"She is—was—a friend of my mother. I had no reason to doubt her sincerity."

Mitch and Orville didn't comment. Both mouths gaped open. "What's the matter? Why are you reacting like that?"

Orville regained speech first. "Did you say *friend*? Of your *mother's*?"

Aubrey blinked several times, not getting it. Why was that significant? "Yes. They go back to my mother's early days in L.A. Heidi was a bit player on a detective series in the nineties. They met at some party my dad had been invited to through his ties to the industry. He hated those events, but my mother thrived on them and went into a major snit for weeks if they didn't go." The two eyed her as if she'd just announced Heidi Buxbaum was really a man.

In a very quiet, studied tone, Mitch asked, "Did your mother send Heidi to you?"

"I'm not sure. I guess I assumed that was the case. Is it important?"

Orville began to rub his hands together. "Is it important? Think about it. If your mother recommended you to Heidi, it's highly likely that Heidi told her what she was planning."

"I suppose that's possible. But how does that help us?"

Mitch groaned. "If she described the project to your mother the same way she did for you, you've got yourself a witness. Your own corroboration."

Her mother? Good grief, the last thing she needed was for her mother to testify on her behalf. "I don't want my mother involved in this."

Mitch and Orville stared at her, as if her words weren't registering.

"I don't think we have any choice," Mitch said. "So far, she's the only person who can confirm your side of the deal."

She clenched her hands. This just couldn't happen.

"Why don't we give her a call?" Orville suggested. "Put her on the speaker phone and we'll all talk to her."

"No!" She sprang from her chair. The thought of talking to her mother right now had her pacing the room.

Orville turned to Mitch. "What's the problem? Why won't she call her mother?"

Mitch watched her pace before replying. "She and her mother don't get along."

"Are they at least speaking to each other?"

"Yeah, though I don't think she's told her mother where she is." He shared what he knew about Iris Appleby with his friend, including her local roots.

"Aubrey, you don't have to reconcile with your mother. All we need is her testimony, if it backs you up," Orville told her in a matter-of-fact tone.

She pivoted, hands on hips, eyes blazing. "No, Orville. I'm not bringing her into this."

"But . . . ."

*

Mitch had been observing Aubrey's tantrum, marveling at her stubbornness. If it had been anyone else going through Aubrey's problems, she would have been the cheerleader, urging them to acknowledge their feelings, confront their worries. Definitely a case of being able to dish it out but not take it.

"Give us a couple minutes, Orville." Mitch said.

"Huh?" Mitch nodded his head toward the door, and that he got.

When it was just the two of them, Mitch pulled her over to the chair she'd occupied earlier. "Sit. Relax. Let's talk about this from a different angle."

Still breathing fire, she complied.

He hauled another chair over to face her, and once seated, took both her hands in his. They were ice-cold and trembling. He should have done this sooner. She needed comforting. He liked the idea of being the one to do it.

"I think I've got this figured out." He kept his voice low to calm her. "I don't think you're worried about putting your mother on the stand, if it came to that. And as much as it would cost you for her to find out about this Heidi fiasco, you could deal with that too." He raised his eyes to look into hers. Moisture again pooled there. He had to take this slowly, step by step, regain her confidence. "Am I tracking so far?"

She nodded, looking down at her hands inside his.

He gave them a squeeze and felt the tension lessen.

"I think you're afraid to ask her for help."

Though her head remained bent, he could tell by the flickering of her lashes that he'd hit his target. She didn't say anything, but from the slight movement of muscles tightening around her lips, he knew she was thinking through his theory.

"Look at me, Aubrey. Is that it?"

She bit a lip and nodded again. "You think that's crazy, don't you. And Orville will too." Her voice remained soft, but her words were clear and defiant.

He lowered his head to hers, attempting to capture her gaze. "Believe me, I know what it's like to need something so bad from your loved ones and not be able to ask for it."

That got her attention. Her face came up, eyes wide. "You mean about practicing law?"

"Yes. Except with me, it's fear of letting them down. I think it's something else with you." He was walking a tightrope here. She had to remain focused on her issues, not his, even though she seemed eager to talk about him.

More tears. She swiped at them with one hand. "I . . . I'm afraid she'll refuse." Her voice was barely audible.

He filled his lungs with a long, deep breath, steeling his heart for the next part. Seeing her go through this painful self-discovery was slashing his gut, but it had to be done. "Worst case scenario, what if she does?"

"Then I don't have a case."

"You don't have one now. Nothing ventured, nothing gained."

"She won't care."

His voice rose. "So she doesn't care. Why does that matter so much?"

She blinked several times. "She's my mother. She should care."

"But you don't think she does, do you?"

She gulped back a sob.

Just a little further to go. She was tough, but sometimes the toughest skins protected the softest souls beneath. "That's been pretty much the case throughout your life, hasn't it?"

She hung her head, eying the floor. "Nothing I do is enough for her."

They sat there for several minutes, Aubrey staring at the carpet, hands in his, Mitch just watching her. "Why do you feel you have to satisfy her? She's the mother here."

She straightened in her chair and withdrew her hands.

He'd pushed too hard.

But she surprised him. "If she's satisfied, maybe she'll love me." Having said that, she slumped back into the chair again.

He'd never met Iris Appleby, but at that moment, he wanted to throttle her for the head job she'd done on her younger daughter.

"Okay for me to come back?" Orville stood in the doorway, pulling at his shirt collar. "No AC out there. Couldn't even get into that closet where you keep the bottled water."

"The door's closed?" Mitch asked, raising an eyebrow in Aubrey's direction.

She held up a hand. "Don't look at me. Won't make that

mistake again."

The moment was over. Damn! He'd just about reached the breakthrough he'd been aiming for until Orville's untimely reappearance. Couldn't blame the old guy, though. The garage got pretty hot during the summer months.

"Make any progress during my absence?" Orville inquired innocently.

"I shed a few more tears, but I'm still adamant against bringing my mother into this," Aubrey said, rising. "Actually, I think we've reached a stalemate, fellas. I need that break."

Mitch shrugged, and Orville sank into his chair, mopping his brow. The sound of beating on a nearby door caught them all up short.

"The break room!" Mitch and Aubrey cried out simultaneously.

"We'd better check it out," Mitch added. He grabbed a key from his desk, then dashed off, Aubrey and Orville right behind him.

The banging grew louder the closer they got to the break room. Reaching the door, Mitch demanded, "Who's in there?"

No answer.

Scowling, Mitch inserted the key, twisted it, and tried the knob. "Stand back, you two. No telling who's there." He pushed inward, mentally preparing himself to confront whatever.

The last thing he anticipated was a gangly, frightened teenager with braces.

*

"Paige?" Aubrey cried.

Paige ran into her arms, burying her head in Aubrey's chest. "Oh, Aunt Aubrey! I'm so sorry."

They hugged and kissed while Mitch and Orville, hands in pockets, stood by, shuffling their feet, looking otherwise perplexed and uncomfortable.

Finally, holding the child away from her, eyes narrowed, brow wrinkled in confusion, Aubrey asked, "What are you doing here? And how did you get here?"

Paige bit down on her lip, eying Mitch and Orville skeptically. "Uh, could that wait a bit? I'm starving." Looking directly at the two men, she added, "Who are these guys?"

Aubrey wanted answers. Her niece was on the lam. But having seen something in the child's eyes—fear? apprehension?—she put her questions on hold long enough to play along. For the moment. She went through formal introductions. The two men, though a little more than curious, as well as frustrated by the interruption, made a big deal about shaking Paige's hand, finding her something to eat. In short, not frightening her.

While Aubrey and Paige made sandwiches, Orville poured lemonade, and Mitch scavenged for chips, fruit, and cookies. Like an expedition on safari, they lugged their provisions to Mitch's office where, with the help of the throw from the davenport, which Mitch spread on the floor, they enjoyed an impromptu picnic.

Paige didn't appear any too anxious to begin her story, and Aubrey wasn't ready to push, so Mitch and Orville carried the conversational ball, kidding each other about the days when Mitch clerked for his old friend.

Sandwiches consumed, lemonade downed, Aubrey was about to begin her inquisition, when Orville interrupted, doing it for her. "So, young lady," he said in his best courtroom voice, "you've been fed, we've all become fast friends, and I've heard more than I ever wanted to about customizing motor coaches. Time to come clean with us."

Paige looked to Aubrey, eyes beseeching her for help.

The child had a talent for grabbing Aubrey's heart in her hands and twisting it. But not today. "I couldn't have said it better myself," Aubrey added. "C'mon, Paige. Spill."

"But . . . do I have to talk it about it in front of strangers?"

"We passed that stage when you ate part of my second sandwich," Mitch joshed.

Paige looked from one to the next, apparently gauging her chances of stalling a bit longer. Then she gave a deep, melodramatic sigh as only a young female teenager can deliver. "O-kay," she said petulantly. "First of all, I was worried about you, Aunt Aubrey."

"Me?" Aubrey hadn't been expecting that one.

"Well, yeah. The last time we talked, you had to run because you were burning this place down." Dramatic pause while Paige surveyed the room. "Still standing. Guess you lucked out."

"We did not have a fire," Aubrey said briskly.

"Just a little smoke," Mitch added.

"Well, I didn't know. And Mom and Grandma didn't know a thing about it, either."

"You asked them if I'd been in a fire?" Aubrey's voice rose and she didn't care. One more mark against her on the home front.

Paige crossed her arms. "Of course not. I know what kind of grilling they put me through when I've messed up. I simply listened and asked a few questions."

Aubrey gulped down a breath of air, relaxing slightly. "Okay, you're right. I should've called you back. Why didn't you call me like you've done several times already? Why did you think you had to come here and check things out in person?"

"I . . . uh . . . "

Inspiration flashed. "Something's happened between you and your mom, right?"

Paige dropped her gaze to the floor. Uncrossing her arms, she clasped her hands and began wringing them. "I tried to wait, like you told me, Aunt Aubrey. Really, I did."

"Wait?" Aubrey tried to recall their last phone conversation and the subject of waiting.

"Remember? I wanted to push Mom to let me go along on tour with her and you told me to give her time before bringing it up again."

"The tour being the reason why your mom needs a motor coach and your aunt is decorating it?" Orville inserted, attempting to catch up.

Paige turned her attention to the older man momentarily. "Yes. My mom's a concert pianist. She's reviving her career after several years of raising me and arguing with my dad."

"Paige! Watch the attitude," Aubrey chided. "So, what happened?"

"I heard Mom making arrangements with a couple of her friends to make the whole trip with her. In addition to the two people she asked along for the first few weeks."

"She thinks she can sleep five people in that thing?" Mitch was incredulous.

"That's my sister, Mitch. More optimistic than practical."

He just shook his head.

"Anyway," Paige cut in, attempting to reclaim the stage, "I thought I'd better remind her that I wanted to go along before she invited anyone else."

Aubrey had a pretty good idea what was coming. "And your mom was less than thrilled. Right?"

Paige nodded. "She told me she was tired of my complaining about being left behind. And I accused her of trying to get rid of me."

Aubrey rolled her eyes. "Oh, Paige. You know your mother. Push her, and she goes all weepy."

Paige sulked. "Just once, couldn't I be the one to break into tears and pout?"

Reaching out, Aubrey pulled the child into her arms and began gently stroking her hair. "You're not made like that, hon. You're strong. You speak up when something's bothering you, and then take action to correct it. Your mom's not like that."

Aubrey looked up to find Mitch staring at her, a strange expression on his face. Before she could figure out what it meant, though, Paige demanded her attention again.

"You're defending her?" Her young voice rose in a whine.

Aubrey paused a moment, trying to find the right words to

salve the child's feelings. "I'm not defending her, Paige. I'm trying to explain her to you."

Paige gave her a defiant look. "And you know her so well? She's on your case as much as she's on mine!"

Paige was an expert at pushing the right buttons. "Sisters do that to each other, Paige. I'm sorry you haven't had that experience as an only child. Your mom strikes out at you in areas where she feels most vulnerable, just like Grandma does with me."

Just like Grandma? Where had that come from?

"Hmmm . . ." Mitch put in.

She caught him giving her an inscrutable smile. What was with him?

Then it hit. The words and advice she's been dishing out to her niece shifted into a vision of her own reality. Gasping, she put her hand to her mouth to cover the shock.

*

"Aunt Aubrey? Are you okay? I didn't mean to hurt your feelings."

Taking her by the hand, Mitch pulled Paige away from Aubrey's embrace and turned her over to Orville. "She's fine, kiddo. Finally. Thanks to you," he said, watching Aubrey intently. "Orville, why don't you two go raid my fridge upstairs. There's a gallon of Rocky Road ice cream in there just waiting for you."

"But . . ." Paige protested, confused by the change of subject.

"No buts about it," Orville intervened. "When Mitch deigns to share his private stash of Rocky Road, we jump at the offer." Before the girl could object further, he swept her out of the office and upstairs to the proffered bowl of ice cream.

"You handled that like a pro. I'd swear you were already a mother yourself or a psychologist," Mitch said as soon as they were alone.

Aubrey shook her head in disbelief. "Maybe you think so. Did you hear the lines I fed her? I almost had myself believing them for a moment."

So they were going to play it that way? Damn. He'd hoped he finally had her. Actually, he did. She just wasn't admitting to it. "Uh-huh. Had me going there. I almost believed you talked yourself into understanding your own mother-daughter relationship."

She eyed him warily, as if trying to decide if he was putting her on. "Yeah, well . . . "

They stood there facing each other for several beats.

Aubrey broke the silence. "Can you believe that kid? Running away from home like that." She blinked. "I've got to call Jenna. She must be worried sick." She reached for her phone.

Before she could punch in her sister's number, Mitch caught hold of her wrist. "We need to find out how she got here first, or your sister will spend more energy reacting to that than dealing with her daughter." As soon as the words were out, he realized how deep that actually sounded. When had he gotten so smart?

"Good thinking, although I don't relish the idea of questioning Paige further."

"Need some help with the cross-examination?"

She raised an eyebrow. "You'd do that for me, Counselor?"

"You make me another sandwich like that concoction you and Paige put together and it's a deal." Yeah, yeah. He was getting sucked in. Willingly. But Aubrey's family was growing on him. And he had another reason. He wanted Aubrey to listen more carefully to her niece's story. It included parallels she had yet to fully understand.

At Mitch's suggestion, they moved the inquisition to his kitchen where Paige and Orville were just finishing their ice cream. In the intervening time, the two of them appeared to have grown closer, at least one would think so to hear their banter.

"Sure I can't talk you into another, Orvy?"

"I've never finished off two bowls of ice cream in one sitting in my entire life, young lady. I'm going to pay for this on the scales tomorrow. It's all your fault."

"You didn't have to accept the dare, you know."

"And let you consume all of Mitch's ice cream?"

"I stopped at a bowl and a half."

"Any left for us?" Mitch asked, peeking into the container. "You weren't kidding. You two are major porkers." At that, the tense atmosphere seemed to break and they were simply three adults and a teenager enjoying each other's company over ice cream.

Mitch took advantage of the mood to extract from Paige the story of how she traveled from California to Iowa. Like she'd told Aubrey during that memorable phone call, she'd found the McKenna's address on a slip of paper her mother had left on her desk. She'd used the Internet to pinpoint the exact location and order herself an airline ticket to Des Moines and a bus ticket from there to Burlington.

"How did you get from the bus station to this place?" Orville asked, having been drawn completely into the saga of Paige's travels.

"You didn't hitchhike, did you?" Aubrey asked with concern. "Tell me you didn't do that, after all the warnings you've been given."

"You think I'd admit it if I had?" Paige leaned over and patted her aunt's hands. "No, I walked. It was a nice day. Hot. And humid. Boy, this place is humid! I had my map from the Internet and got within six blocks before I had to ask for directions."

"When did you get here?" Mitch remembered that they'd been closed down for two days after the smoke incident. Surely the child hadn't broken in while they'd been exiled to the other coach and Debbie's?

Paige appeared reluctant to part with this piece of information, choosing instead to fiddle with the empty can of pop she'd just consumed.

"Tell us when you got here, Paige," Aubrey urged.

"Two days ago. I was going to walk in and announce I'd arrived, but I heard you and Mitch arguing, Aunt Aubrey. I didn't want to make more waves for you, so I decided to look around. I found

Mom's trailer. At least it had a bunch of our furniture in it."

"What have you been doing for two days, child?" Orville asked.

"Well, first I took a long, long nap. Walking around in all this Iowa heat was the pits. So I collapsed in the trailer's bedroom closet and fell asleep."

"Motor coach," Mitch corrected.

"Huh?" The information went right past her.

"Never mind," Mitch said.

Aubrey and Orville stifled chuckles.

"You couldn't have slept for two days," Mitch interjected, "so what else have you been up to? I've been here most of that time and never suspected you were around."

Paige examined her fingernails.

"You don't seem very interested in providing us with details. Have you been hiding from us the rest of that time?" Mitch asked.

Paige continued to gaze at her hands. "Uh, yeah, I suppose so."

"Hiding?" Aubrey nearly choked on her ice cream. "That's why I thought I smelled your cologne the other day! You'd just been there."

"Close call," Paige conceded.

"And the sound of a door closing earlier! That was you also," Aubrey surmised. "Why did you stay hidden so long? Wait a second. You didn't come here to help me, did you, young lady? This is pay back for your mother."

All three stared at each other, unsure whether to throttle the child or burst out laughing.

Paige watched their reactions, looking from one to the next. "Okay, okay, okay. But it serves her right. She won't take me with her in her precious *motor coach*," emphasis for Mitch's benefit, "so I decided to enjoy it on my own."

"I need to let your mother know you're here and safe," Aubrey said, rising.

Paige jumped to her feet too, throwing herself in her aunt's arms. "Not yet! Please not yet, Aunt Aubrey."

Aubrey appeared to steel herself from Paige's pleas. "You've been gone for over two days. Your mother must be frantic."

"She thinks I'm staying with a school friend. She has no idea I took off."

"Oh boy, oh boy," was all Orville could say.

Mitch simply shook his head in disbelief.

"That does it. Will you two guys entertain my niece while I find my cell phone?" Aubrey asked. She didn't wait for them to respond. "The sooner I get hold of my sister, the better. Though what I'm going to tell her, I have no idea."

*

"Paige is there with you?" Jenna asked in a skeptical tone. "In Iowa? Now?"

Aubrey reclined in one of the visitor chairs in Mitch's office, having decided she needed some privacy to deal with her sister. "That's what I said. I called you as soon as I got all the details."

"That's ridiculous. Paige has been staying with a friend from summer school the last few days. She's called me and everything."

"She has her cell phone with her, Jenna. She called from here."

"But why? How did she even know how to find you?"

Aubrey reminded her sister of the mailing labels she'd left out for anyone to see, especially her prepubescent, highly intelligent daughter. Jenna didn't seem to be absorbing the information until Aubrey mentioned how Paige had used the Internet to make her escape.

"She did what? How?"

"She had your credit card information and simply keyed it in like you would."

"Let me talk to her." An order, not a request.

Aubrey hedged. Jenna needed time to calm down. "She's not here right now."

"Where is she? How could you possibly let her out of your

sight after all this?"

Leave it to Jenna to go on the offensive. She'd just been told her child had run away, lied to her about staying with friends, and made significant charges on her credit card, and her response? Blame her sister.

"At the moment, she's upstairs eating ice cream."

"Eating ice cream. How . . . cozy. She pulled this stunt, and you're treating it like a picnic. You have no idea how to deal with children, Aubrey."

"I, I . . . " Stammering. Good grief. And her heart was pounding in her ears. Why wasn't she telling her sister where to get off?

"Get her on the phone. Right now."

"Jenna, I don't think—"

"You haven't been thinking. You run away from your problems and leave Mother and me to cover for you. Now you're making light of my daughter's same lack of maturity."

"That's not . . . She was worried about me. After the smoke alarm went off . . . "

"Smoke alarm? There was a fire? Tell me you didn't have something to do with it."

"I was frying hamburger when . . . "

"You? Cooking? Aubrey, have you lost your mind? You're their guest and you repay them by burning down their place? What about my motor coach? It's still okay, isn't it?"

"It's fine. We had to take it outside for a couple days . . . "

"Outside?"

"The fire chief thought . . . "

"Fire chief!" Jenna was nearly screaming.

"The fire chief thought we should get it away from the smoke, that's all."

"That's all?" Pause. Jenna seemed to be thinking through what she'd just heard. Finally, her voice slightly less agitated, she asked, "Are you done with the coach yet?"

"Well, no. But we're making good progress."

"It is going to be finished on time, isn't it? You know how much I have riding on this tour. There's no room even for a few days' delay."

Aubrey debated how to reply. Yes, she was behind. But she thought she could catch up.

Aubrey's hesitation was all Jenna needed to continue her tirade. "Are you messing up that job the same as you did Heidi's?"

"No . . . I . . . "

"This is how you repay me for helping you escape Heidi's wrath?"

Only I didn't escape it, Jenna. "No, of course not. The coach is coming along fine."

"Really? It doesn't sound like it. It sounds like you're taking a vacation in the Heartland, and now allowing my daughter to join you."

The diatribe continued. Aubrey could have taken the cell upstairs for Paige, but she deliberately stayed away, preferring to protect her niece from her mother's anger. Funny, it was only an hour ago that she was attempting to convince Paige that Jenna wasn't all that bad. Fool!

Finally, Paige wandered into the room, her face wrinkled in contrition. Holding out her hand for the phone, she said, "My turn."

Aubrey no longer had the emotional strength or spirit to keep talking. Jenna had done a pretty good chop job on her. She handed the phone to Paige and stumbled out of the room.

She collided with Mitch, who'd been hovering outside the door. "Watch it, sweets!"

"Oh, Mitch. My life is a train wreck!"

He held her away from him slightly, squinting. "Why? Because your niece took flight from her flighty mother?"

She gasped slightly, surprised by how well he read her sister. "I let Jenna get to me. I knew better. But I had to protect Paige. Run interference."

He lifted her chin with a hand, and rather than the sparks his touch had elicited previously, ripples of contentment streamed through her.

"Because you identify with the kid?"

She didn't answer. Her soul felt raw, as if it had been scraped away by one catastrophe too many. Had she not felt so vulnerable, she might have turned away, fled from Mitch's perception. She'd feared such intimacy earlier. But she was weak. She needed comforting. And Mitch could make things seem better. She let him draw her into the sanctuary of his arms.

"What's Orville doing here?" Graham asked from behind them.

Mitch gave her a look that said *hold on*, and turned to face his brother. "He's been helping me with Aubrey's case."

"Case?" Geoff asked, coming up behind Graham. "What's going on?"

Her voice barely a whisper, Aubrey said to Mitch, "Can you take it from here?"

He gave her a squeeze, then, turning to his brothers, replied, "Remember the hunting lodge Aubrey told us she turned into French pastry? It seems the owner takes issue with her sense of style."

"Back up a second there, bro," Geoff said. "What was that about Orville helping *you* with the case? Are you lawyering again?"

"Again?" Graham added. "You never sat for the bar."

"That's why Orville's here," Mitch said.

Both men studied Aubrey, still ensconced in Mitch's embrace.

Back at Mitch. "How's it look?" Geoff asked.

To Aubrey, Mitch directed, "Go to the kitchen, get some water and sit down. I'll update the guys. Let Paige handle her mother. The kid's got more energy than all of us."

"Paige?" Both men asked.

Mitch pushed Aubrey off toward the second floor.

The last thing she heard as she went up the stairs was Mitch saying, "Looks like we have another house guest."

CHAPTER SIXTEEN

Mitch filled his brothers in on the Buxbaum suit.

"I don't get it," Geoff said, after hearing about Aubrey's escape to Iowa. "Didn't the client, this Buxom woman, sign some sort of agreement holding Aubrey harmless for her work?"

Mitch didn't want to rat on Aubrey, betray her lack of judgment to his brothers.

Orville, making his way down the steps, handled that for him. "This is a somewhat extraordinary situation. Family friend who wanted to keep everything informal so there'd be no incriminating evidence in her divorce proceedings."

"How is she?" Mitch asked, once Orville had joined them at the garage level.

Orville's expression went grave. "I don't like it. She's still functioning, walking and talking. But she looks like she's going to implode at any moment. What happened? I thought she was in control of this situation with her niece."

Mitch updated him on Aubrey's conversation with her sister.

"You mean the kid is Jenna DiFranco's daughter?" Geoff asked, having listened in.

Mitch and Orville nodded.

"Does that make us legally responsible for this runaway?" Gray wanted to know. "I've dealt with this DiFranco woman. Pushy, persistent. A real harridan. No wonder Aubrey looks like she's been run over."

"That's my mom, a real Mac truck," Paige said from the corridor.

Mitch introduced her to his brothers. Afterwards, he asked, "What did she say? Do we need to put you on a plane back to the West Coast?" Strange, he was trusting this precocious fourteen-

237

year-old who'd been lying to her mother the past few days to give him a straight story.

"She's okay with my staying with you guys, if it's okay with you?" She raised her brows hopefully, apparently afraid they might turn her out.

"Uh, for how long?" Gray cut in. "For the next hour, a day, a two-week vacation?"

Paige turned her attention to the oldest McKenna brother. In the blink of an eye, hers, Mitch saw the child's opinion of his brother change from open interest to guarded hostility. Gray had a real knack with kids.

"I didn't mean to barge in. I just needed to get away from my mom."

"And teach her a lesson or two," her new friend, Orville, added.

"Yeah, that too," she agreed begrudgingly. "She told me to sit tight. She's coming to get me. I'm supposed to feel guilty at that because it means she's leaving her precious rehearsals."

"Your mother's coming here?" Mitch asked, a sharp pain drilling into his temple.

Paige nodded her head.

"When?" Gray asked, a little too anxious.

Paige turned hooded eyes his direction. "Soon, I guess. She didn't say. And she needs to get back home right away to get ready for her tour."

Gray moved over to Mitch, taking his arm. "What're we going to do? She could be here within hours."

"Chill, Gray. It's not like we've kidnapped her. Paige says she has permission to stay here. Temporarily."

"So," Paige interjected in an authoritative teenage voice, "we don't have much time to work on Aunt Aubrey's case. We should get crackin'."

"What?" all four men exclaimed.

Paige looked at Mitch. "I heard the three of you talking earlier, before you discovered me. I was listening out in the hall."

"You mean eavesdropping?" Gray supplied.

Paige glanced at Gray, glared, then turned back to Mitch, her expression softening. "Anyway," she continued, once again intoning her flare for the dramatic, "I think I can help."

Four pairs of male eyes, opened wide, stared at her.

She gave them a shy smile. "I sort of listen at doors around home, too."

*

The group reconvened in Mitch's office, with Paige holding court.

"Okay, young lady," Orville said, pulling a chair up next to hers, "you've got our interest. Now tell us what you know."

Paige leaned into the group, like she was addressing fellow conspirators. "Well, this Heidi lady has been calling Mom for days. I took some of the messages. She wanted to know where Aunt Aubrey was."

"You didn't tell her, did you?" Mitch cut in. Then another thought hit. "Is that how she knew where to send the notice of suit?"

Paige gave him an offended look. "No. Despite what my mom thinks, I'm not a kid. I knew enough to keep my mouth shut."

"Then I wonder how . . . "

"That would be my grandma's doing. She came over the day before I took off, wanting to know where Aunt Aubrey was."

"And you told her?"

"That I hadn't heard from Aunt Aubrey since she said the hamburger was on fire. I was so worried, I thought maybe Grandma could help."

"So you gave her the address?" Mitch asked.

"To help me find out about Aunt Aubrey. I didn't think she'd give it to that Heidi lady."

"Are you sure she did?" Orville, always the advocate of fairness, asked.

Paige slapped her hands on her thighs, appearing to relish the role of ringleader. "I heard the call. Mom was still at rehearsal and Grandma thought I was in my room. But I hung around outside the door, concerned she might call Aunt Aubrey. She really went ballistic when I first told her Aunt Aubrey's location, and I was afraid Grandma was going to ream her."

Mitch got up from his chair, came over to her and bent down so he could look her in the eyes. "What exactly did your grandmother say to Heidi Buxbaum? Do you remember?"

The girl tilted her head to the side, as if trying to recall. "She didn't sound very friendly, though Grandma tends to be a bit, uh, short with everyone. I heard her say something like, 'here's where she's staying. Now you deal directly with her from here on and don't call me again.'" Paige lowered her voice, apparently adapting her grandmother's tone.

Still on his haunches, Mitch shot a glance at Orville. To Paige, he said, "And that was it? She remained cold and businesslike throughout?"

The girl nodded.

"I don't get it," Gray said. "The woman would have found Aubrey eventually. Why do we care that she found out through Aubrey's mother?"

"We thought she could corroborate for Aubrey that Mrs. Buxbaum not only knew how the cabin was going to be decorated, but deliberately ordered it up that way."

Mitch faced the group. "But if she was the one who tipped off Heidi about Aubrey's whereabouts, it might indicate she's in cahoots with the woman."

Over her shoulder to Mitch, Paige said, "I don't think Grandma would do that, especially if she thought it would hurt Aunt Aubrey's business. Grandma's pretty proud of her success, even though she rarely tells Aunt Aubrey."

"You don't say," Orville said. He gave Mitch a knowing look. "Aubrey seems to be unaware of her mother's support. Tell us more, young lady."

"I overheard Aunt Aubrey telling you not to get Grandma involved," the girl began. "She's has this *thing* about Grandma. Aunt Aubrey's so smart and creative, but if Grandma even suggests something be done differently, Aunt Aubrey caves every time."

"Have you ever heard your grandmother discuss Heidi Buxbaum otherwise?" Mitch asked.

Paige screwed up her face. "Maybe. A few months back, I overheard Grandma and Aunt Aubrey talking about her."

That got Mitch's interest. "You don't say. What did you hear?"

"Aunt Aubrey said this Heidi lady was being so cooperative. She'd told her the sky was the limit for her furniture budget."

Mitch slammed a fist into the palm of his other hand. "Bingo! What do you think, Orville?"

Orville was smiling that smile Mitch remembered from the old days. The one that emerged when he'd just started to sense a case tipping their direction. "I'd say, turn your computer on, Mitch, so we can take this down word for word. We've struck pay dirt."

By the time they'd finished up their notes on the case, Mitch was beginning to wonder where Aubrey was. He needed to tell her they'd had a break in the case, something to raise her spirits since her call to her sister. He found Gray and Geoff stretched out in the living room watching sports news. No sign of Aubrey or the other two.

"Orville's treating us to dinner tonight," Geoff told him. "He took Paige with him to help carry things."

"And Aubrey?" Not finding her there was worrisome.

Gray glanced toward the kitchen. "She was in the kitchen when I saw her last."

Mitch headed back to the kitchen to look again. No Aubrey. "How long ago was she here?"

Geoff broke his concentration on the sports scores. "Ten, fifteen minutes ago."

Returning to the living room, Mitch said, "And you just let

her leave?"

Both brothers turned curious gazes his direction.

"We were supposed to tie her up?" Geoff asked.

"Of course not! But she's in a terrible state. No telling what she'll do."

"Hey, Mitch," Orville called out, coming into the room, arms loaded with packages. "What's with Aubrey?"

Mitch jumped at the question. "You saw her?"

Orville handed the bags of food to Gray and Geoff. He motioned for Mitch to follow him to the windows facing the street. "She's sitting out there in what I presume is her rental car, doing nothing, staring straight ahead. Car trouble?"

Mitch checked for himself. "No, I don't think so. Did you talk to her?"

"I wanted to, but Paige told me Aubrey probably needed her space."

"Why's she out there? It must be over ninety degrees today." Tiny sharks of apprehension nipped at his gut. Tell him it wasn't so. Turning back to Orville, he asked, "Did you happen to see if she had anything in the car with her? Like luggage?"

"Luggage? No, I don't think so. Wait! I think I saw a duffel bag propped up against the back door." Comprehension struck. "She's not leaving?"

Both men exchanged worried looks.

"Who's leaving? Aubrey?" Geoff asked, returning from the kitchen.

"She didn't say anything about that to us," Gray added.

Mitch debated what to do. His head told him to get the hell out to the front and pull her out of that car ASAP. His heart told him something else. "I think she's considering another escape from her problems."

Orville frowned. "She was doing so well."

"Well, go get her, Mitch," Gray said.

"What do you think, Paige?" Mitch asked. The girl had remained silent, which, for as short a time as he'd known her, seemed out of character.

She stood there, her forehead scrunched up. "She's debating whether to stay or go. You could go talk her into staying, but next time? Who knows?"

"Pretty deep, kiddo. Especially coming from the current queen of flight," Mitch said.

That energized her. She stood straight. "Hey! I'm not running away from my mother or my problems. I was running *to* my mother's tour bus."

"Touché, my young friend. Think we should leave her there to come to her own decision?" Mitch asked.

"She could take off, head back to L.A., Mitch," Gray said.

"Worse yet," Geoff added, "to parts unknown."

Mitch shot a look at Orville. What was his advice?

Orville raised his bony shoulder in a shrug. "It's your call, Mitch."

He knew what that had to be, though his stomach clenched at the thought. "You're right. Thanks." In the kitchen, he stopped at the fridge briefly before charging down the stairs.

*

Aubrey stared at the dashboard without really seeing it. She should get going. Soon they'd notice she'd left and start looking for her. She had to be gone by then. It should be so easy. Her world had come crashing down on her. And the one bright spot, her blossoming relationship with Mitch, was probably doomed too, since she didn't want to involve her mother in her defense. She'd been about to take a chance, to believe in the possibility of a happily-ever-after. Her, the loser who couldn't seem to get her act together, even for the man she loved.

Loved? *Oh, c'mon, Aubrey. You made love to him all of twice. That's all.*

She leaned down to turn the ignition, but her hand wouldn't budge. What was this? Escaping from escaping? She'd reached a new low.

She tried again with the same result.

Might as well face it. Her inner self was trying to tell her something. Did she dare listen?

Engrossed in her head talk, she didn't see the form come up to the driver's side until she heard the gentle rap on the window. She turned to find Mitch there, eying her patiently.

Damn! No chance for a clean getaway now.

"How's it going?" he asked after she'd rolled down the window. He tried for nonchalance even if she was seated in a closed car in ninety degree heat without the AC on.

"I needed to think. Too many people inside."

He nodded. "Understandable. Only will get more crowded when your sister arrives."

She almost jumped out of her seat at the reminder. For a few minutes, she'd managed to forget the impending doom. She didn't know what to say.

He stuck his hand through the open window. It held a bottle of spring water. Icy cold. She could see the beads of condensation on it. "Here. This is for you."

"Water? Thanks. Is that why you're here? To make sure I'm not dehydrating?"

"I thought you might want it for your trip."

"Trip?"

"That's why you're out here, isn't it?" He raised his brows. "You're planning to take off. Leave your cares behind."

He'd caught her dead to rights. But that didn't mean she had to admit to it. "Why would you think that? I told you I just needed some space."

"Like the 2,000 miles between here and the West Coast? Or are you heading somewhere else this time?"

She started to deny his theory but caught herself. He knew exactly what she was up to. "Okay, what if I did think about skipping town? It wouldn't be the worst thing in the world to happen to you and the guys."

"And the motor coach?"

"You don't need me anymore. All the inventory's here and the contractors are lined up for the rest of this week and next."

"Really? You know how bad I am at the interior stuff. How am I going to handle that?"

"Geoff and Graham can help. Heck, my sister'll be here soon. She can do it herself."

"And the bonus for getting it done on time? You think she'll be ready to part with that once she sees the state things are in? You said she already accused you of making a mess of it."

"I'll call her when I get where I'm going and explain. I'll tell her your company had nothing to do with it."

He started to reply, then put his hand to his back and straightened. "Whew! This is getting uncomfortable. Mind if I join you?"

He didn't give her a chance to refuse. He moved swiftly around the car, opened the passenger side and climbed in. "That's better." He stretched his back.

"Why did you do that? I was about to drive off. Oh, I get it. That's why."

"You'd leave without saying a proper good-bye?"

Why didn't he chastise her for fleeing? "And that would be?"

He pulled her across the seat into his arms and kissed her. Thoroughly. Passionately.

When she came away from him, she sought meaning in his eyes.

"I can't let you go thinking you're a failure and unable to redeem yourself." His voice had gone very low and breathy.

"Thanks." His support overwhelmed her. Even though she was running away.

With the tips of his fingers, he tilted her chin upward. "I don't think you should leave. You need to start facing your problems. And I'll be here to help you. Along with Orville and Paige and my brothers."

She started to cut him off, but he moved his fingers over her lips. "Shhh. That's what friends do. They give advice, sometimes even when it hasn't been requested, like now. You're the one who's shown me that."

"But . . ."

He held up a finger to silence her again. "I'm not going to try to stop you. This has to be your decision. Because if you decide not to go, you have to stand and fight for yourself."

"Fight?" Her voice was a husky whisper.

"You said before you were afraid your mother wouldn't care enough to help you. I think the real issue here is whether you care enough about yourself to stay and fight. You certainly go to bat for everyone else, including me. Now, turn all that energy and determination on yourself."

"Me?"

"You know what else I think?" he continued. "I think you've already made that decision, or I would have come out here and found pavement where the car is." He drew her into his arms and kissed her again, sending waves of heat rushing through her that had nothing to do with the temps outside the car.

"See ya." He opened the door, sprang from the car and moved off to the firehouse.

He believed in her. Even if she was stupid enough to go through with her getaway.

The realization left her breathless. The key still awaited her in the ignition. She'd touched it but didn't turn it. Uh-huh. If that wasn't a clue to her next move, nothing was.

*

Mitch returned to the living room, where the others were still gathered.

"Well? What's the story?" Gray asked.

He didn't know what to tell them. He thought he'd gotten through to her, but he wasn't sure. "She said she needed some time away from everyone to think things through."

Orville furrowed his brow. "Outside? In this heat?"

Mitch chuckled. "Yeah. Can you believe it? After all her complaints about the humidity, she's out there in that overheated car trying to make sense of her life before her brain fries."

Geoff walked over to the window and looked out once more. "Still there. Do you want me to keep an eye on the car?"

Mitch fought the temptation to say yes. But this had to be Aubrey's decision all the way. Standing watch at the window wasn't going to help her. "No. She'll be in sometime."

They watched a ball game for the next half hour. Orville napped in the easy chair and Paige wandered off to a corner of the room to listen to music.

"Finally!" a voice said from the doorway. A female voice. "I've been looking all over this place for everybody. I was ready to check the infamous break room."

Aubrey was back. The old Aubrey. The one with the coastal chip on her shoulder and the inability to leave well enough alone. The one he loved. Mitch breathed a sigh of relief.

"It's about time you showed up," he said. "We've got a motor coach to decorate."

*

"That's exactly what I was thinking," she said with a smile as she entered the room. "I had some planning to do, and I've heard that heat makes the brain work better. So I tested out the theory."

"Did it work?" Gray asked, playing along.

She considered for a moment, then chuckled. "Nah, mainly, it made me thirsty." She held up the empty water bottle. "I had this to get me through 'til it ran dry." She looked at Mitch. "Someone seemed to know exactly what I needed."

"So what's our first move?" he asked.

"Do you know these guys?" She held out a business card. "I arranged for this outfit to do new wall treatments. But they're not scheduled for a few days. I could really use them and the carpet layers here tonight. I'm hoping that finishing the coach before the deadline may cool Jenna's anger."

"I know this outfit," Geoff said. "Went to school with one of the partners. I'll call him."

"That leaves the carpet layers to me," Gray said. "Got their contact information?"

She pulled out her cell phone to check. "Thanks," she said, writing the telephone number on a sticky note. "I could also use some help clearing stuff out."

"Let's get moving," Mitch said, in response.

"What about us?" Orville asked, indicating himself and Paige.

She set them about preparing the meal they'd brought back from the deli. Then they all went into warp speed with their various tasks.

Gray got lucky with the carpet people. They were anxious to get the job finished so they could take off the rest of the week for an auto show in Chicago.

Geoff didn't fare as well. The so-called friend from high school turned out to be the older brother. Then he got an inspiration, Peggy. After he'd recruited her and she made a few strategic phone calls, they were in business.

Once drafted to finagle her friend's involvement, Peggy wanted to be part of the fun as well. When Debbie heard what was afoot, she volunteered her services also, which turned out to be providing strawberries and shortcake for dessert. Tommy came along for the ride, not realizing Paige had joined them. It took all of five minutes for him to develop a giant-sized crush on the *older woman* and for Paige to discover the power she held over the boy.

"This is my mom's motor coach," she told him proudly.

"Wow! Cool!" the boy replied, supplying just the right amount of awe to stoke Paige's ego. "Do you get to ride with her?"

"Nah, not this time," Paige said, sounding like it was no big deal. "Who wants to be on the road weeks at a time when I've got such a cool deal back home with summer school?"

Around eight-thirty, roughly five hours after they started, the new wall treatment and carpet had been installed, and Jenna's belongings looked like they were meant to be there.

Aubrey and Paige were laying out the new comforter on the bed when Debbie called from the front, "Aubrey? Paige? We've got company."

Jenna. They were about to get reamed. Or would the coach deflate her wrath?

"Showtime, kiddo."

Paige gave her a brave smile. "I'm sorry I got you involved in this, Aunt Aubrey."

A little late but well intended. "I can handle your mom about the coach. But you have to do the same about your running away. Don't sell her short. She's frightened about this tour, not sure how she'll do back on the stage after all these years and afraid she'll let you down."

Each squaring her shoulders, the two walked out to face Jenna.

As soon as she saw her daughter and sister framed in the door of the motor coach, Jenna ran over to them, grabbing Paige in her arms. "Oh, Paige, do you know what agony you've put me through?"

Paige let her mother hug her and examine her before replying. "I didn't mean to scare you, Mom. Aunt Aubrey says you have enough on your mind. I just wanted your attention."

Bending down, Jenna cupped her daughter's chin in her palm and looked her directly in the eyes. "You certainly succeeded there!"

"I would have been happy to bring her back to L.A. in a day or two," Aubrey added.

Jenna switched her attention to her sister. "That wasn't necessary. Paige is my responsibility, and I take it seriously." A tinge of defiance crept into her tone.

Aubrey reached out and took her sister's hand. "I know. Neither

Paige nor I ever doubted that. All I meant was that you wouldn't have had to interrupt your rehearsal schedule that way."

Jenna bit a lip. "Thanks. But, as you told me, you have your own business to attend to."

One thing about several hours of flying. It had helped temper her sister's mood. Still, she needed to know that Aubrey wasn't the lost cause she'd accused her of. "Exactly what I've been doing. Want to see your coach?"

Genuine surprise swept across her sister's face. "You're . . . done?"

"Almost." Aubrey tried not to smile too much at her accomplishment. "And I think you're going to be pleased with the result."

Jenna looked in the direction of her coach and started to head over to it.

Aubrey jumped in front of her. "Wait! This is more than my project. The McKennas have done a great job on it as well. Have you met them yet?" Mitch, Graham and Geoff were leaning against the stairs, trying to look inconspicuous, yet protective. Peggy, Tommy and Orville had disappeared, probably upstairs. Debbie was the only one nearby.

Jenna pursed her lips, as if debating whether to be gracious or pushy. Good manners won out. "Ah, yes. The McKennas. Your hosts."

Aubrey thought she detected a note of sarcasm in her sister's statement but let it pass. She needed reinforcements. "Mitch! Graham! Geoff! Come meet my sister."

That was all the invitation Mitch needed. Offering Jenna his hand, he motioned for the other two to accompany him. "Ms. DiFranco, it's a pleasure to meet you in person."

Aubrey marveled at his smooth, charming manner, a far cry from her own first meeting with him. Rather that resent it, though, she was relieved he was helping her fend off Jenna.

"And you're . . . ?" Jenna asked.

"I'm Mitch McKenna, chief mechanic. You've got a great vehicle there, Ms. DiFranco. Say the word, and we'll be happy to take you out for a trial run."

"I'm Geoff. We've talked on the phone, but it's mainly this guy here," he said, indicating Graham, who was last in line, "who's been your contact."

Jenna took Geoff's hand and smiled politely. Then she turned her attention to Graham. "So you're Graham?" she commented, sizing up the eldest McKenna brother.

Graham shook her hand brusquely, stepping forward and back immediately, as if performing a do-si-do in a square dance. He gave a curt smile. "Ms. DiFranco. How did you go for three days without noticing your daughter was missing?"

Blinking, Jenna stepped back herself, apparently at a loss for words.

Aubrey's stomach plummeted. She thought things were back on track with Jenna, then Graham went all prickly. "Paige explained all that. She was supposed to be staying at a friend's."

Jenna gave her sister a hooded look as if not expecting her to come to her rescue. "I just learned of my daughter's . . . change in plans . . . today."

"Uh-huh. Well, you certainly made tracks getting here when you found out she was staying with us. Were you concerned about our ability to watch over her?"

"I simply wanted to see for myself that she was okay," Jenna replied defensively.

"Can we talk about me later?" Paige intervened. "You gotta see your coach."

"Yes, Ms. DiFranco," Mitch added, "we'd really like to show you."

After Jenna had seen the entire coach, Aubrey couldn't help herself. "So? What do you think?"

"I think," Jenna replied, "you got me needlessly concerned that it wouldn't be done on time. Was that so you could look like the great heroine?"

Hearing that, Mitch and the others, except for Paige and Aubrey, backed away.

Aubrey's patience was at an end. "You already claimed that role by giving me this job, Jenna. But ever since, you've acted like you regretted helping me, questioning my ability to finish the job on time, my decision to stay with the McKennas, and now the fact that I served as a haven in the storm for Paige."

"Why shouldn't I? You haven't exactly given me cause to believe in you."

Jenna's words assaulted her heart. But instead of hurting, the arrows angered her. "Just a darn minute, Jenna! Though the term 'screw-up' comes up whenever you or Mother discuss me, I've been doing pretty well for myself. Yes, I made a bad judgment on the project for Heidi Buxbaum. But my mistake was in trusting her."

Jenna released a long, deep, put-upon sigh. "I haven't called you a 'screw-up,' Aubrey. I wouldn't have asked you to work on my coach if I really thought that, sister or not."

"Then why have you been second-guessing me at every turn since you sent me here?"

"Second-guessing you? Is that what you think I've been doing?"

Aubrey crossed her arms in front of her but didn't reply.

"Aubrey?" Jenna took her arm. "Sisters do those things, especially when one has been through the ringer emotionally the last few years and is facing the test of a lifetime."

Darn her! Always thinking of herself. Forgetting that her daughter was there taking it all in. Before her niece could put it together, Aubrey cut in. "Your so-called *test of a lifetime* isn't limited to just you, Jenna. Heidi Buxbaum's attorneys have found me, thanks to Mother, who saw my address on shipping labels you left out on your desk."

"I did?"

"That's how I found Aunt Aubrey, Mom You've been kinda forgetful lately."

"Aubrey, I'm sorry. I had no idea such a minor detail could cause you trouble." Jenna removed her hand from Aubrey's arm.

"Why would Mother tell Heidi your whereabouts?"

"Because Heidi has been pestering her, threatening to embarrass her in front of her precious friends."

"But . . . that's so . . . cold. Even for Mother."

"I don't think she knew it was to help Heidi in her suit. I, uh, neglected to tell Mother all the sordid details other than Heidi's husband had not been pleased with the renovation."

Jenna considered her words. "Where does that leave you? Especially if the coach is almost done. Will you be returning to L.A. soon?"

"Mitch and Orville have taken on her case," Paige said helpfully.

"Mitch? And who's Orville?"

"That would be me, ma'am," Orville said, coming forward to shake her hand. "Orville Drummond, attorney-at-law." He shot a glance at Aubrey. "Sorry, dear, but I thought you could use the moral support." He returned his attention to Jenna. "It seems that Mr. and Mrs. Buxbaum are in cahoots to ruin your sister's reputation and career, Ms. DiFranco."

"Really?" Jenna once again threw a dubious look toward her sister. "Why? It's not like your business is booming yet, Aubrey, so there's no money in it. Does Heidi have some grudge against you?"

Aubrey shook her head. That question had been nagging her as well. "You're right about the money, unfortunately. Aubrey Carpenter hasn't made her fortune yet. And I hardly know Heidi, except through Mother."

Orville moved in a step. "Which is what we were discussing earlier before we discovered our young stowaway."

"That's only on boats, Orvy," Paige said. "Here, I'm the uninvited houseguest."

"Young lady, you definitely need a new hobby," Graham said, elbowing his way into the group. "One that doesn't involve the Internet, airline flights, or your aunt."

Jenna raised a brow, as if trying to discern why this relative stranger had taken such a negative fancy to her daughter.

"As I was saying," Orville continued, "before we learned of Paige's presence, we were discussing how your mother might be able to help Aubrey's case." He went through the litany of charges against Aubrey and the stack of circumstantial evidence building up against her.

Jenna looked confused. "Why not just call Mother and get her here to help you?"

"Eureka!" Mitch exclaimed.

Orville smiled, as though they'd finally found an intelligent life form.

Aubrey watched control of her life slipping away from her. She had no one to blame but herself. And that meant only she could reclaim it. So much for theory. Time for action.

"I didn't want Mother brought into this," she explained to Jenna while looking at Mitch. "I didn't want her to know how I screwed up," she looked back at her sister briefly. "Okay, I can say the word. Anyway, that thought scared me more than the idea of losing the case."

"Hon . . . " Jenna started to say, but Aubrey held up a hand to cut her off.

"And even scarier than that . . . " she took a big gulp, " . . . was the thought of asking for Mother's help and having her turn me down."

"Mother wouldn't . . . and if she did . . . "

Aubrey plunged ahead. "And even if she did, I'd just find another way to fight this."

"Of course you would," Jenna added, finally saying just the right thing.

Aubrey opened her arms to indicate the others who'd gathered around. "And, as you can see, I've got this wonderful crew to help me."

"And me, too, Aunt Aubrey!"

"And me, too," her sister said softly, offering her a hand.

Once the almost-group-hug died down, Mitch said, "So?

Ready to make a call?"

Now? The thought still terrified her. But she was ready for this. If her mother said no, well then, she'd think of a brilliant alternative and not let her mother's refusal get to her.

Debbie hugged her. "Go ahead, dear. You're ready."

CHAPTER SEVENTEEN

All those little details that had been floating through her brain trying to line up since Debbie had shown her the picture of her mother and the clippings suddenly shifted into place, like the focus on a camera. Her mother felt cheated of the dreams she'd lost as a teenager and was trying to live them out through her daughters. But Aubrey's ideas of success and fulfillment were out of sync with her mother's.

She had a phone call to make. "Mind if I use your office?" she asked Mitch, who extended a hand to escort her. When the others started to follow, she turned back, overcome by their support. "Thanks, everybody. But I've got to do this on my own." To Orville she said, "Stay close by, if you would. If I can convince her to testify on my behalf, you'll need to speak to her immediately."

She punched in the numbers on her cell phone with a great show of bravado. For herself. When her mother answered, Aubrey took a deep breath and plunged ahead. In a few sentences, she told her mother about the lawsuit, the evidence against her and about Mitch and Orville representing her.

"You let her talk you into those drastic changes without ever checking on her ownership?" Her mother's voice rose, like she was gearing up for another harangue.

"If I recall, Mother," she said evenly, "Heidi came to me on your recommendation."

"Well, yes. I thought you'd appreciate the business."

"Which I did, even though I was starting to do pretty well on my own. But you told me that Heidi was going through a tough divorce and could really use the pick-me-up she'd get from remodeling her mountain cabin."

Hesitation on her mother's end. Exasperated sigh? "I'm sure I didn't put it like that."

"Not those words, but certainly the thought. When she asked me to keep our agreement off-the-record, even though I knew it was unusual, I went along with it. My decision, but I based it on what you'd told me." Ah, gee, she'd let herself get defensive. She was supposed to be asking for her mother's help, not indicting her. "Okay, forget that. I made a bad mistake trusting Heidi. Now she wants to sue me for it. I need your help to fight her."

"My help?"

"I need you to negate Heidi's claims that I exceeded our agreement. Also, I need you to tell what you know about how she planned to use the project to retaliate against her husband."

She waited for her mother's response, positive it wouldn't be forthcoming.

"Would I have to testify in court?"

Would she have to testify in court? That's what concerned her?

"Perhaps, if it gets that far. Orville hopes our discovery brief will be strong enough that her attorneys will either drop the case or offer to settle out of court for much less."

"Oh."

Disappointment? "Would that be a problem for you? If it went to court?"

The silence continued. What was going through her mother's head? "I . . . suppose . . . I could . . . manage that. I've never been called to the stand before. That's what they call it, isn't it?"

Her mother's voice actually sounded hopeful. Did that mean she was considering the possibility? The courtroom was a bit like the stage.

"Mother, that's terrific! I'll let you speak to my attorney, Orville Drummond. He's the one calling the shots. The *director*, so to speak." Her mother had backed down, well, somewhat, when Aubrey had stood up to her. *File that fact away.* "And Mother—Mom—thanks."

*

When she got off the phone, she returned to the garage only to discover that the others had cleared out.

"How'd it go?" Mitch asked, stepping away from the other motor coach.

"I thought I'd been deserted."

"Peggy and Geoff went out for more ice cream. Gray is showing your sister and Paige around town, since it's still light out. And Debbie is upstairs. Insisted on doing the dishes."

"And you?" She lifted a brow to accentuate her question and walked toward him.

"Me?" He stuck a tool in his pocket. "I'm here because . . . I'm curious about your call."

"Curious, huh?"

He swiped a hand across his mouth. "Your case has a lot riding on her reaction. If she refused to help, we have to find another way as soon as possible."

She arched her brow again, accompanied this time with a tilted head and lowered lashes. "That's it? Interest in my case?"

He offered a slanted smile. "Possibly, I was concerned for you." He waited a beat. "How did it go?"

Finally. He certainly took his time getting to the important part. But now that he'd asked the question, how did she feel about her talk with her mother?

"She agreed to provide the evidence we want. It's not like I beat her into submission. But I didn't let her barbs get to me either. I left Orville getting the details from her."

"Lucky guy."

"Lucky me. To have found you and Orville. I'd probably be on the run again, if you hadn't, uh, brought me the bottled water." She lifted her hand to his face to wipe away a spot of grease streaked across one cheek. The contact shot ribbons of fire through her arm.

He took her hand in his, a smokiness coming into his eyes. "You would have come back on your own. My visit just expedited things."

She narrowed her eyes, skeptical.

"You would have," he insisted. "You would have realized it was time to take control of your life and not let your mother's or sister's or anyone else's opinions sway you."

She squeezed his hand. "Thanks. You helped me get to that place."

He returned her gaze, his lids lowered, the eyes beneath them dark. "Debbie offered her guest room to your sister and niece for the night. I moved your cot into the other coach."

Was there more to that statement? "Thanks."

"The sleeping bags we used earlier in the week are still there, too," he said meaningfully.

"Oh? Maybe they'd be more comfortable?"

"Perhaps. I'll stop by to help you . . . arrange them." He bent down and kissed her forehead. "See you later. I need to check with Orville before calling it a night."

She watched him go, sensing that maybe, just maybe, her life was back on course.

*

Around eleven-thirty, Mitch made his way downstairs and headed to the coach where Aubrey was sleeping. "Aubrey?" he whispered into the dark interior. He'd hesitated at the door only briefly, reminding himself of his vow not to sleep with her again. He wavered between not wanting to hurt her or himself and his desire to be with her one more time.

"Mitch? Is that you?" she called back, her voice raspy.

Decision made, he moved forward, trying to feel his way along the wall. "Pray I don't step on a forgotten bolt," he said in hushed tones, finally reaching her and taking her in his arms.

Something smooth and supple clung to her body. Beneath it, he felt heat. Warmth that begged him to touch and caress. He complied. "Umm. You smell wonderful."

"I tried the coach's shower. Hope that's okay."

"Glad I had the foresight to hook up the water. We . . . uh . . . could try it again?"

She withdrew her head from his chest. "You want to?"

"Maybe later," he breathed. "I like where I am right now. You feel so good in my arms."

"It's getting to be a habit."

He pulled away slightly. "A good one, I hope?"

"Oh, yes."

"Are you sure?" He hated himself for spoiling the mood, but he didn't want her to be the least bit uncomfortable with the inevitable end of their affair. "I've purposely stayed away from you, well, physically, since the other night."

She snuggled deeper, the scent of wildflowers wafting around her. "I've noticed."

"It wasn't because . . . because I . . . didn't want to be with you again. Hell, that's all I've thought about when I wasn't figuring out how to beat Heidi Buxbaum."

"I'm glad to hear that." Her voice was so low, he could almost feel her vocal cords vibrating in his chest. When she nibbled at an ear, swiping the outer ring with her tongue, his body imploded. "Lady, do you have any idea what that does to me?"

"Turn you on, I hope, since that was the intent."

"You admit to being after my body?" His own voice had grown quite husky.

Placing her arms around him, she slid her hands up and down his back muscles, massaging as she went. "Can you blame me? You're quite the specimen, Mitch McKenna."

Though they were both on the floor, her ministrations made him feel like he was floating. "Oh, Aubrey!" He'd planned to take this slowly, enjoy every minute of passion along the way. But her mere presence and the fresh fragrance of her hair and floral scent of her body and that deliciously thin and silky nightgown provoked a much faster, less controlled pace.

Aubrey's mood matched his own. She initiated the disposal of clothing, pulling his shirt away in one swift movement.

Mitch returned the favor, stripping her of her one and only garment.

In the thrashing about that followed, he focused on touch and smell and taste. Her breasts seemed to meld their shape to his grasp, though the nipples stayed firm and supple. As his tongue laved around them, they tasted fruity, like ripe strawberries.

As his hands worked their way downward, the moistness between her legs told him she was just as excited as he. He cupped her mound, thinking he held within his hands everything he needed in this world.

All his good intentions about keeping this relationship light with no strings took flight about the same time as his libido took over. Before succumbing, he remembered how he'd resolved to be the strong one, the one who maintained control, especially of his heart. The hell with it. This was so much better.

They slept in each other's arms, drained. Around five in the morning, as the light coming through the windows brightened the interior of the coach, Mitch awoke, dressed and made his exit. Not before kissing her on the nose first, saying, "Later, sweetheart."

CHAPTER EIGHTEEN

The firehouse took on the appearance of an armed camp the next day. Mitch and Orville holed up in Mitch's office. No one else was allowed in without permission. Aubrey welcomed Jenna's presence. It took her mind off the negotiations and warfare she suspected were being conducted in Mitch's office. They'd shooed her away when she'd tried to interrupt the confab.

Geoff had taken it upon himself to entertain Paige with a game of chess.

Though they'd all feasted on scrambled eggs and sausage for breakfast, her innards felt hollow. A lot was riding on Mitch and Orville's call to Heidi's attorneys.

For at least the tenth time, Aubrey gazed out the coach's exterior door. Still quiet. "Here, Graham," she said, holding out her notebook to him, "you take over as my sister's personal assistant. I'm sure Mitch and Orville need me in there."

Graham accepted the notebook, but not without protest. "Mitch told you to stay put here in the coach and gave me orders to keep you here."

She pulled her most pathetic look. "Surely they're done in there by now?"

"It's only been an hour," Jenna said. "I think you should do as Graham suggests and remain here." She and Graham exchanged amiable looks, like conspirators holding her prisoner.

Aubrey shot a glance at the opposite wall. It appeared closer than the last time she'd looked. The whole room seemed smaller. Her claustrophobia was kicking in again. She had to get out of there, no matter what the orders had been.

"I need some air," she said over her shoulder as she fled into the garage. She got as far as the corridor leading to the guys' offices when Mitch and Orville burst into the hallway, slapping each other on the back, grinning from ear to ear.

"Hey, everybody! Gather 'round," Mitch called out.

"Aubrey! Great news," Orville announced as soon as he saw her.

"What? Tell me."

But Mitch wanted the entire group to assemble. That accomplished, he turned to Orville. "Do you want to do the honors?"

"Don't mind if I do. Your sense of modesty will surely keep you from telling them about the fabulous job you did." He put his arm around Mitch. "Heidi and her husband, Cyril—love that name—reconciled about a month ago. Shortly before you joined us, Aubrey."

"Right, Orville, but we already knew that," Aubrey reminded him.

"Yes, dear. Just setting the stage. Their reuniting involved Heidi selling her husband a bill of goods that she was your victim. She claimed she was completely taken in by your guile and desire to get ahead in the business by dumping a ton of overpriced antiques on her."

Aubrey opened her mouth to protest but realized Orville had launched into lawyer-speak and was laying out their case.

Orville continued, "He must not have believed her at first, until she put together this lawsuit, complete with the trumped up testimony of a couple associates."

Geoff motioned for him to speed it up. "Why do you both look so triumphant?"

Orville took his time leading up to the big reveal. "Her whole case depended on her credibility, which was helped by her so-called witnesses, and by the fact that you ran off and didn't face the music, Aubrey."

"Okay, but we knew that, too," she said.

"All it took, plus Mitch's ability to convince them we had the goods on her, was to swiftly refute her story and show that you hadn't actually run off."

"And it worked?" Graham asked.

"Oh, boy, did it work!" Orville said. "Once Mitch mentioned that Heidi had discussed her plan of retaliation with your mother, her attorneys couldn't drop the case fast enough."

"Drop? As in . . . it's over?" Did she dare hope for that much?

Mitch came over to her and took her hand in his. "That's right. I told them we were filing a countersuit for slander, since she was well on her way to tarnishing your reputation."

"Oh, Mitch, I'm happy to let it end here." The realization that it was over was overwhelming. Her throat constricted, she could barely mouth the words, "Thank you."

He squeezed her hand. "See what happens when you let people help you."

When further words failed her, Paige interrupted, smiling at Mitch. "You are good! Just like Aunt Aubrey told you. You really should go back to the law."

*

Though the words were out, Mitch couldn't believe he'd heard them. And hoped desperately that his brothers hadn't, either. He fought the urge to look at Aubrey. He had to steer Paige away from the subject, cover it any way he could.

"What's this?" Graham asked.

Damn! The innocent words of a child had just toppled his carefully constructed world.

"You want to be a lawyer now?" Geoff asked. "Sit for the bar?"

Though Aubrey appeared surprised by her niece's revelation, she wasn't coming to his rescue. In fact, the look in her eyes seemed to be urging him to come clean with his brothers.

Why should he expect her help, other than the fact that he'd just saved her bacon from Heidi Buxbaum and spent an incredible night with her in his arms?

This couldn't be happening now. Not when he thought everything was under control. Blood pounded against his temples. And his stomach retched. His body was telling him he couldn't avoid it any longer. But he could try to defuse it. "I just helped Orville with Aubrey's case. That's all."

"You said Orville wanted you to come work for him," Paige persisted. "You know, be his partner. Eventually take over the business."

The child had just stuck a dagger in his gut. And each succeeding assertion from her twisted it deeper.

"You thinking of leaving us, Mitch?" Geoff asked.

Paige apparently didn't catch the drift. She continued, "Don't worry about that. He said he couldn't let you guys down."

His brothers simply stood there staring at him, questions and hurt written in their eyes.

Finally, Aubrey came to his rescue. "Uh, Paige, this is between Mitch and his brothers. Maybe the rest of us should clear out and let them talk." She grabbed her niece's hand and gestured for Orville and Jenna to accompany her.

Paige turned back to Mitch, her forehead wrinkled in concern. "What's wrong?"

Mitch released a gigantic sigh. "You only repeated what you heard. Your aunt's the one who brought this on."

Geoff and Gray turned to Aubrey. "Mitch is going to work for Orville?"

Before she could reply, Mitch cut her off. "You couldn't just leave it alone, could you?"

She started to say something, but Mitch held up a hand. "I told you, not once but several times, this was my business. To leave my brothers out of it."

"I . . . " she attempted to get in.

"Hey, Mitch, I'm sure Aubrey . . . " Gray interjected before

Mitch raised his hand again.

Mitch turned angry eyes on her. "I've put up with your meddling and interfering with my affairs ever since you got here. I even thought some of it was cute and maybe even perceptive. But I've got my limits. And now you've gone past them."

"But I . . . " she tried again.

"Good thing for you that the case has wrapped. You can finish your sister's coach, but all bets are off between us. I'm revoking the sleepover clause. You'll need to stay somewhere else for the rest of your time here." With that, he stomped off to their living quarters upstairs.

*

Aubrey stood motionless, with the rest of them staring back at him in shock.

No one spoke. Aubrey's heart pounded in her abdomen, nausea growing. The room grew close, as if the ground had opened beneath her and sucked her in. She wished it had.

Jenna touched Aubrey's chin, tilting it upwards. "Are you okay? You've gone completely pale."

Orville put a grizzled hand on her shoulder. "It's okay. He didn't mean it. He just needs time to realize that."

"I don't think so, Orville. He was livid. I trespassed on his private life."

"What did you do, Aubrey?" Graham asked. "I've rarely seen Mitch that agitated."

She looked from Graham to Geoff. Both shot her quizzical expressions.

"I found out something about Mitch when I first arrived," she explained. "And ever since . . . ever since . . . I kept bringing it up."

"What?" they both asked in unison.

"That's for Mitch to tell you. Paige overheard us arguing about when that should be."

Paige threw herself into Aubrey's arms. "I'm so sorry. Mitch has been so cool. I didn't realize he would go off the deep end when I said what I did. I didn't mean to hurt him or mess things up for you."

Aubrey hugged her niece to her, stroking her hair. "I know, sweetie. I wish you'd kept this knowledge to yourself, but maybe now that it's out, it's for the best."

Graham took her hand. "We'll give him a few more minutes to cool down, then Geoff and I will make him tell us what you won't."

As Graham and Geoff started up the steps to their living quarters, Geoff turned around and called out to Aubrey, "Don't leave, like he told you. Let us find out what's going on."

*

Mitch ripped off his knit shirt and threw it in a wad onto his bed. The action felt good. He stripped off the rest of his clothes and did the same. He needed a shower anyhow. Time to think, away from everyone. And maybe the hot water streaming from the shower head would cover up the moisture welling in his eyes and let him continue to believe he was a strong, virile male who was impervious to the charms and shortcomings of a West Coast interior decorator.

He let the water run, so it would build up steam, not unlike his own sad state of affairs. When he did duck under it, he had to lean into the wall to keep himself from beating his hands against it. Did she ever listen to him? Was it so important that she fix his life that it made up for barging into his business?

He had no idea how long he stood under the hot, rushing water. He finger pads showed shrink lines when he finally turned it off and toweled himself dry.

"Mitch? You in there?"

It was Geoff. Mitch didn't want to answer, but that was stupid, because he was sure his brother had heard him closing the shower door. "I don't need company, Geoff."

"Gray and I are your partners as well as your brothers. You need to talk to us."

"And we don't like the way you treated Aubrey," Gray added.

Aubrey? Had she sent the guys to make amends for her? *Too late, lady. You blew it. You can't keep manipulating me.*

"Come out here. It's just the two of us. We both drew the short straw."

A minute later, hurriedly dressed, Mitch stepped into his bedroom. Geoff was seated on his bed gathering up the dirty clothes.

Mitch grabbed the bundle and quickly stuffed it in the nearby hamper. "Okay, I'm here."

Gray rolled his eyes, as if forcing himself to deal with his brother's surly mood. "The Mitch McKenna we've always known, despite his inadequacies at housekeeping is, above all, fair. He gives people the benefit of the doubt."

"So?"

Gray sat back in the room's only armchair. "You didn't need to treat Aubrey that way. How was she supposed to know her nosy niece had overheard a private conversation and didn't have the sense to keep it to herself?"

Mitch knew his brother was right, but he was still very angry at Aubrey for bringing this to a head. It was his life. It wasn't up to her to decide what he told his brothers about his private needs and desires and when he told them.

Geoff leaned forward. "So, little brother. What's put you into this snit? Aubrey? Her niece?" He paused for effect. "Or . . . having to talk to us?"

Geoff was almost as perceptive as Aubrey.

And Gray just as tenacious.

No way was he going to get out of this without opening up to them.

"She didn't tell you anything after I left?"

Geoff stretched his legs in front of him, crossing one over the other. "She told us she'd been urging you to tell us something. She said the rest was up to you."

"And that she had no idea Paige had heard you talking about it," Gray added.

Geoff demanded, "Tell us what everyone else seems to know already."

"Something about going to work for Orville Drummond, I believe," Gray said.

Though he felt trapped, their love and interest penetrated his struggle to keep them ignorant of his problems. Even before he began to speak, he could feel the stressed muscles around his forehead begin to relax. Deep down, he'd wanted to do this all along. But the fear of hurting them had kept him silent.

He pulled his chair closer. "Remember how prickly I was around Aubrey at first?"

Both nodded but remained silent.

"Besides her 'I've-come-from-a-planet-smarter-than-yours' snobbery, I was afraid she'd see through me."

Geoff blinked. "See through you?"

Mitch went on to explain about his ineptness at interior decorating and how that part of the job had come to be such an irritant to him. His weak spot. By some huge cosmic coincidence, Jenna DiFranco had taken care of that. "About the same time, Orville called me in." He outlined Orville's offer. "Then Aubrey got involved."

"How'd she do that?"

"I . . . uh . . . sorta told her," he admitted.

The other two exchanged meaningful glances.

"Because she made you?" Geoff asked innocently.

"No, of course not! We got to talking. More than once. She's easy to talk to. And I found myself telling her things, private things, that I haven't shared with anyone else."

"Uh-huh," Graham said. "She didn't force you to tell her and she wasn't the one to tell us. So what's the beef? What, besides being what appears to have been a very good friend to you, did she do to make you angry with her?"

"What hasn't she done?" Mitch heard his voice rise. What had she done, actually? She'd insinuated herself into his life, gotten under his skin, and now had him so worked up because she'd made him finally confront his brothers.

"You're the attorney, or at least you aspire to be, so you tell us," Geoff demanded.

Mitch started to reply, then realized what his brother had just said. "You're okay with that?" he asked softly, not daring look either of them in the eyes.

Though not one to be demonstrative, Gray took his hand. "To do the thing you've dreamed of since you were a kid? Of course we are, dummy! When you signed on with us, you told us it didn't matter that much to you."

"We were foolish enough to believe you," Geoff added, taking the other hand. "Gray and I were so focused on making this place a success, we didn't see beyond that."

"A stranger and family friend caught it. I'm sorry we were so dense," Gray said.

"No, guys, I wouldn't have had it any other way. At least until now."

"I know what you were doing," Geoff told him. "It overwhelms me how much you've given up to help me through my illness." He choked on the last part, his eyes misting over.

"And you got me through my failure at architecture. I really wanted this company, and you helped make it a reality." Gray's voice sounded just as poignant.

Mitch withdrew his hands from his brothers' grasp. "So you're kicking me out?"

"Isn't that what you want?" Gray asked.

"Sorta. For now, only part time. Orville's fine with my

continuing to work here for a while."

"And if we've already found someone to be our mechanic?" Gray asked.

"We have?" Geoff arched a brow. "Who?"

Gray smiled. "Me. I planned to do that part before you signed on, Mitch."

Mitch had to chuckle. "That was fast. I didn't realize how dispensable I was."

"You know that's not the case, bro," Geoff said. "We needed you these first few years while we got on our feet. And we still need an attorney."

"You got it!" Mitch shook first Geoff's hand, then Gray's.

As they pulled apart, Geoff said, "We've got the mechanic part covered, but that still leaves us needing an interior decorator."

Gray gave them a knowing smile. "That's right. But don't we already have someone who could handle that part?"

Geoff gave them a conspiratorial grin. "We do. What do you think, Mitch?"

What did he think? His life had taken a new turn, a turn he'd wanted for so long. And his brothers not only understood and accepted it, but actually seemed to relish being on their own. Go figure. But Aubrey had. She'd known this was what he had to do long before he did.

And as her reward, he'd turned on her and accused her of meddling in his life.

"I think there's a meal of crow waiting for me downstairs. Thanks for the chat, guys," he said, taking their hands again. "I'm late for an apology."

*

Mitch felt a spring in his step as he raced down the stairs in search of Aubrey. He heard voices coming from Jenna's motor coach.

Inside, he found Orville and Paige playing chess and Jenna and Aubrey in the back bedroom.

"We're almost done with Jenna's inspection," Aubrey said tersely, not quite looking at him. Her face appeared mottled, pale with blotchy red spots.

"Paige and I have a five o'clock flight. We'll be leaving soon," Jenna added.

Paige and Orville looked up from their game, curious but silent.

"Please stay on a few more days, Jenna. You've hardly had a chance to visit," Mitch said in his most hospitable manner.

"Thank you," she replied, checking out her sister, "but I need to get back to rehearsals."

"Don't leave on my account. I'm here to apologize. I'm sorry about my outburst."

"Mitch," Paige said in a tiny voice, "I'm sorry too. I was so excited about Aunt Aubrey winning her case, I didn't think when I let it slip about you going to work for Orville."

"It's okay, kiddo," he said, patting her head. "That discussion with my brothers was long overdue. Both you and your aunt were smarter than me to realize that."

His words prompted Aubrey to raise her head and look at him, eyes narrowed.

He spoke directly to her. "How about you? Could we go somewhere and talk?"

"I need to finish here with Jenna. She needs to get on the road."

"Couldn't she could spare a few more minutes?"

"I heard your apology. There's nothing more to say."

"Yes, there is."

"You told me you want me out of here. I'm trying to comply with your wishes."

He lifted a strand of her hair. "Please, Aubrey. Give me a chance to explain."

Aubrey exchanged looks with Jenna, as if seeking her opinion.

Her sister shrugged.

"Look, I'm parched. Come with me for a bottle of water. We can talk on the way."

Aubrey brushed his hand away from her hair and continued to stand there, not moving.

"Oh, go ahead, Aubrey. You owe him that much after what he did for you," Jenna said.

"Yeah, Aunt Aubrey. Give Mitch a chance," Paige added.

"Oh, all right!"

He dragged behind her long enough to whisper to Jenna, "Give us ten minutes. Then come spring us from the break room." He caught up with Aubrey, put a hand on her back, attempting to steer her toward the break room, but she shook free of him.

Once there, he grabbed a bottle of water, offered her one, which she refused, and took a few sips. All the while, he frantically framed his closing argument. He'd never argued a case in court before, but he desperately hoped what he'd learned in law school would help him now.

"I told the guys about Orville's offer."

She gave him a guarded look from where she stood across the room. "Good."

"And I told them about wanting to take him up on it."

"Uh-huh."

"And how I felt about working here."

She lifted a brow at that. "Really?"

He grinned. "Yeah. All the things you've been urging me to tell them, I did."

She crossed her arms in front of her and looked at him expectantly. Like there was more.

"And like you kept telling me, all hell didn't break loose. They were quite supportive."

"That shouldn't have come as a surprise. They love you, Mitch, and would do anything within their power to help you realize your dreams."

She was talking in more than one-word replies. Encouraging. "You knew that. I didn't."

She shifted her gaze away from him.

"Okay, maybe I did. But deep down. In a place I buried the same day we buried our father, which I feared revisiting." He sipped more water. His throat really was parched. "Know how I pushed you about what would happen if you asked your mother for help and she refused?"

She nodded.

"I had my own doubts about how my brothers would react to my wanting to go into the law. And what I'd do if they weren't supportive."

She continued to stare at him, not replying.

"I knew I was going back to the law, eventually, with or without their backing. I didn't know how to deal with the guilt of leaving them if that happened. I owe them so much."

"But you've more than paid them back for all the help they've given you over the years."

"I know that . . . now. But think about your own situation. Even before I pushed you into it, you knew you didn't owe your mother anything. You had to be desperate enough to test it."

He didn't know how to proceed. Well, he did, but it was hard to tell a woman you loved her when she was standing ten feet away, arms crossed, one hip jutting out. They stood there, neither saying anything. Aubrey stared at the floor, Mitch watched her stare.

Finally, she broke the standoff. "Thanks for telling me. I'm glad things went well with your brothers." She moved toward the door. "Good luck with your law career."

She was leaving? He had so much more to tell her. He slipped between her and the door, and before she had a chance to protest, slammed it shut.

Eyes wide, she exclaimed, "Why did you do that?"

He tried the doorknob. True to form, the door jammed. He turned back to her, trying not to appear too smug. "I'm glad we didn't jump right into making the changes to this room that you suggested. I'll call the guys, if your claustrophobia returns. I've got my cell with me this time. But we've got some things to work out, and I don't want you running off."

Her face was screwed up in a skeptical expression. "Things? What things?"

"Why don't you sit? This may take a few minutes."

She rolled her eyes but complied. "Okay, guardian of the cell phone. Let's hear it."

"If I'd known getting Heidi Buxbaum off your back meant the return of the 'Attitude,' I would have thought twice before making my call to California."

She eyed him for a few beats as if barely tolerating his presence. "So we're back to Square One, are we? I have 'Attitude' and you don't have the time of day for me."

He expelled a heavy, frustrated sigh. This was not going well. He'd brought her in here to make things right, not botch them up more. "Whoa, back up, lady. Sorry. What I meant to say was . . . I want you to stay."

"I don't think so, Mitch. You've made amends for blowing up at me earlier, but how do I know it won't happen again?"

He came over to her, placing his hands on her shoulders. "I guess you're going to have to trust me on that."

She drew back. "I thought I could trust you before. I thought . . . after last night . . . that things . . . " She let it go at that.

He pulled her back to him. "Things are, oh, hell, Aubrey, I don't know how to say it any other way. I've fallen in love with you."

Her eyes rounded. "You . . . ?"

"I love you. I knew it when I went out to the car to keep you from running off. And when I asked you to stay just now, it wasn't just to finish Jenna's coach." He'd said it, out loud, of his own volition, and he'd meant it. Attitude or not, he wanted this woman.

*

275

Aubrey fought to remain steady on her feet, despite the fact that he was holding her in his arms. He loved her! And he wanted her to stay. All their polite talk about keeping it light, no commitments, no regrets. They'd been kidding themselves.

He looked her in the eyes. "Well? I've sorta gone out on a limb here. Care to join me?"

"I thought . . . but I . . . " She stopped herself. There was only one way to put it. "I love you too, Mitch."

He pulled her into his embrace. "Thank God! I was afraid you'd never say it."

"So was I," she breathed out, in between kisses. "You called me a meddler. I don't think I've ever pushed my way into someone's life as much as I have yours. I cared about you from the beginning and couldn't help myself."

"Meddling . . . schmeddling. Whatever you want to call it, don't stop. Ever. I want you in my life, L.A. Lady. If I join Orville, there'll be a part-time interior decoration job here. But if I have to, I'll follow you to the Coast."

"*If* you join Orville? I thought that was a done deal."

"Not without you."

"You'd do that?" He'd not been willing to follow Dianne. He must really . . .

His eyes grew cloudy, clouds she could lose her worst fears in. "Yes, I would. We've only known each other briefly, but in that time, you've made me happier than I've ever been."

She laid her head on his shoulder. "Oh, Mitch. That's such a beautiful thing to say. I've never been in love before. This is for keeps."

"Then all is forgiven?"

"All is well with the world."

"Then let's go tell our world what we've discovered." He flipped open his cell and punched in Geoff's number. "Damn! Battery's run down. I never let that happen, but my mind's been elsewhere. You're not getting claustro yet, are you? I told your sister to come rescue us in a few minutes. It won't be long."

"I can tolerate a few more minutes." She raised her lips to his and the two of them returned kiss for kiss. In the clinch that followed, she reached down to her slacks pocket and turned off her own cell phone. No, a few more minutes locked away with the love of her life couldn't hurt at all.

About the Author

As a former human resources analyst, Barbara Barrett combines the passionate stirrings of love with the reality of job demands in her contemporary romances. A member of Romance Writers of America, Barbara spends part of the year in Florida and the other half in her home state of Iowa. She is married with two grown children and six grandchildren. When she's not writing, she's learning more about interior design and cooking. Or playing her new passion, Mah Jongg.

In the mood for more Crimson Romance? Check out *Once Upon a Wish* by Pam Andrews Hanson at *CrimsonRomance.com*.

CPSIA information can be obtained at www.ICGtesting.com
Printed in the USA
LVOW072301060313

323097LV00014B/318/P